Mills &

A chance to read and collect some of the best-loved novels from Mills & Boon—the world's largest publisher of romantic fiction.

Every month, four titles by favourite Mills & Boon authors will be re-published in the *Classics* series.

A list of other titles in the *Classics* series can be found at the end of this book.

Violet Winspear

THE TOWER OF THE CAPTIVE

MILLS & BOON LIMITED
LONDON · TORONTO

All the characters in this book have no existence outside the imagination of the Author, and have no relation whatsoever to anyone bearing the same name or names. They are not even distantly inspired by any individual known or unknown to the Author, and all the incidents are pure invention.

The text of this publication or any part thereof may not be reproduced or transmitted in any form or by any means, electronic or mechanical, including photocopying, recording, storage in an information retrieval system, or otherwise, without the written permission of the publisher.

This book is sold subject to the condition that it shall not, by way of trade or otherwise, be lent, resold, hired out or otherwise circulated without the prior consent of the publisher in any form of binding or cover other than that in which it is published and without a similar condition including this condition being imposed on the subsequent purchaser.

First published 1966
Australian copyright 1980
Philippine copyright 1980
This edition 1980

© Violet Winspear 1966

ISBN 0 263 73447 1

Set in 9/10 pt. Linotype Baskerville

*Made and printed in Great Britain by
Richard Clay (The Chaucer Press) Ltd,
Bungay, Suffolk*

CHAPTER ONE

VANESSA pushed shaking fingers through her hair and stared across her bedroom at the bamboo blinds flapping at the windows. Through the slats, weirdly, menacingly, stole the thud of jungle drums, drowning out the usual evening creak of cicadas and rustle of palm fronds ... then, bringing her heart into her throat, there echoed through the plantation house the harsh crack of a revolver shot.

For interminable seconds Vanessa was welded where she stood by fear—fear of who might be down there in the hall —then love and anxiety overcame her panic and with her uncle's name on her lips she raced along the gallery to the stairs, an endless swoop to the hall, where she gazed frozenly at the tall figure in a combat jacket over khaki trousers who had just stepped out of her uncle's study. Her feardrowned eyes slipped from the nerve kicking hard in his jaw to the revolver that hung down in his right hand ...

'You—*señor*!' The words scraped Vanessa's dry throat as she thrust past him into the study. Wedges of shadow stood in the corners of the room, the veranda doors gaped wide open, and in the bright pool of light shed by the desk lamp a grey-haired figure lay slumped, unbreathing under the hand she touched to his clay-cold face. 'Uncle Len, speak to me,' she implored, like a frightened child. 'Darling, are you ill—?'

'Come, *señorita*,' hands closed over her shoulders and she was impelled away from the still figure in white drill, led out firmly to the hall. 'Come, we must leave as quickly as possible. There is nothing to be done for Señor Carrol, and I have a launch awaiting us by the river bank.'

The words made no sense to Vanessa as she jerked free of the imperative hands. She didn't feel her lightly clad shoulder hit against the wall, for like a small trapped creature she hardly knew whether she faced friend or foe in this moment that was straight out of a nightmare. She glanced up wildly from the revolver he had thrust into the waistband of his trousers, heard him say: 'Your uncle died of a heart attack, Miss Carrol. I merely winged a prowler who appeared on the veranda.' Then he abruptly loomed much closer, and though Vanessa believed what he had said, she stiffened against the wall. Their eyes locked, and he spoke with a cutting edge to his deep, alien voice: 'The rebellion has broken out with a vengeance, as you can hear, and it is necessary that you accept my assistance. You will do so voluntarily—or the other way.'

'What do you mean—the other way?' she breathed.

'Must I really be more explicit?' His teeth snapped whitely in a brief, unkind smile. 'Are you not woman enough to know what I mean? Perhaps not! Your good uncle was my friend and I intend to snatch you away from Ordaz, with or without your co-operation.'

His lean, dark hands leapt, took hold of her and jerked her from the wall to which she had glued herself. She heard him mutter almost in her hair. 'Time is running away fast, *chica*, and I do not wish to use brute force in order to get you through the jungle. Listen, the drums grow nearer!'

She shuddered at the quickening drum thuds, felt snakes of sweat crawling down her back, and knew from the pressure of the lean hands right through the silk of her blouse that Don Rafael de Domerique *was* capable of using brute force in order to get her away.

'Uncle's workers won't hurt me, surely?' she gasped.

'Not in their right senses, no,' he rejoined. 'But they are now drugged with hate and the mad promise of their leader, and this is no time for me to describe what crazed terrorists do to their white victims.' And even as he spoke Vanessa was being whisked across the hall, through a door and into the seething tropical night.

Over everything hung the heavy, almost overpowering scents that rose out of dense thickets of bamboo and creepers as Vanessa and her escort blundered on through the half-mile jungle belt that separated them from the river. Thick ropes of lianas lay like traps across their path, while every now and again the Don's arms sliced into huge webs that held unmentionable hairy-legged horrors, and though Vanessa's heart quaked inside her upon these occasions, she knew as well as he that undisturbed spider-webs meant that their path was at least clear of machete-armed terrorists.

At last, after half a lifetime, they were scrambling through a tangle of sappy growths at the river's edge and the Don was swinging her to the boards of his moored launch. His hand impelled her down a flight of steps to a small cabin, where she sank on to the bunk in the darkness, uncontrollably shivering, listening as above on the deck she heard the powerful motor spring to life and they shot away into the dark silk of the river.

Relief was a thick, saline lump in her throat as she sat forward and cradled her body with scratched arms. Just in front of her there was a ring of grey that slowly formed into a porthole. It was open, and a breeze fanned her face and carried the thud of native drums.

The rebellion had been building up for days. Just a week ago a coffee plantation further inland had been sacked and burned. Don Rafael had turned up at Ordaz only hours afterwards, grimly full of warning that the situation was worsening and they would be wise to pack up and let him take them across to Luenda, the island on which he lived. But Lennard Carrol had known no other world but his plantation for almost thirty years and he had refused to budge. He had wanted his niece to go to the island, but like him she couldn't believe that their workers were preparing to turn on them. She had thanked the Don for his offer of help, but had chosen to remain at the plantation.

'I hope you will not regret your obstinacy, Miss Carrol.' Through the veneer of the *hidalgo's* sophistication there had suddenly glinted the metal of the dominant Spaniard. He wasn't accustomed to being opposed by a mere woman, and in a cutting voice he had added: 'It seems to me that you British have the misguided courage, that too often you put your trust in hope, and then when it is too late you pay with your lives.' His angry eyes had flashed to her uncle. 'Señor Carrol, will you not insist that your niece accompany me, here and now?'

'Uncle Len,' her fingers had bitten urgently into her uncle's arm, 'you've said again and again that the workers will stand by us.'

'I believe that, Don Rafael,' her uncle had looked firm, adding with his whimsical smile: 'I'm afraid our women won't be forced against their will, anyway, especially when they have red hair.'

'*Es muy joven.*' A deep shrug of the square shoulders, a carved look about the lean, swarthy face. 'You have my telephone number. Do not hesitate to get in touch with me should trouble arise.' Then with a curt bow he had turned and stalked out of the house, leaving Vanessa wildly hoping that she had seen the last of him.

During the week that followed she and her uncle had carried on with their various duties as though the brewing storm had little to do with them. They were the Carrols, rendered inviolate by their many kindnesses to their coffee workers. The wives of the men never hesitated to come to Vanessa with the troubles afflicting their children and she was ever ready with help and advice. It just wasn't believable that she and Uncle Lennard were going to reap treachery out of the goodness they had sown.

But by dinner time this particular evening there hadn't been a servant left in the house. After a scratch meal, barely picked at, Vanessa automatically cleared the table. Her uncle said he'd get his papers ready—just in case. 'Pack a few necessities, my dear,' he added. 'I'll try to contact Rafael de Domerique by phone. He'll help us if he can—it seems after all that he knows these people better than I.'

That was what had broken her uncle's heart and snapped it out like a failing light, that all his years of being a fair and benevolent employer had gone for nought. He had trusted his workers, but like children resenting parental control they had turned on him.

The launch throbbed like Vanessa's heart. She grieved silently and tearlessly for the uncle with whom she had lived for the past four years. Twenty-one now, she had been left parentless by a car accident just as her schooling had ended. Her uncle had invited her to share his home and she had not hesitated to come out to the coffee plantation just above the Ordaz River, where it widened out into one of the Central American lakes embracing the edge of this tropical zone of cacao, bananas, dense mangroves and rubber trees.

Luenda lay a number of miles off the coast of Ordaz, a brilliant scimitar cutting into the Caribbean at its tip, its green and jungly hilt jutting towards the Equator. The powerful, wealthy Domerique family had lived there for centuries, for it was a Spanish protectorate, pouring much of its yield from oil and tropical agriculture into the pockets of the man who had rescued Vanessa. She shivered, hot and cold in her green blouse and brown linen skirt, staring across at the porthole through which she could now see the writhing tongues of flames, leaping above the dark mass of the jungle. She knew that it was her white, gracious home that was burning, searing out of her life everything she had grown to love.

Then she stiffened, her moist hands clenching together as rope-soled shoes padded on the steps leading down to the cabin and Don Rafael came into the small enclosure. He struck a match and lit a pot-bellied lamp. His movements were deft and deliberate, his face was a swarthy carving above the sudden flare of light. She guessed he had fixed the motor dead ahead for Luenda.

'I can remain but a short while—you are all right?' he demanded.

There was a stony remoteness about him as he regarded her, it seemed not to occur to him that she had seen the burning plantation and was needing comfort—or did he know it and did not give it in case her courage dissolved into tears?

Her eyes were dark with nightmare thoughts, ringed by the fatigue of abused emotions even as she nodded in answer to his question.

'It was blind and foolish of you to ignore my warning of a week ago,' he said. 'Just a few more minutes and I should have been too late to get you away.'

'I—I know, but I couldn't leave Uncle Lennard. He was

all I had——' She pushed wearily at the thick, sweat-streaked copper hair that lay tangled above her grey-green eyes. Her cheekbones showed sharply, her mouth was without a tinge of colour. 'He was so confident that common sense would prevail in his "people", as he always called them. Why, *señor*, did they turn on us?'

'Because they have been incited to it by promises of the riches of the white boss-man. It will go on happening, but you must put the memory of it behind you. My family waits at Luenda to welcome you, and you may stay with us for as long as you wish.'

'You're so kind to say that, *señor*.' A ghost of a smile moved her colourless lips. 'I—I can never repay you——'

'Who is asking for repayment?' His autocratic face assumed a mask of cool displeasure. 'We have never been *simpatico*, Miss Carrol, but that is no reason why I should leave you to the unrestrained savageries of a band of rebels. You Englishwomen, in my opinion, exhibit rather too much independence, but in the last resort you are but women.'

His words hammered her temples, and each second the tremors that shook her were getting out of control. A warm hand pressed soothingly against her head, his lean fingers sank deep in her hair. 'There, it will soon be over, *pequeña*. Give way to it, let yourself shake—forget the stiff British upper lip.'

And clenching the sleeves of his combat jacket, she trembled helplessly in his arms, racked for long moments by nervous reaction. When at last it receded, he went to a wall cabinet and took out a bottle and a glass. Saffron liquid glinted in the light of the lamp, burning her lips when he tilted the glass against them. It was a strong brandy and it helped, a long measure that left her drugged and quiescent on his bunk when he returned to the deck of the launch.

She lay there with heavy-lidded eyes, a light quilt drawn over her legs. He had slipped her sandals from her feet, lowered the lamp and told her to try and get some sleep. It would be several hours before they reached Luenda.

As she was carried out to sea to an unknown island, she let her mind float back to the plantation and the occasions when Rafael de Domerique had dined with Uncle Len and herself. How excessively foreign he always looked in his immaculate white dining kit, a suggestion of lost and pagan continents about him with the topaz candlelight reflecting in his jetty eyes, and flickering over the lean, haughty planes of his face. His politeness towards her had never held anything she could really put a finger on, but she rarely felt at ease in his presence.

Once he had dined with them when a party of young geologists had been present. They had flirted harmlessly with her, the only female at the party and wearing the apple-green chiffon that went so well with her colouring, and after dinner they had put records on the gramophone and she had partnered the men one at a time. The aloof *hidalgo* had smoked one of her uncle's Havana cigars and looked down his high-bridged nose at the noisy horseplay when Jack Conroy had proceeded to demonstrate one of the crazy new dances from England.

'The darned man has no sense of humour!' had flashed through Vanessa's mind as she caught his glittering dark glance upon her, and egged on by his obvious disapproval of Jack's antics she had smiled gaily at the young geologist and gone with him, unresisting, into the moonlit garden. They had talked about mineral deposits, as it happened, but from that time on Don Rafael had seemed to regard her as rather empty-headed. '*Es muy joven*,' he was to say of her not long after that party. 'She's very young.'

And because she was young, and he made her feel at a disadvantage, she had impetuously ignored his warning of the danger which had built to such a horrible climax tonight. No wonder he was coldly furious with her! If she had agreed to go to Luenda last week, Uncle Len might have decided to go as well. He might not have suffered that killing heart attack. The shattering loss of her uncle swept over her again, and turning her face into the bunk pillow she wept herself into an exhaustion that finally found relief in sleep.

Some time later there were footfalls on the steps outside and a hand pushed open the cabin door. Dark eyes swept the girl on the bunk, lost to the world in her exhaustion, her coppery hair strewing the white linen of the pillow, the stain of tears on her cheeks.

'Ah, you are awake!' At once his mask of aloof politeness was back in place. 'Soon now we will be at Luenda, therefore if you wish to make yourself a little more presentable you will find washing facilities through this door,' he indicated it with a sweep of a lean hand on which a crested ring of a medieval design caught her eye. 'I will be on deck, Miss Carrol. You will no doubt enjoy the beauty of the lagoon which lies below the *castillo*.'

Something in his manner was faintly hurtful and she watched with bewildered eyes as he swung round and left her, then anger washed over her. Was it to be expected that she would be bandbox-fresh to meet his family after their flight through the jungle? All she possessed in the world was this torn blouse and creased skirt, the rest of her belongings had been looted or burned.

Chilly, arrogant Spaniard, she disliked being dependent upon him as much as he resented the fact that she was. His initial offer of assistance, of course, would not have involved him to this extent had she accepted it, and he had obviously made it because of his liking for Uncle Lennard. They had got along remarkably well despite the vast difference in their ages, and it had always amazed Vanessa that her uncle could regard Don Rafael as though he were another British planter instead of a black-browed Spanish patrician who lived as his fierce Colonial forebears had, in a *castillo* on an exotic island.

She sighed, slipped achingly from the bunk and went into the adjacent washroom. She flicked open the porthole curtain and grimaced at her scarecrow reflection in the mirror above the wash-basin. Any man, she supposed, could be excused a look of rejection from that apparition, let alone the high and mighty Don Rafael de Domerique with his fastidious tastes.

Water gushed into the basin under the rather angry twist of her wrist, then she peeled off her blouse and skirt and after washing she didn't hesitate to use briskly on her hair the silver-backed brush lying on a nearby shelf. Her hair crackled under the manly bristles and after she had clipped back the copper swathes, she dressed again, wrinkling her nose at her crumpled clothing but unable to do a thing about it. She also felt rather naked without a dab of lipstick, and she stared for a long moment into her own eyes in the mirror. There was nothing left, she thought drearily. The flames of hell had whipped across her life and now she must go it alone.

Shoulders braced, she walked into the cabin and mounted to the deck, where she caught her breath at the vivid scenery that met her gaze. Sunrise had flown out of the arms of dawn, daylight had come, and as the launch was manoeuvred through an opening in the pink and amber peaks of a coral reef, there sprang into view the most beautiful sight of Vanessa's life. The lagoon beach was a barrette of pearl edged by the opalescent sea, the crests of coconut palms were haloed by the spreading sun, while a little further back casuarinas stirred their lacy foliage in the silky trade winds. Above the beach rose a bastion of cliffs, dominated by the chiselled ramparts and golden-rose walls of a castle out of a medieval romance.

'It's utterly splendid, *señor*!' Vanessa's eyes glowed silver-green in her still rather drawn face. 'You must love it with every beat of your heart.'

'It is like a tapestry, eh, Miss Carrol?' He turned to look down at her. 'The stone for it was quarried here on Luenda many, many years ago, and though the *castillo* is entirely of Castilian design, it is that remarkable golden-rose stone that softens its outlines and gives it such a pleasing aspect.'

'The Castillo d'Oro,' she murmured. 'I could never have believed that such a place existed outside a book of fables. The sun gilds its turrets and it is indeed a golden castle.'

'I have a goddaughter, the orphaned child of friends I once had, who has another name for it.' His flawless teeth glinted in a rather caustic smile. 'She refers to the *castillo* as the Torre de la Cautiva, the tower of the fair captive. She is of a romantic turn of mind, you understand—you and she might have interests in common.'

There was a note of satire in his voice, echoed by his eyes, into which Vanessa looked directly a moment before he returned his attention to guiding the launch to a small landing jetty. The dazzling sunlight, slanting across his face, had shown Vanessa that she was mistaken in thinking his eyes were jet-dark. As cornelians reveal themselves suddenly in stone so had startling flickers of gold lighted up in Don Rafael's eyes. She couldn't repress a little shiver, for it was as though she was being warned to prepare herself for quick-changing facets in the character of the man himself.

She stood tense beside him as they neared the jetty. He had removed his khaki jacket and she saw that he was wearing a fine linen shirt with short sleeves. His arms were corded and powerful with dark hair on them; where his shirt lay open at his firm throat there was a glimpse of deep chest muscles. Vanessa guessed he had snatched time to use that razor she had noticed in the washroom, otherwise his forceful chin would have been carrying a strong dawn shadow. She knew herself a pale contrast to his swarthiness, and found she was irresistibly comparing him to the Spanish buccaneers who had roved the Caribbean in bygone days. It was that in him which fluttered a flag of alarm in a woman, that look handed down from forebears who had plundered what they couldn't win by other means!

'Look!' He swept out a hand and she saw that a couple of natives had appeared near the jetty, having come round from a ridge of rocks where they had evidently been fishing with hand-spears. They had dumped their silver haul down on the pearly sand and were waiting with wide grins for the launch to slide in against the jetty.

One of them caught and made fast the coil of rope which Don Rafael tossed to him, while the other man assisted Vanessa off the launch. Her legs felt jellified after the rocking motion and as she went down the steps to the beach she was very conscious of the scrutiny of the bronzed Indians. She noticed the barbaric beauty of the dark faces, knew from the high cheekbones and thin, curved lips that a measure of Spanish blood ran in their veins. Many of these Indians were descended from the slaves owned by the first Spanish settlers, and when these two addressed as *compadre* the man who had brought her here, she guessed them to be two of the many people he employed on his plantations and in the plants processing the fruit, spices and perfumes said to abound on the island.

He followed her to the beach, lithe and animal-graceful as the Indians. 'As you can see, Gallito and Perico have been fishing,' he smiled. 'They wish to toast some of their catch for us. They will cook them over a coconut shell fire, a most delicious meal when these small fish are not long out of the sea. You would like this, Miss Carrol? You must be feeling extremely hungry, and I set out too rapidly for Ordaz yesterday to think of taking food on the launch.'

She had not thought about eating until this moment, now she realized that her body was feeble this morning because she needed food. The demands of facing life without her uncle were reclaiming her from the nightmare of last night, and as she admitted that she was hungry, she also knew that she welcomed the respite that breakfast on the beach would accord her. To arrive destitute *and* enfeebled at the *castillo* might put her at even more of a disadvantage, for if the rest of the Domerique household were as strong-willed as the master, then she was going to need her wits and strength if she was to hold her own.

Don Rafael acquiesced to the Indians' invitation, and one of them proceeded to build a fire of the sun-dried coconut shell while his companion cleaned the fish and laid them across cane to cook in their own juices. Soon a most delectable aroma was drifting to Vanessa's nostrils, for she awaited the meal sitting in the shade of the casuarinas, the talking trees as she knew them to be called. Don Rafael had fetched plates, forks and a pair of tumblers off the launch and now with expert swipes of Perico's machete he beheaded a couple of coconuts and filled the tumblers with the pale, sweet milk. The fish, crackling and golden-brown, were served up not many minutes later, after which the Indians disappeared among the plumy tamarisks to eat theirs, leaving their *compadre* and his guest to breakfast in privacy.

Vanessa had often gone on picnics back at Ordaz, but

never had the food tasted quite like this. She ate hungrily the slices of roast breadfruit with the crunchy little fish, washing down the delicious mouthfuls with coconut milk.

'That was *bueno*, eh?' Don Rafael gave her his aloof smile and handed her a silk handkerchief so she could wipe her lips. 'I fear I cannot offer you a cigarette—ah, of course, you do not smoke! It is wise of you not to have succumbed to the habit, but I am myself a smoking fiend for these.' He took from a pocket of his jacket the gold case in which he carried his lethal-looking cheroots. The other end of the case was fitted with a lighter and after kindling one of the slim, dark cylinders he sat with his shoulders at rest against the trunk of one of the trees, smoke drifting enjoyably from his thin, well-cut lips.

One of the Indians came for their soiled breakfast things, giving Vanessa a shy smile and a bow when she said, '*Muchas gracias*,' for the meal she had really enjoyed. He then padded away on bare, leathery feet to the water's edge where he crouched singing as he washed the crockery.

'What does he sing about, *señor*?' she asked, for her knowledge of the Spanish language was confined to a few short phrases.

'That the sea is like love, both cruel and beautiful,' Don Rafael replied suavely. 'Gallito and Perico are brothers, good, simple fellows whom I employ to do odd jobs about the estate of the *castillo*.'

'You have no fears, *señor*, that what is occurring at Ordaz might one day occur here on Luenda?' She eyed him enquiringly.

'The fear of rebellion here is fairly remote, Miss Carrol. Luenda is cut off from the revolutionary elements pervading the mainland, and then again our life here has feudal qualities which are curiously satisfying and perhaps only possible on an island which has known only Spanish rule since the sixteenth century. We, like you English, are natural colonists, you know.'

And there the likeness ended, she reflected as she sifted the fine sand through her fingers and gazed towards the shimmering opalescence within the embrace of the reef. It was a Spaniard, according to rumour, who had stirred up the trouble at Ordaz! The hemlock bitterness of it all was gripping her again, while the uncertainty of her future loomed like a dark shadow in the brilliant sunshine of Luenda.

Then she gave a start as a hand pressed her shoulder and hard fingers burned through a rent in the silk of her blouse. 'Last night you were angry, shocked and frightened, *muchacha*, and when the blood is hot from all these the pain is less. Now it jabs, eh? Now you are facing loneliness and wondering why an unkind fate has placed you in the hands of the arrogant Spaniard from the island of Luenda?' The dark steel of the Don's eyes was magnetic, holding her gaze against her will. 'Time, Miss Carrol, will dull the edge of your pain, and you must be thankful that you have your life. That is *afortunado*, eh?'

'Of course I'm grateful for my life, *señor*, but I can't think what I'm going to do now—now the plantation is no more and my uncle is dead. I'm totally untrained for an office job, as yet, and if compensation is eventually paid for the burning of the plantation, it won't be for ages——'

'You are not to concern yourself with money matters.' The man beside her spoke curtly. 'I fully realize that right now you are without means. What does it matter? You are my guest, and as such——' There he broke off and his eyes narrowed as he regarded the sensitive flush that played over her face. 'Is it such a hard thing for you to do, to accept the hospitality of a man who had the friendship of your good uncle? He would wish this, and be thankful that it was into my hands that you fell last night.

'*Madre mia*,' a smile of derision flickered on his lips, 'have I treated you so badly?'

'I—it isn't that, Don Rafael!'

'It is that you cannot like me,' he mocked. 'Well, we must not let the personal enter into this. You are but a child who is alone and in need. There is no more than that to the matter.'

But there was! Vanessa's gaze followed the scintillations of small, vivid birds through the honey-warm air into the whispering foliage of the casuarinas. There was the memory of that brooding look his eyes had held when she had awakened suddenly on the launch. The natural chivalry and protectiveness of the Spanish *hidalgo* warred within him, she was certain, with a reluctance at finding himself the guardian of an English girl, one whose closest relative had died last night, leaving her totally adrift.

With the best possible grace, however, she was obliged to accept his hospitality. She had at least the consolation of knowing that as soon as the British authorities learned of the sacking of the plantation, wheels would be set in motion to put things right for her as far as money went. Then she could return to England, independent once more of Rafael de Domerique—still an unknown quantity despite the fact that as a friend of her uncle's he had drifted in and out of her life during the past four years.

Friendships between men, she reflected, were largely founded on a mental basis. That could not be when it came to men and women, the fact of their every difference must enter in, making friendship in the purest sense an impossibility. Always at Ordaz she had known that she could never be friends with the man who would dictate the course of her life for the next few weeks.

With his eyes narrowed against the intermingling of brilliant sky and pearly sand, he said, pleasantly, as though addressing a tourist: 'I think you will like the town of Luenda, Miss Carrol. We have here an unchanging atmosphere which is at once peaceful and exciting ... like true love, which holds those qualities from its beginning until its end.'

She felt a startled little leap of her pulses that he should say, and think, such a thing. With that faintly cruel mouth of his, he seemed of the type who would love with violence. She could be wrong, of course, but all the same she didn't envy the woman upon whom his fancy might already have settled. She would undoubtedly be beautiful, because in his dark, smouldering fashion the *hidalgo* of Luenda was a fine-looking man. And how she would be envied by the other *señoritas*, installed in that golden castle, waited on like a queen, possessed by this man who must represent to them all that was desirable in a Spanish male...

At this point Vanessa's reflections were cut off short. There was a sudden thunder of hoofs as a rider appeared round that bend of the beach. Long raven hair flew wildly, then vivid as a dark woodcut against a blue background the black streak of glistening coat and wild eyes was checked by a jerk on the reins and sent spinning into the air on its hind legs. An oath broke from Don Rafael and in a second he was on his feet and confronting the girl on the horse. Boyish in a checked shirt and breeches, the girl might have been sixteen or seventeen. Her exotic little face was set with enormous, long-lashed, defiant eyes.

His nostrils flaring and ice ridging his words, the *hidalgo* broke into a quick spate of Spanish. The horse jibbed as he was speaking and out shot one of his lean hands, fastening on the bridle and holding the sweating beast steady as he finished reprimanding the girl. She glared down at him. The pair of them were angry as back-arched cats.

'I repeat that I will not have you riding wild like a *gitana*.' Don Rafael had switched abruptly to English, as though even in the midst of his anger he was conscious of discourtesy towards his English guest in using a language she could not fully understand. 'Your mount is a highly strung thoroughbred, Barbara, not a circus performer. Look at him, quivering with nerves ... much more of this and I shall forbid you to ride at all.'

'Forbid? It is a favourite word of yours, *padrino*.' The girl tossed her tempestuous head and cast a glance in Vanessa's direction. She had a clear golden skin and would have been quite lovely if her mouth had been less sullen. 'You are the English girl from Ordaz, is it not so? You are different from what I expected—your hair is alight in the sun and you have eyes the colour of smoky emeralds. Is it English to look as you do?'

Vanessa caught her breath, amused, vexed and a little embarrassed all together. Thoroughly British and reserved in her own responses, she was disconcerted by the Latin tendency to say outright what sprang into the mind. Yet could it be that only on Luenda were these people less inhibited than elsewhere? In all the four years she had known Don Rafael, he had never until this morning talked openly of a thing like love, or sprawled on the sand and tucked into fish and breadfruit accompanied by coconut milk.

Still showing an aloof disapproval of his goddaughter's behaviour, he introduced Vanessa formally to her, Barbara del Quiros.

'Are you coming to stay at the *castillo*, Miss Vanessa Carrol?' The girl spoke impudently, but after her dark eyes had flickered over Vanessa's torn and creased attire, she added: 'We are of a similar build, so I shall be able to lend you something to wear.'

'That's kind of you, Miss del Quiros.' The girl after all was less bad-tempered than she had at first appeared, while a rapid glance at Don Rafael showed Vanessa that he, too, was pleased by the offer.

He put lean fingers over the girl's and pressed them. 'Miss Carrol has suffered the loss of her good Tio Lennard, *chiquilla*. Also her home has been burned, therefore she will certainly be our guest for a while. Be kind to her, eh? You are both children in a way, and perhaps it will do both of you good to play together.'

Barbara smiled, then, as she gazed into his eyes from the scarlet saddle of her black horse. '*Que gran caballero!*' She tapped his shoulder with her riding-crop. 'One moment the ice-cooled Spanish steel of his temper for Barbarita, now the velvety persuasion. *Padrino*, I would not be the woman who loves you, you are too terrible in your anger, and in your tenderness overwhelming.'

'You speak with an effrontery I would permit in few other people, Barbarita.' His teeth flashed white. He was irritated rather than angered this time; a little unsure of how to handle this girl, Vanessa realized. 'But this business of riding Matador until he sweats. I will not have that,' he sternly rebuked her.

'He enjoys it,' she argued, putting a hand against the horse's glossy neck and giving it a stroke. 'But the truth is, I saw the launch approaching from the *castillo*, then when you did not come I was worried—you see, I have a fondness for you, *padrino*, though you are such a bully.'

'Miss Carrol and I have breakfasted here on the beach. My two Indians toasted some of their catch for us.' He turned his head, blue-black in the strong sunlight, and looked directly at Vanessa. 'You are feeling a little better now you have eaten, eh?'

She nodded. Gone, thankfully, was that deathly feeling of not caring what came next in the scheme of things. The shock of losing her uncle would take some getting over, but now she had faced up to her unavoidable dependence upon the *hidalgo* of Luenda she realized that she was quite looking forward to seeing the interior of his golden-rose *castillo* —the tower of the fair captive, as his goddaughter called it. Is that how Barbara del Quiros regarded herself, as the Don's fair captive? As Vanessa put back a strand of copper hair and quizzed the girl, Don Rafael added:

'I will send one of the Indians to the *castillo* for a car. The climb from the beach to the headland is a tiring one, and you are still looking dazed and tired, Miss Carrol.'

He walked down the beach, tossing the stub of his cheroot from him, his deep-toned Spanish drifting back to Vanessa as he spoke to one of the Indians.

'You do not like the *compadre*, do you, Miss Vanessa Carrol?'

Vanessa turned sharply to look at Barbara del Quiros. Barbara laughed and flicked a fly from her horse's neck. 'It is plain that you dislike being here, on the island which he partly owns, no longer your own mistress but compelled to obey him.'

'You put it rather strongly, Miss del Quiros,' Vanessa retorted. 'I am here only for a while—and I have no intention of taking orders from Don Rafael. I—I'm a guest, not an employee.'

'You are proud, I think,' Barbara smiled. 'Perhaps to be an employee of Don Rafael's would suit you better?'

'I think it would!' Vanessa agreed vehemently, and wondered if there was a possibility of employment for her on the island. Lost for a moment in her thoughts, she absently prodded a spiky sea-urchin with the toe of her right sandal.

The tide was now crashing in against the coral reef, dashing its spray in silver shafts through the golden meshes of the sun. Against that background stood framed for a long moment the man who had brought her here. He was gazing fixedly at the breakers, shattering in jewelled shards on the peaks of the reef that guarded his private lagoon.

What was he thinking as he stood there? That the sea was cruel and beautiful ... like love?

Abruptly he swung round and trod deeply in the glittering sand as he came back towards Vanessa and his goddaughter. The sun gilded him—the vigour and vividness of the man struck at Vanessa like a blow.

Here on Luenda he *was* different! He was the master ... not the guest who treated her with a distant politeness.

CHAPTER TWO

THE sun was dazzling on the crested Silver-Cloud Rolls as it swept between a magnificent pair of gates and ran along an avenue of flame-petalled flamboyant trees.

Vanessa, deep in the embrace of dove-grey upholstery, was conscious of the Don's appraisal as she swivelled to gaze at the fiery trees from the rear window of his car. 'Everything on this island, *señor*, is more so than anywhere else,' she just had to say. 'The place is real, I suppose? I'm not asleep and dreaming it, am I?'

'Do you perhaps wish, *señorita*, that the island and *I* could fade into a figment of your sleeping subconscious?' He spoke in those clipped, half-mocking tones she had come to know from his visits to Ordaz. When she looked at him, a smile was twitching the edges of his lips. 'Come, we are not recent acquaintances who hesitate to cross foils. I invite you to attempt a thrust through my guard.'

'How magnanimous of you, *señor*!' She caught her breath as there thrust through her a desire to do just what he suggested. 'You feel you can be generous, I suppose, because you have all this, a *castillo* and half an island, while I have nothing at the present time but my writhing independence. Don Rafael, if you really are generous, then you'll find me a job of some sort while I'm here.'

'So? Already you are asking for employment?' One of his black brows arched sarcastically. 'What would you prefer to do, Miss Carrol, pick cotton, pack citrus fruits or sort spices? Then again there are the perfume factories—ah, but I am forgetting, you are more acquainted with coffee production. Perhaps you would prefer to assist with that side of things, eh?'

She flushed uncontrollably at the cool scorn in his eyes, and locked her bottom lip between her teeth. Oh, lord, what an ungrateful creature she must seem to him! Last night he had risked possible death in order to save her, yet here she was rejecting what he had done even as she drove with him to the refuge of his home ...

'I admire independence, Miss Carrol, but you carry yours to rather exasperating extremes,' his words bristled with thorns and she winced at the prick of them. 'All British women cannot be as opposed to a helping hand as you appear to be. There must be one or two who appreciate the *hombrada* in men?'

'I—don't know what the word means,' she admitted, and she couldn't stop herself from shrinking into a corner as he suddenly loomed near, the spread of his shoulders blocking light from the window, the glitter and glint of his eyes and teeth making him look angry enough to bite.

'It means manly impulse,' he crisped. 'It is a thought of the most painful that my *hombrada* of last night was resented by you, such a pity that my name is not Smithers, Brown—or Conroy. From men so named you would doubtless accept aid and comfort as a mere matter of course, but with me there must be this clash of temperament, absurd constraint and burning in the British heart because for a while you will be under obligation to a foreigner. A week ago I attributed your reluctance to come to Luenda to love of your uncle. Do not misunderstand, I am not disputing your love, but I realize now how deep goes your dislike of me.' He snapped his fingers, cynically. '*Ello no importa,* but I have put myself in the place of your good uncle and whether you like it or not you are my concern until the authorities settle matters for you with regard to the razing of the plantation.'

'I—I could get in touch with the British Consul,' she heard herself say, rather wildly.

'You may certainly do so,' he agreed suavely. 'No doubt your passage to England will be paid, but you will be obliged almost at once to find work—for which you have said you are as yet untrained. My good girl, be realistic and sensible! I have said that my home is yours—throw my offer back in my teeth and I shall not forgive the insult.'

Vanessa cast a quick look at him and saw from the set to his imperious features that he was in deadly earnest. He withdrew to his corner of the seat and turned his gaze to the window, while Vanessa stormily wished that it had been Jack Conroy who had whipped her away from Ordaz. She could have shrugged off her obligation with a lighthearted: 'Thanks for helping me out of a spot, Jack. You've been a brick.'

But she most certainly couldn't say that to Don Rafael de Domerique. He felt he owed her his protection on account of the regard for her uncle, and to cross him over the matter was obviously an affront to his code of honour. Darn the feudal notions of the Spanish!

The tunnel of flame trees suddenly widened and the Rolls swept into the paved forecourt of the Castillo d'Oro and purred to a standstill at the foot of a semi-circular stone stairway. The chauffeur opened the door beside Vanessa and she stepped out, followed by her host. They mounted the steps and the Don stood beside her as she took in with wondering eyes the panorama which the *castillo* commanded. 'The first Don Rafael to live on Luenda was a man who liked to be looked up to,' her companion remarked, a note of amusement in his voice.

Her glance was drawn as though by a magnet to his face, stamped with a similar autocracy, she thought.

'You like what you see of our island, Miss Carrol?' he asked.

'It's beautiful, *señor*.'

'*La isla esta bella*, you would say in Spanish, *señorita*. I must teach you our language, I think.' A flickering smile. 'Then you will perhaps feel yourself more at home with us. At home,' he savoured the expression. 'Invented by the British for proper use by the foreigner. Ah, you British, so clever and shrewd, such excellent opponents in a battle— but are you warm at heart, I wonder?'

Vanessa met the mocking brilliance of his eyes, her loyalty stung. 'Yes, *señor*—in our own restrained fashion.'

'The sun has to break through the snow, eh? And the snow, I fear, lies deep in patches.'

She was saved further argument with him, for behind them the great arched door of the *castillo* was opened and a uniformed footman melted to one side as the Don put light fingers at Vanessa's elbow and ushered her into the immense hall. An expanse of mosaic flooring swept ahead of them. A double staircase rose from the centre of the hall, enriched by filigreed ironwork and jewel-toned *azulejos* set into the facings of the steps.

'We will go to the *sala*,' the Don said, and they mounted the staircase to the first gallery, where tall doors were swung wide by yet another footman. Vanessa, nerves tensed, preceded her host into a room with a wide sweep of windows, a high gilded ceiling and silk-textured carpets. Dark mahogany threw into attractive relief several elegant, damasked sofas and chairs on silvered legs.

There were two people in occupation of the *sala*, a man who glanced up from a newspaper and a woman who turned gracefully from one of the windows. The softly clinging material of her dress was in one of those neutral shades so becoming on a classic brunette, while at her right hip a wing of drapery was held by a jewelled scimitar brooch.

'So at last you return, Rafael?' She held out a slender hand and looked only at him, yet Vanessa knew that the velvety brown eyes had skimmed her from head to foot without missing a detail of her dishevelment.

The *hidalgo* ran a smile of sudden startling charm over the woman's lustrous coiled hair, graceful white neck and upraised face which Goya might have put on canvas.

'Rafael, we have been much concerned for you,' she scolded him caressingly. 'Why did you go alone to Ordaz?'

'A man alone who knows his own mind is often more effective than an army, Lucia.' He carried her hand to his lips and touched them to the tapering, diamond-weighted fingers. There was also a gold ring of alliance on that elegant right hand, and Vanessa realized that this seductive female was none other than the Señora Lucia Montez, the young widow to whom the Don had sometimes referred in conversation with Uncle Lennard. Her much older husband had died a year ago, and Don Rafael was gazing down at her as though she alone occupied the island with him.

With flattering reluctance he relinquished her hand. 'I am gratified that you have been concerned for my safety, Lucia,' he murmured smilingly, 'and I am sure you will forgive me for not divulging the reason for my abrupt departure from the beach party yesterday. My private secretary had orders not to speak of it until this morning, when I was confident I would be on my way home.'

'Now you are back safe and sound at the *castillo*, Rafael, your folly is naturally forgiven.' The *señora's* warm voice, as it issued from her wine-red lips, held more than a hint of how much she was prepared to forgive him. 'It has been plain to me for days that you were much concerned for your friend Señor Carrol, and for his young niece, of course.' A smile in Vanessa's direction. 'Ah, but where is the *señor*?' she added.

The *hidalgo* shot his dark, direct glance at Vanessa, then in rapid Spanish he explained what had happened at Ordaz. Lucia Montez listened with a very sympathetic air, while the young man who had been reading now stood beside his chair, eyes as dark as the Don's fixed upon Vanessa. He was of an agile build, with a slim, debonair moustache, and his left arm in a black silk sling. His cream tussore suit was set off by a tan silk shirt and a matching handkerchief in the breast pocket of his jacket. He might have been in his late twenties, which made him several years younger than the other man.

'You have my deepest sympathy for your loss, Miss Carrol,' he said in English, when their host ceased to speak.

'Thank you, *señor*,' she murmured, thinking he looked less aloof and easier to get along with than Don Rafael, who stepped to her side and, with his fingers at her elbow, formally introduced her to the dashing Spaniard, Ruy Alvadaas, and the *señora*, who graciously smiled and yet could not stop herself from glancing at the lean brown fingers which barely touched the pale skin of Vanessa's arm. The *señora* was evidently on the possessive side!

'Come, let us make ourselves more at home.' The Don's left hand swept in an inviting gesture from Lucia to a brocaded sofa, while his other hand whisked a chair into position for Vanessa. 'Will you pour drinks for us, Ruy? Can you manage?'

'But of course,' the other man smiled. 'My hand grows easier each day, and I use this sling merely to rest it.'

'And because it acquires for you the *simpatia* of the *señoritas*, eh, Ruy?' Lucia Montez looked directly at him and laughed low in her throat.

'*Verdadero*,' he admitted, with an easy shrug of his shoulders and a glance towards Vanessa, who sat near a window with a ray of sunshine burnishing her copper hair. She caught the complimentary glance and gave Ruy Alvadaas a pale shadow of her former lively smile.

'You will in future be more careful of car doors, Ruy,' the Don said crisply to the man he had introduced as his cousin. 'You will take a sherry, Lucia?'

'A glass of your delicious Lágrima, please, Rafael.' Señora Montez settled herself into the embrace of the sofa, beside which a low arabesqued table held a silver and crystal cigarette box. She put back the lid and took one of the cork-tipped cylinders. Directly she inserted it between her lips, the flame of the hammered, eagle-shaped lighter was at the tip of it. As she put back her smooth head and expelled smoke, she looked long and deep into the Don's eyes.

He replaced the lighter, then turned to Vanessa. 'What would you like to drink, Miss Carrol?' he asked.

She looked at him and her mind was blank. Couldn't he see, she thought tiredly, that what she really wanted was to be alone, not sitting here in his impressive *sala* a bedraggled foil to the well-groomed poise of Lucia Montez?

'Perhaps a little cognac for the *señorita*,' he said to his cousin. 'For me a bacardi, if you please.'

Ruy Alvadaas had slipped his left hand out of the sling and was busying himself at the cabinet on which stood various crystal wine flagons and decanters. He brought over the drinks on a tray, and Vanessa cupped her glass of tawny cognac and made polite answers to the questions put to her by the *señora*. She had lost everything! Why, how terrible —but how fortunate that Don Rafael had reached the plantation in time to save her life.

'You are a hero, Rafael.' The brown eyes treated him to a look that must have melted right through to his masculine bones.

'Nonsense, Lucia! Luck plays its part in these matters.' He smiled at her, seated now, his long legs stretched out in front of him as he sipped lazily at his long glass of ice-cooled rum, lime juice and grenadine. 'It was Miss Carrol who had to draw on her courage—I could so easily have been El Zorro, the leader of the rebellion. It is said he is a Spaniard.'

Vanessa saw from a twitch to the edge of his mouth that he was bantering, but she also knew that he was obliquely referring to that moment outside her uncle's study, when she had thought for a fearful flash that he was an enemy rather than a friend.

'Please to drink your cognac, it will do you good,' he urged her, almost gently.

Like a weary child she obeyed him, sipping without tasting, and very aware of the scrutiny of the elegant widow. 'You have not been to Luenda before, have you, Miss Carrol?' she said.

Vanessa shook her head. 'I had heard of the island, of course. Don Rafael talked of it on his visits to—to my uncle.'

'Señor Carrol and myself had business interests in common,' the *hidalgo* interposed suavely. 'It is no more than my duty as a man who had his friendship to provide a refuge for his niece.'

Lucia received his explanation with a smile that said she understood—perfectly. She turned graciously to Vanessa. 'If there is anything you require, my dear, then do not hesitate to approach me.'

'You're very kind,' Vanessa answered politely, while in her mind she rejected the thought of accepting charity from this woman. There had been no spontaneity about her offer, and Vanessa glanced at him to see whether he would touch one of the pampered hands in gratitude. At that precise moment a scarlet-tinged black bow of a butterfly winged into the *sala* and made straight for a creamy hibiscus blossom with a hint of flame edging its petals. Vanessa saw the keen flash of the Don's eyes as they watched the butterfly curvet into the air above the flower, then resettle to probe the petals once again, its colour or perfume making it more interesting than the exotics that companioned it. The Don's firm lips twitched slightly, as though his alien sense of humour was tickled, then as Vanessa wondered if he would glance at Lucia Montez—for wasn't the hibiscus the flower of love?—there was a tap at a leaf of the tall doors and they opened to reveal on the threshold a thin, middle-aged woman in a severe black dress.

Don Rafael rose to his feet and went over to her. They spoke together for several minutes, then he came tall and dark to Vanessa's side. 'An apartment has been prepared for you, Miss Carrol,' he said. 'No doubt you wish to go to it right away?'

'Yes, please!' She was famished for privacy and a warm bath.

Ruy Alvadaas rose to his feet as she did. 'I look forward to seeing you later on, *señorita*.' He gave her a smile and a bow, and as her lips moved in an answering smile, she felt rather than saw the frowning look the Don swept over his cousin's face.

The debonair Ruy was evidently a bit of a lady-fancier, but the master of the *castillo* need not worry, Vanessa reflected tiredly, that she wanted a flirtation with his relative, charming as Ruy seemed. She doubted whether she'd be here long enough for that, and Latins, in any case, simmered too much beneath that aloof and courteous surface of theirs. She had no inclination to be caught in the stormy undertow of a Latin's passion!

Don Rafael accompanied her as far as the next gallery, where her apartment was evidently situated, and the woman in black paused a few steps ahead, her hands clasped in front of her, the lacquered darkness of her hair drawn back in a knot from a rather severe face.

'Concepcion will ensure that you are given all that you require, Miss Carrol.' The Don's eyes took in the weary smudges under Vanessa's grey-green eyes. 'Rest as long as you wish. I will have luncheon brought to you.'

'You're very kind, *señor*.' Vanessa spoke sincerely, for there was kindness in this man despite his alarming exterior, iron code of honour, and inborn certainty that women were rather helpless, often flighty and continually in need of male guidance.

'*Esta es su casa, señorita*. Rest and sleep—and remember that while we have good memories of those we have loved, they never completely die for us. *Adios!*' His lean fingers pressed her wrist, then he strode away along the carpeted corridor to the stairs, but he didn't go down them, he walked under an archway that presuambly led to his own apartment.

Vanessa's bdroom was vast and high-ceilinged, the bed hewn out of mahogany with a damask-draped headboard and tall baroque posts.

After being shown the sumptuous adjoining bathroom, redolent of the rose essence Concepcion had scattered lavishly into the pink-lined tub that was filling with steamy water, Vanessa assured the woman that she had all she needed and was finally left on her own.

As she heard the bedroom door close, she felt her nerves limply relaxing for the first time in hours. She tiredly shed her ripped clothing, cooled her tub-water, then lowered her aching body into the lapping fragrancy. There was a rubber headrest, and she lay with closed eyes while the ache soaked out of her body if not out of her heart. A long time later she rose out of the scalloped, oyster-pink shell that was sunk deep in the pale green tiles of the floor, and towelled off. A glass-topped toiletry table held flagons of various crystals, dusting powder and cologne. A lavish patting of the cologne left her feeling petal-cool, after which she slipped into the soft silk robe Concepcion had laid ready for her. There were also a small pair of matching mules, and as Vanessa brushed her hair she wondered if Barbara del Quiros had supplied them.

Feeling refreshed and a whole lot more civilized, Vanessa walked into the big bedroom and across the thick carpet, a mosaic of muted colours, to the latticed balcony laced with sun-bright ramblers. She sank down into a contour chair, pulled the silken robe over her slim legs, and brooded with her eyes upon the lizards who basked on the hot balcony paving, jade images but for their pulsing throats.

Ordaz seemed a million miles away, but grief still lay like a stone in her heart. Her uncle had become the father and mother she had lost in her teens. A gentle, understanding, humorous man who had known, despite his bachelorhood, exactly how to be a parent.

Oh God! She rose restlessly and walked to the parapet of the balcony, which she gripped as though she were drowning. Why had she rejected so blindly the offer of sanctuary and accommodation which might have saved her uncle's life? Why hadn't she been sensible and insisted that he come here to Luenda? Tears burned in her eyes, fell over her lashes and rolled slowly down her cheeks. Then to the left of the *castillo* there arose on the warm, somnolent air the sweet and sombre chime of chapel bells. Vanessa listened to them as the sun dried her tears, and they brought the inevitable realization that what had to be, had to be.

The coffee plantation had been not only her uncle's livelihood, it had been his home, his world, the wife that had never come into his life. Had he been persuaded to tear himself away from it, his heart would have been left behind with the well-tended coffee bushes with their satiny green leaves, the spicy aroma that hung about the plantation day and evening, the piano he had liked playing, the books he had enjoyed reading....

Vanessa sighed and relaxed her painful grip on the parapet. When the chapel bells ceased to tumble, she returned to her bedroom and drew the jalousies together behind her. The room was dimmed, but a gorgeous Spanish throwover was a splash of colour on the bed, bright in contrast to its frame and the stepped dais on which it stood. She ran her fingers along the heavy silk fringe and let her mind drift to the Spaniards inhabiting the *castillo*.

They were proud and subtle, she thought. Disdainful

in the face of danger. The men as lithe as panthers, with a snap to their tempers and bred-in-the-bone ideas about the part women were meant to play in life's scheme.

The women?

Vanessa recalled the magnolia skin of Lucia Montez, her dark rose mouth and brown eyes that could look bold as well as mysterious. She was certainly a man's woman, utterly feminine from her gemmed earlobes to her narrow, high-arched feet. Yet despite her femininity she was not the sort to be unnerved by life; she obviously liked men and enjoyed their homage and admiration while retaining that quality considered so essential by Latin males, a charming acceptance of their authority.

With small teeth gnawing her bottom lip, Vanessa glanced at her own tear-stained, faintly rebellious eyes in the mirror of the dressing-table. She twisted one of the glass rods out of a perfume flagon and held it to her nose. Mmmm, haunting and exclusive! The kind of perfume a man of discrimination would like on a woman he desired in his arms ...

There her thoughts scattered as the door opened and a head came poking round it. 'Good, you are not yet sleeping, *cara mia*!' Barbara del Quiros entered with a smile and an armful of clothing, which with a clank of gold coins on a wrist chain she tossed to the bed. 'There you will find a couple of day dresses and one you might wish to wear at dinner this evening. Also I have provided some lingerie and stockings—ah, and I must remember to let you have a pair of evening shoes. We are both small-footed, I see.'

'I'm grateful to you, Miss del Quiros.' Vanessa's smile, however, was constrained, for to be of an independent nature and then in a matter of hours to find yourself dependent upon the generosity of strangers is hard to take. Thank goodness this girl was near her own age and in no way patronizing!

'The *compadre* will no doubt arrange for you to buy clothing of your own, but in the meantime these things will help——' There the girl broke off and stared inquisitively at the tide of sudden colour that swept up Vanessa's slender neck to the roots of her hair.

'He will insist,' Barbara grinned, perching on the side of the lounger and selecting a custard-apple off the fruit platter. 'It is *curioso* that you do not like him. Many women have pursued him—do you not find him exciting?'

'It's just that I—I like to be independent,' Vanessa replied.

'Do not be too much that way with the *compadre*,' his goddaughter advised amusedly as she nibbled the creamy flesh of the fruit in her hand. 'He is very much a Spaniard, let me tell you, with a devil and an angel in him, and like most of our men he likes to believe that women are helpless as lilies. Spanish women know this to be a fairy tale, but they in their turn wish to be kept in hot-houses and tended with care. You women of England do not like this, eh? You demand to be treated as the equals of men?'

'Women are their equals, in my opinion.' Vanessa needed to occupy her hands, and she started to hang in one of the deep wardrobes the dresses which Barbara had lent her.

When she turned from the wardrobe, Barbara was regarding her with her dark, vivid head on one side. You are a new one on me, her pose seemed to say. But then, Vanessa reflected, it was more than likely that this girl who lived in a *castillo* on a Spanish island had not had much contact with Europeans and the outside world.

'It may certainly be true that women are the equals of men,' the girl said, 'but it is wiser to let men think otherwise. We would lose so much if they accepted the view that we are as capable as they. The homage and protectiveness would die out of them. Had you a *novio* back at Ordaz?'

'A boy-friend?' Vanessa shook her head as she folded the lingerie and stockings into a drawer. 'My uncle and I were quite content with each other's company.'

'But surely there would have come a time when you wished to marry?' Barbara dropped the dark stone of the custard-apple into an ashtray on the lounge-side table. 'A life without the love of a husband must be very dull, and there can be no children. I want to be loved, and there must be much *hombria* in the man.'

Vanessa smiled as she turned from the chest of drawers. The word Barbara used was undoubtedly connected with the one Don Rafael had come out with on their drive from the beach to the *castillo*. These people, it seemed, attached a great deal of importance to daring and virility in the male of the species. Head slightly bent, she fingered the apple-green robe that glimmered softly round her slim body. 'Do I thank you for the loan of this negligée, Miss del Quiros?' she asked.

'Please to call me Barbara, for I am going to call you by your first name.' The girl looped tanned arms about her knees and smiled now without a hint of that sullenness Vanessa had noticed down on the beach. Evidently *'el gran caballero'*, as she called her godfather, was rather more bossy at times than she liked, but fundamentally she seemed to have a sunny, easy-going temperament. Her dark glance roved over Vanessa. 'No, the robe is not one of mine. Silk is manufactured at one of Don Rafael's factories, so it is possibly a sample garment made up from the silk. The colour is most suitable for you.' Then with a hint of most unexpected shyness, the girl added: 'You look as though you have stepped out of a Velazquez canvas with your copper hair, emerald eyes and buttermilk skin.'

Vanessa caught her breath at the compliment and involuntarily tightened the sash of the robe. The frankness of these Latins was disconcerting to say the least! 'You'd be right if you were talking about Señora Montez,' she laughed.

'La viuda' wears paint,' Barbara retorted with devastating youthful cruelty. 'I have never seen *her* straight out of her bath. Then, I think, her skin would be quite sallow. Vanessa, do you consider that I am *bonita?*'

'Surely you have a mirror in your bedroom?' Vanessa teased. 'Of course you're pretty. That's probably one of the reasons why your godfather doesn't want you cantering about the island like a boy.'

'It is very true that he would have me behave with more decorum,' a shrug of the slim shoulders, laughter in the vivid dark eyes. 'What happened is that my *dueña* had to return to Spain to tend a sick sister, so I am free to roam like a *gitana*. The Don will soon find another gaoler to accompany me everywhere, but for the time being I am enjoying myself. *Que hombre!*'

Yes, quite a man, Vanessa silently agreed. Half corsair, half overlord who took his responsibilities very seriously. Tenuously there stole into her mind a picture of Lucia Montez held close in his masterful arms. She was lovely and exciting in a way Barbara was as yet too young to understand, with everything in common with the *hidalgo*. His autocratic blood, and most important of all the Latin temperament—which was ice over fire.

'Your eyes have grown dark and you are thinking of Ordaz, are you not, Vanessa?' Barbara's voice was sympathetic. 'I had better leave you to rest, otherwise my *padrino* will be scolding me again. I will see you later, eh?'

Vanessa nodded, and after the door had closed on Barbara, she sank on to her bed and willed herself to go limp. She turned her face into the silken pillows, her mind a chaos of intermingling scenes that threatened to give her no rest. But sleep finally dropped a curtain over her disturbed mind and she drifted away from an awareness of the strange turn her life had taken.

She awoke suddenly several hours later and saw through the mosquito netting now swathing her bed that someone was entering the room. It was the severe-looking Concepcion, carrying in her hands a tray on which stood various dishes under silver domes, a coffee pot and a cup on a saucer. Concepcion set down the tray and opened the jalousies, then she looped back the muslin bed drapes. 'You have slept well, Señorita Carrol?' she enquired politely, banking the pillows behind Vanessa's shoulders and standing the tray across her lap.

Vanessa gave her a smiling nod and lifted a silver cover from several crisp rolled tortillas. 'Thank you for letting down my mosquito netting,' she said. 'I'm afraid I forgot it.'

The tall, thin woman in the long black gown was turning away towards the door, now she glanced round with an enquiring expression in rather hooded, unemotional eyes.

'It was not I who arranged the netting, *señorita*,' she replied in a voice that matched her eyes. 'I have not been in your room since leaving you four hours ago.'

Her English was heavily accented but perfectly understandable, and Vanessa stared at her a moment, her fingers clenching with an unconscious rigidity on the neck of the tabasco container. 'It must have been someone else,' she shrugged. 'Perhaps Señorita del Quiros.'

The woman inclined her dark head, then went silently away, closing the door as though she feared that the faintest click would cause discomfort to the *compadre's* guest.

Vanessa poured coffee into the pale green cup and added cream from the little silver pitcher. The pain of remembering was with her again and had to be fought, therefore she tackled gallantly the crunchy tortillas, button mushrooms that melted in her mouth, and buttery potato ring with spinach in the centre. Her sweet was a banana fluff set with dices of pineapple and sections of tangerine, but she ate without being aware of taste and finally set aside her tray with a feeling of relief.

Her arm brushed the netting as she settled back against her pillows and again she briefly wondered who had entered while she slept and swathed her head against the possible intrusion of a mosquito. These people were certainly thoughtful of their guests, and yet it was still galling to Vanessa's independent spirit that she was being forced to yield her will to Don Rafael de Domerique's. No other man had yet managed that, for she had valued her freedom at Ordaz, her position as mistress of an attractive home whose master was her easy-going uncle.

With her hands clasped behind her head she studied the richly ornamented ceiling above her bed, especially the passionate Spanish faces of the knights and their ladies.

Love, she thought driftingly, was to be fulfilled to the very core of your being. Joy, suffering, tears, laughter ... these were the chiselled facets of the gem that was true love. Did she want to feel such terrors and wonders and tribulations? She supposed she did, and that was why a lukewarm alliance with one of those geologists or doctor visitors to the plantation had never appealed to her. After working for long stretches in the jungle and then coming again into a civilized home, any woman seemed angelic to them, and Vanessa had always known that those quick infatuations had to be cooled down and discouraged before she got involved in something that would never have brought a deep and lasting bliss. Only a sense of being at a man's beck and call and of doing her duty rather than offering every cell and fibre to his demands ...

Deep in thought, she hadn't heard the door tapped upon and opened, and a prolonged shiver ran over her as a deep voice said: 'Concepcion informs me that you have slept. Are you now feeling more rested, Miss Carrol?'

Vanessa's glance flashed round and there by the door stood Don Rafael with his hands in the pockets of a dressing-gown of rich, sombre silk. His hair was slicked back to a raven smoothness from his broad forehead, and as always his gaze was impossible to evade under the strong arching of his brows.

'Yes, thank you,' she replied, polite as a schoolgirl and feeling not unlike one with her copper hair still tousled from her nap. Slim, tensed in the ornate bed on its stepped dais, she was also intensely aware of her bare state under the silk robe and it was all she could do not to snatch the Spanish throwover around her and hide prudishly from the detached scrutiny of this man as he strolled to the side of the bed.

His glance took in her luncheon tray—late lunch, for the clock showed that it was past four o'clock—and he deliberately lifted one of the domes to see how much she had eaten.

'I—I did my best,' she said defensively.

'So I see.' He gazed down at her, a disconcerting glimmer of amusement in his eyes. 'You find this room to your satisfaction, Miss Carrol?'

'It's very beautiful,' she was edging together the folds of her robe and resenting in her every fibre the shyness aroused in her by this tall, imperious man who probably thought of her not as a woman but as a teenager like his goddaughter.

'This was always my mother's bedroom.' He seemed not to notice the heightened colour in Vanessa's cheeks. 'It is one of the finest in the *castillo*, but perhaps you appreciate more modern furniture and embellishments?'

'Not in a *castillo* setting,' she smiled slightly, softening towards him because of that reference to his mother and the look of gentleness it had brought to his mouth.

'But the bed intimidates a little, I think.' Amusement again lit sparks in his eyes as they dwelt on her. 'Is there not a fable about a princess who was irritated by a mere pea all the way through a layer of mattresses? I read such a tale as a boy, and there was an illustration you very much resemble, perched as you are under that filigreed canopy.'

Her fingers clenched on the throwover even as she smiled at the remark, for she was being told in a humorously roundabout way not to be so prickly with him, to relax, for he was really not an eagle about to swoop on a doe. It was all very well for *him* not to think of himself as an eagle, but with that haughty nose, those flecked-jet eyes and that imperious mouth—well, he was bound to be overpowering in a girl's bedroom!

'So, you smile a little and look less tense.' His left brow flickered teasingly. 'You invariably betray an awkwardness in my presence which intrigues me, I must admit, and I can only surmise what is passing through your mind. Come, you should be thankful that it was I who snatched you from danger last night. You might think that the adoring Mr Conroy would accept a mere thank-you for his services, but I assure you he would not. There are few knights in shining armour, *chiquilla*.'

'I'm well aware of that, *señor*,' she retorted, bristling anew at his reference to Jack Conroy, whose visits and letters to the plantation had been airily pleasant and in no way adoring. It was an added annoyance that the Don seemed aware that she had favoured Jack and enjoyed his friendship. Darned officious Spaniard! He needn't think he was controlling her life! Her eyes flashed silver-green and she said recklessly: 'In what coin do I pay *you* for my life, Don Rafael—the same as that you think an Englishman would expect?'

For a moment there seemed utter silence in that beautiful room with its glowing ceiling, then all at once Don Rafael was bending over Vanessa, one lean hand gripping a bedpost, his eyes glittering so close to her that she could count the small lines that rayed out beside them. For electrically charged seconds the Don pinned her on his dark steely gaze like a butterfly—she writhed inwardly that he should be aware of the fear that hammered her heart.

'You flatter yourself, Miss Carrol,' he drawled at last. 'What might appeal to a young colt like Conroy is not necessarily to the taste of a man who has seen more of the world and its diversions. The warmest fires often grow out of green wood, it is true, but you are still green wood as far as I am concerned.' He straightened, his hands returned to his pockets, his regard became cool. 'All I ask in return for your life is that you remain here at the *castillo* until you are able to return to England in a position of independence. I am insisting upon this as a friend of your good uncle. It is for his sake that I keep you here—you comprehend?'

Humiliated by what she had said to him, she nodded and wished he would leave her alone, but he blandly enquired if Barbara had brought her the promised clothing. Ah, that was excellent. The dresses would suffice until she felt in the mood to go shopping.

'Don Rafael,' she broke in huskily, 'I don't wish to impose on your generosity more than I have to. I don't suppose I shall be here all that long——'

'Nevertheless you will need articles of clothing of your own.' Her argument was swept away as though it had never been, and after strolling to the balcony doors for a possessive glance out over his immediate territory, he turned to survey the room with that cool arrogance of his. Above him, depicted by the brush of a sixteenth-century artist, were faces that held his same look of proud hauteur with a leashed emotionalism behind it. Had love of a woman yet touched the heart of the *hidalgo*? Had that curt mouth ever softened to tenderness and whispered the sweet inanities that lovers whisper? Vanessa somehow doubted it, though *la viuda* Montez was obviously fascinated—not to say determined.

'Now you are rested,' he said, 'I suggest that you dress and join my goddaughter in the garden. You will find her an amusing and diverting companion, and solitude at this time can bring you only despondency.'

Lost in her thoughts, Vanessa was staring at him, and a quick frown drew his straight brows together. 'You will do as I instruct, Miss Carrol.' Having given his orders he strode to the door, treated her to a detached bow, then was gone. Vanessa slowly shivered as though a cold wind had passed over her, and as she slid off the big bed she told herself that as soon as possible she would get in touch with Jack Conroy and see if he could lend her some money so she could stay at an hotel. Being under obligation to Jack would be easier to tolerate than feeling herself a virtual prisoner at the Castillo d'Oro.

Her teeth bit down on her underlip, for out on the balcony she had noticed that this suite of rooms was set within a tower of the *castillo*, and there was a cool look of ruthlessness about Don Rafael de Domerique that was far more noticeable on his own territory than it had been upon his visits to Ordaz.

CHAPTER THREE

VERY gradually Vanessa was absorbing the emotional shock of losing her uncle, and the following days at the *castillo* were made easier for her by the company of Barbara del Quiros. The girl had an audacious tongue at times, and plenty of impatient, nervous energy, but she kept Vanessa from brooding as, probably, no one else could have done at this time.

Some mornings they swam, others they took gallops along the beach after Vanessa had been provided with a mount. Frothy wavelets ran to the edge of the sands as the two girls cantered side by side, colourful fishing craft were silhouetted against the sun-dusted sky, while sea birds winged through the sparkling air. It was an hour to which Vanessa looked forward, and it wasn't entirely spoiled when now and again Don Rafael appeared out of the blue and joined them in a gallop. He sat his mount as though he were part of it, and the open-necked shirt he wore with his well-cut breeches made him look carefree and much younger.

That was when you were riding a little way behind him, Vanessa corrected herself when this thought came into her mind. Seen full face he was always typical of the autocrats who had abounded in the colonial days. Despotic, kind in his own aloof way, but a woman's adversary rather than a friend.

Then came a morning when peaceful relations scattered like a spindrift over the tide-way coral. Why, he demanded of Barbara, had she gone out last night without asking his permission? Vanessa felt her pulses jolt for the girl as she recalled the Don's simmering displeasure at the dining table, after he had sent a servant to fetch his goddaughter, only to be informed that she was nowhere in the *castillo*.

Lean and angry, his black brows joined in a bar above his eyes, his glance had dwelt for a menacing instant upon Vanessa, as though he suspected her of knowing his goddaughter's whereabouts. Then cloaked again in his suave courtesy he had turned to answer a question put to him by Lucia Montez.

It had been an uncomfortable evening altogether. Sociable Ruy Alvadaas had gone off somewhere for the weekend, and Doña Manuela, the Don's elderly grandmother, only joined the family for dinner upon special occasions. Vanessa had escaped to her room after coffee in the *sala*, and though Don Rafael had still looked ready to pounce with a question, he had refrained and coolly bowed her out of the door, watching, she sensed, as she hurried across the hall and up the stairs away from him. His displeasure had a way of lingering like a whiplash. Uncalled-for anger upon this occasion, for Vanessa's friendship with Barbara did not extend as yet to complete confidence. The girl invariably had plenty to talk about, but she rarely talked about herself.

When Vanessa heard Don Rafael throw his question across at his goddaughter, she let her mount drop a few paces behind them. It was a private matter, this business of Barbara's absence from the *castillo* last evening, and Vanessa neither understood nor appreciated the rigid Spanish rules that single women were expected to follow. Always to have a chaperon with them when they took an outing; never to do anything without first asking permission of the master of the house. It was feudal! Crying out for rebellion on a girl's part.

Though she tried not to listen, she heard a rapid exchange of angry words ahead of her. There was in Barbara's manner a hint of defiance touching despair as she half faced round on her black horse and argued with the man who was determined to control her life. Then all at once rising emotion got the better of her Latin temper and she lifted her plaited riding-whip and brought it down upon the lean hand stretched to her mount's bridle. A livid mark sprang across the coppery skin and as the Don involuntarily released his grip on the bridle, Barbara flicked her horse's flank and he bounded away.

Vanessa saw the Don's lean figure tauten like steel the

instant before it cuts into action, then with a savage movement of his hand he swung his mount so he was facing her. 'I had better not ride after the foolish child,' he crisped. 'Now tell me, Miss Carrol, you have no knowledge of where and with whom she went last night?'

'None at all, *señor*.' Vanessa sat upright in her saddle, and though his eyes were glittering so fiercely, she braved them to defend Barbara's actions. 'In my opinion a girl of Barbara's age is entitled to a bit of freedom, and I can quite understand her revolt against your insistence that she be chaperoned everywhere and kept on leading strings like a child. It's—why, it's humiliating!'

After she had said this a short silence hung between them. The coppery skin was stretched taut over his blade of a nose, his finely wrought cheekbones and angular jaw, and yet what Vanessa felt was a curious excitement rather than apprehension. 'Women have a habit of airing what is in their minds, and you are certainly no exception, Miss Carrol,' he finally said. 'So you think it right that the child who is in my charge should slip out of her home in the late hours, obviously with the intention of meeting a man?'

'Why obviously, *señor*?' Vanessa cut in. 'She may have gone for a moonlight swim, a late stroll, a visit to a girl friend.'

'She may, indeed,' he allowed. 'But permit me to say that I know my goddaughter rather better than you, and that demonstration a few minutes ago, the using of her whip on my hand, was sheer female fury that I had guessed correctly that she was in the company of a man last night. A man, moreover, of whom I would not approve.'

'Barbara's young and pretty,' Vanessa fought back, 'and it's perfectly natural she should want friends of the opposite sex. Your feudal outmoded system of segregating your young girls and keeping them from mixing with young men is asking for trouble.'

'Yes, we have been doing this for a long time, Miss Carrol, but the result has not been a spate of disastrous marriages as in your country, where girls select a husband regardless of parental wishes or the young man's prospects.

You will not agree, *señorita*, but the parents or the guardian of a girl are often the wisest judges of her character and the kind of man she should marry, and it must cause much heart-burning to English parents that they have so little say in this important matter.' The Don's unsmiling glance swept Vanessa's face, then he deliberately added: 'Your good uncle confided to me, some time ago, that he had doubts regarding your growing friendship with the young Conroy. Did you know of this, that Señor Carrol was concerned?'

Yes, Vanessa had known that Uncle Len regarded Jack as a bit of a lighthearted rover, but it infuriated her that Don Rafael should imply disapproval of a friend of hers. The young geologist *was* a friend, not someone with whom she was contemplating marriage—and even if she were, it was no business of this domineering *hidalgo*'s!

'My uncle would never have interfered in my life,' she retorted. 'He was tolerant enough to understand that what makes a woman happy is not necessarily a well-ordered life.'

'*Vaya?*' The unusual jetty eyes went narrow. 'You would be prepared to accompany Conroy on his expeditions into various jungles? This, I think, would take a great deal of courage—and love.'

'Of course, *señor*.' She tossed back her hair, secured by a white headband and ripe as a gleaner's sheaf in the sun. 'I wouldn't marry anyone unless I cared a great deal for him.'

'I am inclined to believe that.' All at once the alien voice held a note of tolerance, as though he had no intention of being angered by her emotional peccadilloes, as he probably regarded them. 'You miss your good uncle, *señorita?*'

She glanced down at the glossy arc of her mount's neck and saw the proud mane all blurry as tears rose in her eyes. She fought for composure, won her battle and could again look at her companion. 'It has helped, being with Barbara,' she said. 'Somehow she seems to want my company as much as I need hers. It's important to—to feel needed.'

'With such a sentiment I am in full agreement.' Don Rafael studied her, then added: 'I would like to discuss this more fully, therefore let us go over into the shade of those palms.' He slipped his feet free of hooded stirrups and swung from his Moorish saddle. His lean right hand gripped Vanessa's as he assisted her to the coral sand, after which he secured their mounts' bridles to the slender trunk of a coconut palm.

They strolled, themselves, to the cool shade of a clump of bamboo palms, whose rustlings mingled pleasantly with the seductive murmurings of the sea. Spray blew from the wave crests to the beach, and Vanessa, her gaze bent upon a tentacled jellyfish, felt the brush of the Don's arm as he fired the tip of a cheroot and thrust his lighter into a pocket of his breeches. The aromatic smoke eddied to Vanessa's nostrils, and when she slanted an upward glance at the Don she wasn't quite prepared to find him looking down at her. It was a look, moreover, that seemed to go to the depths of her eyes, as though he searched for something in her that he had not yet found.

'You like what you have so far seen of our island, Miss Carrol?' he asked.

It was with an effort that she withdrew her glance from his and gazed towards the lagoon and the foam-laced reef. She could feel her hands clenching the fibred trunk of the palm against which she leant, and she knew that these glimpses of gentleness in her self-imposed guardian were more rattling than his chilly aloofness, or his biting sarcasm. She told herself irritatedly that she preferred him as she had always known him, slightly dangerous and looking down his imperious nose at her youthful gaucheries. In a purring mood he threw her off balance.

'You do not find Luenda congenial, *señorita*?' he prompted, blowing a blue ring of smoke past her brooding eyes. 'I had hoped that you would do so.'

'*La isla esta bella, señor*. I shall miss so much beauty when I leave.' She perversely hoped that to speak of leaving would shatter his good humour and make of him the adversary she preferred tackling.

'You will not be leaving yet.' He steam-rollered her remark as though it were a gauzy fly, and marched on over the debris with sublime indifference. 'One day soon I must take you to see one of the *viñas* where we grow the grapes for the wine you said made your head whirl the other evening. Last year's vintage was a good one, this year it should be even stronger. The *viñedo* is one of the most interesting parts of the island, for the peasants have undiluted Spanish blood and they make of the wine pressing a true *fiesta*. You have never seen this, eh, *señorita*? The laughter, the singing, the feuds that spring up between the young men when their bold eyes fall upon the same *muchacha*. Life is so simple to be a peasant—one might almost wish——'

There he abruptly broke off what he had been about to say, gave one of his deep shrugs and changed the subject. 'This matter of Barbarita, about which you think I am being so high-handed,' his left hand described a gesture of impatience. 'Let me explain that a friendship between a Spanish girl and a man who is *soltero*—that is a bachelor—is likely to be misconstrued by the islanders as a courtship. Our rules of courtship are not to be played around with, also I have private plans for Barbarita which do not include this casual *novio* she has found herself.'

Vanessa glanced at him and saw that he was looking at his most forbidding. Impossible, she reflected, to imagine him as a peasant who cultivated grapes, crushed them in the great vats and made bold eyes at the golden-skinned girls, one of whom he would like to love and make his wife...

But no, this man could not marry out of his class, nor indulge in dreams of doing so!

The Don had evidently been watching the various expressions chasing across Vanessa's face, for he said with a touch of irony: 'Are you comparing the rigidity of our codes with those of your own country? Are you thinking that we are unjust to our women because we chaperon and guide them? Let me assure you that Spanish women are not unhappy in their imprisonment, as you probably think of it. They like to be cherished.'

'Cherished, yes,' Vanessa returned, 'but not bullied.'

'You think me a bullying man?' The lift of a black brow. 'You think I am harsh towards Barbara? In Spain she would be kept under much more rigid supervision than here on the island, for she is without *pariente* and due to inherit quite a fortune when she comes of age. That is why I cannot permit further meetings with this young man. They must be—how would you say it?—nipped in the bud.'

'Forbidding a girl to do something is asking for opposition, *señor*.'

'I am aware of that, *señorita*.' Somewhat impudently he stroked into place a devil's peak of hair which, she had noticed before, was inclined to spring up when a breeze got at his black head. 'Most Spaniards have cognizance of the female psyche, that is why I agree that it is important to a woman to feel needed. You have this need, while Barbarita has need of a chaperon. Employed by me in this capacity, you would have the authority to veto outings of which I would not approve.'

In the interval of silence that followed his surprising offer, Vanessa heard the drumbeat of her pulses, the crying of big-winged birds fishing beyond the reef and above her the quake of palm fronds. This was what she had wanted, wasn't it, employment of some sort and the security of independence? Why then didn't she say at once that she would be glad to take on the job?

Then she gave a start as she felt long fingers close over her left shoulder and the pressure of a thumb in the fragile hollow below her collarbone. 'I must soon hire someone to act as Barbara's *dueña*,' the suavity had gone out of the Don's voice and it was cool again, 'and you will recall that you were asking for employment within an hour or so of your arrival here. You talked of your writhing independence, as though I had it impaled on the point of a pin. *Ventredieu*, you manage to pack much independence into a small package!'

Exasperation mingled with the ice in his voice, and Vanessa was almost certain that he fought a compulsion to give her a shake. He had moved closer while talking, and she felt a constriction in her chest at his nearness, a difficulty in breathing ... a molten something was streaming from his touch into her very bones. She clenched her hands and felt her teeth locking together. She prayed for him to let go of her.

He must have felt her feverish desire to be released, for his fingers gripped, then relaxed and were gone. As she edged away physically and mentally from that moment of intimacy, he said, in a caustic tone of voice: 'Rest assured that the dislike is not all on your side, Miss Carrol. I have disliked you, often, upon my visits to Ordaz, but we are at the moment talking business and I had the impression that you had developed a feeling of friendship for my god-daughter. Am I mistaken, after all?'

'Of course I like Barbara.' If she emphasized the words, she felt justified in view of his frankness. 'But I don't happen to think that I'm cut out to be a policewoman.'

His nostrils went blade-thin, while the muscles tautened about his mouth. 'You have nerve, of an irritating kind,' he crisped. 'You think I will not lose my temper completely with you because you are the niece of Lennard Carrol, but circumstances have proved already that you are not inviolable because you are that rarity, that gem among women, an English Miss.'

'You—brute!' she gasped, and never had she felt such an itch to slap a face. Dislike of him raged through her; from the ridge of his black brows to his arrogantly booted feet he was an object she had to get away from, quickly, before she treated him to the satisfaction of the tears prickling her eyelids. She turned, took several steps, then froze as there slithered down the trunk of a bamboo the chequered length of a snake. It weaved its head, hideously, only inches from Vanessa's pallid face, then a cry broke from her as a steely arm locked itself about her waist and she was plucked backwards against the Don's hard chest. The plaited thong of his riding-whip cracked against the snake with deadly precision and as it fell to the sand a booted foot crushed down on the nasty head. The chequered body writhed, then went flaccid, and the pressure of forearm muscles relaxed against Vanessa's ribs to let her catch her breath.

'Was it venomous?' she gasped.

'Dangerous enough.' Then with easy strength, and before Vanessa could thwart the intention, the Don swung her up into his arms and strode with her towards their tethered mounts. As he put her into the saddle of her chestnut he looked directly into her eyes and broke into his slow, irony-tinged smile.

'Not many of us, you see, can be completely independent, Miss Carrol,' he said. 'You needed my help just then, as I need your assistance with Barbara. Not to police her, I assure you, but to be her companion and friend.'

Vanessa met his smile and suddenly felt confused. Darn him! He made himself detestable one minute, then switched on the coaxing charm and threw out of gear all her previous reactions to him. She gripped her bridle, as though she needed its support. 'I've always been under the impression, Don Rafael, that you regarded me as rather flighty.' A nerve flickered under the diffident smile upon her mouth. 'Doesn't one need dignity to be a *dueña*?'

'I would not expect dignity of one—so young.' His jetty gaze dwelt on her slender neck and arms, pale in contrast to the fumed-oak look of his throat and forearms. Vanessa had long since given up hope of acquiring a tan, blaming her inability to do so upon an ingredient in her skin which wouldn't co-operate, despite her sunbathing sessions on the veranda of the plantation. Catching the Don's scrutiny, she felt a tide of warmth creep up her neck into her cheeks. What was he thinking, that a spot of responsibility might help her to grow up?

But, with a sweeping gesture that took in the beach, the sea, the distant jutting of mountains, he said: 'Does the tragedy of Ordaz make you feel guilty about enjoying the beauty we have to offer? Is that why you are opposed to the idea of staying here? This would be understandable, but time was meant to veil the bad things that happen to us, *chica*.'

The scenic beauty and peace of Luenda did throw into

relief the stark awfulness of what had happened at Ordaz, but there was an underlying reason beyond guilt and sadness that made Vanessa feel restive about remaining on the island. It was as though—absurd notion—she were in some kind of danger from which she had to run before it caught up with her.

'I am not asking you to make up your mind right away,' the Don lightly pressed her hand. 'Think about it, and if you continue to have reservations about the undertaking, then I shall look elsewhere for a chaperon. But bear in mind that Barbarita would prefer, and possibly respond to someone nearer her own age. Someone, moveover, who understands that it is not all roses to be young, that there are many thorns to stab the vulnerable, unsophisticated feelings.'

'Yet, knowing this, you'll ruthlessly forbid Barbara a friendship she must want badly,' Vanessa argued. 'She defies your authority to go after it.'

'I shall not ruthlessly forbid it, Miss Carrol.' He looked sardonic. 'Barbara defies me now and again, but believe it or not she has an affection for me, and she knows I have a concern for her happiness. I assure you it will not be necessary for me to be—ruthless.'

'Your definition of the term might be vastly different from mine,' Vanessa shot back at him, thinking him a lean inquisitor as he stood there beside her mount; the hand Barbara had whipped was stroking her mount's glossy neck, the sun struck raven glints from his hair and revealed the topaz flecks in his deeply set eyes. A wincingly attractive man, but not a comfortable one.

'Often one has to be cruel in order to be kind, Miss Carrol.' He shrugged, then took a glance at his crocodile-strapped watch. 'I have an hour to spare before I begin work with Carlitos, my secretary, therefore I suggest that we make our way to a nearby *venta* and take breakfast there. It will be an experience for you, a not unpleasant one, I promise.'

'Breakfast—at a *venta*?' she echoed. 'But won't they wonder at the *castillo* where we have got to?'

'The master of the *castillo* makes his own time.' Suddenly his smile was teasing as he swung into his own saddle. 'We have breakfasted *alfresco* before. Do you remember?'

Yes, she remembered. He had talked of the beauty and cruelty of love upon that occasion. For these Spaniards it seemed to hold too much of the latter emotion for it to be a comfortable experience; by tradition their marriages were arranged, they did not fall headlong in love, or run off together. A suitable fiancé was selected for a girl and when in due course she was considered emotionally ready for marriage, the ceremony took place. Vanessa had heard that such marriages were often an enormous success, but what of girls like Barbara who rebelled against the system? Those who found love with a passing stranger, yet were forced to give him up in order to gratify the wishes of parents, or a guardian?

It was a monstrous system, Vanessa decided, her green eyes flashing as she cantered round a groin of rock in the wake of the Don's black horse. And that man had his gall, asking her to take on the job of restraining his goddaughter's natural instincts! Of ensuring she toed the Domerique line until his cold-blodded private plans were ready to be revealed. No doubt he had a suitor lined up for the girl, someone blue-blooded and rich—not unlike himself.

Vanessa's grip so tightened on her mount's bridle, that he tossed his head and gave a snort. The Don turned at once to say over his shoulder: 'Ride carefully just here, *pequeña*. This is no longer part of my private property and the beach is not kept clear of rock.'

'Very well, *señor*,' she replied politely, 'I'll go carefully.'

Very carefully, she added to herself. Which meant that she'd not rush to make a decision about this job he had offered her. It could be that Barbara had more need of her than she had at first realized.

An ancient cart track led up from the beach to the *venta*, whose white-washed walls showed rough and sun-scaled through rents in purple and saffron cloaks of wistaria and allamanda. A Moorish archway led into the cobbled courtyard, where chickens grubbed and husky little donkeys browsed between the shafts of thatch and seaweed carts.

On the *ajotea*, the flat roof, family linen bleached in the sunshine. Beneath the green fan of a bush palm sat an old lady in black, her face as shrivelled as a brown pea, rocking with her foot a basket-cradle that presumably held a baby.

As the two riders trotted into the courtyard, she slowly took a clay pipe from her mouth and gazed towards them as they dismounted. When she said: '*Quién esté ahi?*' Vanessa guessed her jetty beads of eyes to be sightless.

Don Rafael gripped Vanessa's elbow and led her across to the old woman. '*Buenos dias*, Maria,' he said. '*Qué tal, señora?*'

In the exchange that followed, in that odd way one can sometimes catch the trend of a foreign language, Vanessa gathered that old Maria was going along quite well and that her baby grandson was the joy of her twilight.

'*Me alegro*, Maria.' Don Rafael shot a smile down at the tawny baby boy who played so contentedly with his toes. 'You have a fine *muchacho* of a grandson. He takes after your son in looks, I think, but he has Paquita's smile.'

'That Paquita,' the old woman gave a nod of satisfaction, 'she is a good wife, *gracias a Dios*, and such a mother. My Ramon was never so happy as now.' A gnarled brown hand sought the Don's and pressed it. 'It was you, *compadre*, who worked the miracle for those two. They would never have found this happiness if you had not paid for Paquita to have that operation. Now my Ramon has his son, who is called Leon Rafael for you, *señor*.'

'Ah, if I have a *muchacho* named for me, then I must make him a gift.' Don Rafael withdrew a wallet from the hip pocket of his breeches and extracted several banknotes, which he put into Maria's hand, adding quietly: 'It is better not to tell Ramon, who considers still that he is in my debt. Buy small things for the boy whenever he has need of them, and keep this a small secret between us, eh?'

'You have your good mother's generous heart, *compadre*. Bless you and yours!' Old Maria pressed her wrinkled lips to his gift, and as she stowed the notes into a capacious pocket of her black dress, she watched his face above her just as though she saw the forceful dark features, the slashing brows and breeze-peaked hair.

Suddenly she said: 'I think you have a little heartache, Don Rafael. I sense it in the atmosphere.'

'Come, Maria,' he broke into a laugh, 'are you trying to make me believe in your gipsy magic?'

'Laugh away, *mi amigo grande*, like all the men, but these eyes of mine are not as blind as eyes that can see.' Then, with a disconcerting suddenness, those sightless eyes were turned upon Vanessa, standing so quietly where an avocado tree hung its green fruits above her head. 'You have brought a pretty *turista* to see us, Don Rafael?' old Maria asked.

He turned to look at Vanessa, and unexpectedly she coloured beneath his gaze. Strange, but it had never occurred to her to wonder whether he regarded her as pretty. Not that she thought herself pretty. In her own estimation her cheekbones were over-pronounced, her mouth too wide, and her chin had rather an obstinate set to it.

'Perhaps you are a clairvoyant, Maria,' Don Rafael quirked a wicked left eyebrow at Vanessa. 'I do have a young *inglesa* with me, and the heartache you sense is hers. A fortnight ago she experienced a very sad loss, now she stays at the *castillo* for a while.'

'You have my sympathy, *señorita*,' Maria said, 'and I bid you welcome to the Venta Riera.'

'*Gracias, señora.*' Vanessa put her hand into the gnarled one that was held out to her, but Maria didn't shake it, she proceeded to trace with a fingertip the lines criss-crossing the palm. After several tense moments the old woman gave a throaty chuckle. 'A saint could not persuade this one to do what goes against her will,' she murmured.

Vanessa felt herself go warm and cold there beside Don Rafael, too polite to withdraw her hand from Maria's, but wanting to with every nerve in her body. There was no knowing what this elderly gipsy might reveal, and *he* could understand every word of her Spanish, while Vanessa had to snatch at a word here and there and make what she could of the disclosures.

Her eyes lifted to the bland face of the Don, who said, rather wickedly: 'Do you wish me to translate, *señorita*?'

'N-no——'

'I think I should. It is all very interesting.' His eyes were glinting with laughter. 'Maria says that you have much love to give, but that you will not give it willingly. This, she adds, is because you are *inglesa* and therefore cool—on the surface. Your lifeline is long but not always smooth, holding the promise of three events which will give you much happiness. One of these events looms near, it is the biggest—it may already have happened...'

The rest was not quite so significant, and when Maria's bony fingers let go of Vanessa's, she stepped away on rather tremulous legs. She couldn't quite take all this light-heartedly. The blind palm-reader, the white-walled seclusion of the *venta*, the clutching scents and sounds all around, created a mood that was both enchanting and unnerving. And Vanessa, after all, was female and therefore vibrantly responsive to the occult and what lay in her stars.

She believed Maria! She knew it could all happen, the bursting free of the love she had not yet given, the joys and tribulations that would flower out of that love. It was exciting, and weird, and suddenly she wanted to hide the expression in her eyes from the man who had seemed to mock it all. She knelt on the grass beside the basket-cradle of young Leon Rafael, whose big sparkling eyes, and pink gums gnawing at a toe, were enough to steal any girl's heart. 'You brown imp,' Vanessa chuckled, when he abandoned his toe and decided that her thumb looked tasty. 'Yes, you're eatable yourself, you rogue.'

'You understand not a word, but you enjoy it, eh, cheeky one?' Don Rafael put down a hand and stroked the black fluff on the baby's head. 'This is a woman who speaks to you, *chiquito*, and though all your life you will make eyes at such pretty mysteries, you will never quite understand them.'

Then with that easy strength Vanessa had already sampled, the Don took her by the shoulders and swung her to her feet. 'It is unwise to kneel in the grass,' he said. 'It might have concealed another *bête noir*.'

Vanessa brushed at the knees of the riding trousers Barbara had lent her and tried, nonchalantly, to ignore the fact that the pressure of his hard fingers still lingered on her shoulders. So gentle with a child, so tough with a woman! Did this man dislike women, though he felt their attraction? '*Señor hidalgo—bienvenido!*' exclaimed a voice, and Vanessa glanced up and saw a plump young woman coming across the courtyard. She wore a blouse of hand-worked lace tucked into a black skirt. Gold hoops swung from her ear-lobes, and her hair was drawn back sleekly from a smiling face set with a pair of lively dark eyes.

'*Buenos dias*, Paquita.' Then in slow English, the Don added: 'Miss Carrol and myself have just been admiring your handsome son. He is a child to be very proud of.'

Paquita gave the Don an eloquent look, then, gold hoops swinging, she gave her son a loving hug. 'Not to eat a toe, *querido!*' She laughingly took a crunchy *rosco* from her apron pocket and inserted it into the gummy young mouth. 'He grows so fast, and eats so well,' she added proudly. 'Soon he will be helping Ramon at the *viña*.'

'Work proceeds well at the *viña*?' Don Rafael looked interested. 'The foreman at my own *viña* promises a record vintage.'

'Ramon is also of that opinion, *señor hidalgo*.' Paquita crossed herself with the unselfconscious fervency of Latins. 'This has been a *bello verano* for us, is this not so, *madrecita*?' She affectionately pressed the bent shoulder of her mother-in-law, who sat puffing drowsily at her clay pipe, immersed in memories of the past as the young become lost in dreams of the future.

'*Ay*, Paquita. The grapes grow sweet in the sun.' A smile climbed over the wrinkled old face. 'When the grapes are sweet, there is love in the air.'

Only the old, and only the young, dare to say such things. The poetry of the wise and the innocent, indescribably moving, so that Vanessa felt a prickling along her arms and her scalp, just as one does when stirred by certain pieces of music.

Beside her Don Rafael spoke in Spanish to Paquita, then he leaned down towards old Maria and informed her that he and Señorita Carrol were going to eat breakfast in the garden.

She nodded, bemused by the sunshine and her elderly contentment. '*Ah, bueno, muy macho. Hasta luego, señor.*'

'*Hasta luego, señora.*'

Vanessa echoed the Spanish words, which sounded so much warmer than their English equivalent, then she and Don Rafael followed Paquita around the side of the *venta* to the garden. The *comedor*, it seemed, was occupied by several rough carters and Paquita did not consider it proper that the *señor hidalgo* and his guest should take breakfast in their presence. They passed a colourful water-walk with an archway of water falling into a long stone trough, fed, Vanessa was informed, by the sweet-water stream that gave the *venta* its attractive name. Circular, wrought-iron tables stood beneath the dappled shade of trees, and Don Rafael indicated the one beneath a guava laden with crimson bells.

'*Si, señor.*' Paquita flicked the chairs with her apron, then bustled away to fetch cutlery, a tablecloth and a menu.

It was an enchanting spot in which to take breakfast, and Vanessa could feel the warmth and rustic pleasantness getting at her usual reserve with Don Rafael and melting its icicles.

'This menu is in Spanish, so shall I choose for you, Miss Carrol?' he asked.

'Please, *señor*,' she replied. Though it was really amazing the amount of Spanish she was beginning to pick up. She knew, for instance, that when old Maria had wished him goodbye, her *muy macho* had meant that he was much of a man. She fingered her napkin and listened to his deep voice ordering their breakfast. Paquita was obviously bursting with curiosity, and Vanessa hoped to goodness she wasn't putting her in a romantic bracket with the Don. Hadn't he said that the islanders were quick to regard an association between a bachelor and a single girl as a courtship? But then he was the *hidalgo* and probably permitted a shade more licence than the other men—licence he'd take anyway!

Paquita promised the speedy arrival of their first course, and added that she would bring their *viño* at once.

'Wine—at breakfast?' Vanessa exclaimed.

'Most certainly, as I have ordered soft-shell crabs and they go well with the Viño Verde which is a speciality of the *venta*.' His eyes teased mercilessly across the table. 'You say of us Spanish that we live by rigid rules, yet you open wide in shock the green eyes because I order this *viño*. It is better than tea.'

'You've had plenty of cups at the plantation,' Vanessa protested as he pulled a face. 'Why didn't you say you preferred something stronger?'

'Perhaps I did not care to risk being thought even more of an uncivilized foreigner,' he mocked dryly. 'I understand that tea is a tradition in British households, just as wine is so in ours, therefore bear with me and discover for yourself how excellent is Viño Verde with sweet white crabmeat.'

It was delicious, Vanessa had to admit. Astringent on teeth and palate, perfect with the crabmeat, dark brown bread and home-made butter.

Appetizing food and relaxed conversation go together, and though later on Vanessa would look back on this hour with a sense of disbelief, right now she tucked into the various good things that were brought to the table under the guava tree and listened with interest as Don Rafael talked of the estate he had turned into a convalescent home for children. Coins of sunlight dappled their heads and revealed a hint of gold in the green wine. The Don's slender brown fingers turned his wine glass by the stem, his crested ring flashed, and there was a deep gleam of enthusiasm in his dark eyes.

Now and again at the plantation Vanessa had admitted to herself that this man could be a compelling conversationalist, and right now, mellowed by her surroundings and the wine, she welcomed this mood of relaxed friendliness into which they had slipped. It couldn't last, of course. He was still her courteous enemy behind that slow smile that crinkled his eyes. Something would crop up and they'd be fencing again before the day was out.

He had travelled extensively and described vividly the lovely places he had seen. Verona and its astounding frescoes, the fascinating architecture of Portugal, the Acropolis by Greek moonlight. These he had particularly enjoyed, but the island of Luenda was for him the only place on which to live and die. Its people were warm and real, untouched by the worm of discontent which seemed to be eating into the hearts of so many in the outside world.

Vanessa, almost a victim of the Ordaz revolt, was quick to agree that the Luenda islanders were nice folk. The fishermen sang while pulling in their laden nets, the field workers made a fiesta of husking the corn and to a stranger like herself they couldn't have been friendlier. Between Don Rafael and his workers there obviously existed a strong personal tie. He was their *compadre*; they looked up to him, asked advice of him as was their right and gave him a sturdy loyalty without a hint of the servility that too often conceals a festering resentment of the privileges bestowed by wealth.

The inborn authority of the man, combined with a fine business brain and the lean hardness of a matador, made of him, she knew, almost an idol in the eyes of the islanders. *Mi amigo grande*. Their friend as well as the father-figure to whom they could go with their personal problems. His was a big responsibility in a way, one he had shouldered at the age of nineteen when his father had died, and if at times he sighed for the lesser responsibilities of being the peasant owner of an olive-yard or a small *viña*, it was understandable.

He lay back in the chair facing Vanessa's his eyes narrowed against the sun which streamed across his brown throat and winked on a bronze medallion half buried in the hair of his upper chest. He was really just a man, she found herself thinking, despite his possessions and the power he wielded. He could look lazy and abstracted, and sometimes tired. And when he saw handsome babies like Leon Rafael, no doubt his thoughts turned to the marriage he must one day make himself. Would he make that marriage with a woman like Lucia Montez, someone to match his own sophistication? Or would he choose a girl, lovely and uncomplicated, whose main purpose would be to give him several tawny sons to carry on the Domerique name?

Had he succumbed to the enchanting widow? She certainly seemed ideally suited to be the wife of a socially prominent Spaniard, with an exquisite taste in clothing. Seen in one of her classic gowns against the filigreed archways and baroque panelling of the *castillo* she was superbly Spanish. In the topaz glow of the dining candelabra she was also at her best. Her creamy-olive skin and her long, almost Moorish eyes were made for the mystique of candlelight. The slight parting of her dark crimson lips whenever she looked at the Don, the suggestion of an intimate smile, bespoke a degree of confidence on her part that would surely not have been there had he shown himself indifferent to her svelte, brunette charms.

Was he contemplating marriage with *la viuda*? Was that why he wanted Barbara in the care of a trustworthy person, because soon he would be off on a honeymoon?

'Of what are you thinking, Miss Carrol?' he murmured suddenly. 'The revelations of old Maria?'

She shook her head and fingered a red petal which had fallen to the table.

'Have you no belief in the palm-reading powers of the *gitana*?'

'Have you, *señor*?' she fenced lightly, smiling to hide the belief she had felt with her hand in the papery thinness of Maria's.

'I intend to make my own destiny, regardless of the dark powers.' He growled a laugh and got to his feet. He came round to Vanessa and extended a hand to assist her from her chair. Again as beneath the bamboo palms she was close to him, aware of tension in him, as though he forcibly withheld something he wanted to give voice to. Her glance lifted but rose no higher than the forceful jut of his chin. She heard herself say: 'I promise to think carefully about the post you've offered me, *señor*.'

'*Gracias.*' The muscles were taut in his jaw. 'Perhaps you will let me know your decision within the next few days?'

'Of course.' Now they were walking towards the *venta*, past the water-walk, into the hot sunshine. A side-glance at the Don's face showed an abstraction that told Vanessa his thoughts were riding ahead of him, to the work that awaited him. It was also possible that he was mulling over the problem of Barbara, who was no longer a child but a headstrong adolescent who had decided to give him trouble at a time when, very possibly, he had an important personal decision to make. A decision connected with Lucia Montez.

Afternoons at the *castillo* were slumbrous and quiet. Vanessa had never acquired the siesta habit, and while Barbara retired to her room to rest, the British girl explored the *castillo* and enjoyed the many antique attractions it had to offer.

This particular afternoon she came upon a spiral staircase which led up to a door she couldn't resist opening. It was oiled and did not creak as she unfastened it. Ah, she was out on the rooftop of one of the *castillo* turrets. Her breath caught excitedly in her throat and she went to the indented parapet and took in the wide and splendid view. The silence all around had a crystal quality, as though if you moved it would chime, maybe shatter. Now and again a bird winged towards the sea like a brightly shafted arrow, and Vanessa, sensitive to beauty, relaxed into one of the wall embrasures and let herself drown in the shimmering landscape.

She was gazing at the ocean, an aquamarine platter on which the island was set like a lavish waterlily, when a distinct mutter of voices made her glance sharply over her shoulder. The door to the rooftop was set in a wall that branched left and right, forming, she saw, a rectangle that was concealed from the main portion of the turret. Vanessa got to her feet and branched against the parapet, a breeze plucking at her copper hair, she wondered in a quiet panic if she had stumbled on a secret meeting place of a pair of lovers. A wrenchingly vivid picture sprang into her mind, and her throat went dry at the thought of being caught up here, like a Betsy Pry, by Lucia Montez and the Don.

She was halfway to the door that opened on to the spiral staircase when a feminine voice spoke behind her. '*Mierda!*' It was high with alarm. 'It is only you, Vanessa!'

Vanessa swung round. Barbara del Quiros confronted her, tawny-skinned and lovely in pleated white silk, a hand pressed dramatically to her heart. 'Sweet mercy, we had visions of someone else, *cara mia*, and you can guess who I mean!' Barbara put back her head and laughed with relief and a touch of bravado. Then she called over her shoulder: 'It is safe to come out, *guapo*. We are discovered by Vanessa, and I think she has too much dislike of my *padrino* to go to him with tales.'

A man strolled out from the rectangle and joined Barbara. He wore a cream silk shirt with tobacco-brown slacks. His tanned throat sported a gay green scarf, while an impudent smile showed a neat line of white teeth under a slim moustache. Ruy Alvadaas! A thread of shock ran through Vanessa as he took her hand and bowed his sleek head over it. 'From here it is a *vista gloriosa, eh, señorita?*' he murmured. 'You also admire it, as Barbara and I have been doing?'

A pulse beat quickly at the base of Vanessa's throat and she felt surprise grow into anger. Alvadaas was much older than Barbara, with the cynical eyes of a man who had been around, and his insinuation that he and Barbara had been admiring the view was wasted on Vanessa. A streak of lipstick marked his mouth, and in a cool voice she informed him of the fact. A grin flickered his lip, but his eyes were a glittering jet as he took out a handkerchief and erased the giveaway smear. Erased as well was some of the charm Vanessa had enjoyed in a surface fashion, for it hadn't taken her long to realize that he was a gay and flirtatious sponger, tolerated at the *castillo* because his mother and the Don's had been sisters. If Barbara's godparent learned that it was his good-looking rake of a cousin the girl had been meeting on the quiet—plainly, there would be hell to pay!

'I thought you were taking siesta in your room.' Vanessa spoke sternly to the girl, whose fingers were plucking at the flame chiffon encircling her throat. Barbara dragged her gaze from Ruy's face, and a blush ran up her throat to the raven wings of hair that sprang from her temples. She was desperately smitten by the man, Vanessa saw, and so frankly ardent and lovely with her skin that was golden as the tansy buttons Vanessa remembered from a riverbank near where she had lived in England. She used to crush the buttons to have their scent on her fingers ... and no doubt that was how Ruy Alvadaas felt about this wild-growing flower of a girl, shut away from the world as he had known it, in a *castillo* on an island.

Now Vanessa understood, even sympathized, with the Don's anger over Barbara's refusal to disclose her whereabouts last night. To be the guardian of a fiery and increasingly lovely girl couldn't be easy, but all the same Vanessa stiffened her spine and resolved not to get involved. She had plans of her own, that very evening she intended to write to Jack Conroy ...

Then, as Barbara stood silently and eloquently before Ruy Alvadaas and Vanessa saw his dark eyes glide over her young figure, she knew that her letter to Jack wouldn't get written. With a fatalistic feeling she knew, instead, that she would request an interview with Don Rafael.

CHAPTER FOUR

VANESSA was crossing the hall soon after *merienda* when she met the Don's secretary emerging from the study. She seized the opportunity to request an interview with Don Rafael, and Carlitos politely bowed and said he would impart her wish to the *señor hidalgo* when he returned from a business conference.

Dinner at the *castillo*, in accordance with Spanish custom, was always a late affair, and Vanessa was on her way downstairs when the Don came striding from his own wing and fell into step beside her. He briskly informed her that he had arranged to see one of his tenants immediately after dinner, but the interview would not take long and he would be gratified if Vanessa would present herself in his study at ten-fifteen.

'Very well, *señor*.' She spoke as formally as he, and upon slanting a glance at his face she saw his eyes narrowed speculatively, but if he meant to ask a question it was frustrated by Barbara. He and Vanessa had reached the hall just as the girl came flying down the staircase with the grace of a gull, white-winged in chiffon with touches of black to match her hair, which was secured by a high Spanish comb set with seed pearls. She paused in her flight and stood gripping the mahogany handrail. Her dark eyes flashed from her godparent to Vanessa. 'What are you saying?' her look demanded. 'What are you telling him?'

Vanessa returned no message of reassurance with her own eyes. It would do the girl good to squirm a little; she wasn't a child and must know that Ruy Alvadaas was the last man on earth the Don would want her to get mixed up with. Had she been meeting a decent young man of her own age, then Vanessa's attitude would have been far less stuffy. But Alvadaas was a wolf and it seemed that the best way to keep him at bay was to become the girl's shepherd.

The hint of a smile trembled at the edge of Vanessa's

mouth, for the situation held a certain piquancy. It was one she had hardly expected to become involved in when her peaceful existence had been bounded by the plantation and the various household duties and small pleasures which occupied her.

All through dinner Barbara kept shooting sullen and pleading glances across the silverware at Vanessa, who chose to ignore most of them. But she was too soft-hearted to keep on looking unmoved by Barbara's fear and she eventually smiled a reassurance at the girl. She had no intention of telling Don Rafael that she had stumbled on Barbara and Ruy that afternoon, up on one of the turrets for a purpose disconnected with the view. For one thing she didn't trust his temper, and for another Ruy's dismissal from the *castillo* would be bound to make of him a sort of martyred hero in Barbara's infatuated eyes. She might do something foolish, such as running off with him, and if her godfather had to bring her back, forcibly, the relationship between them would be irrevocably damaged. He was obviously fond of the girl, and she of him, and Ruy Alvadaas wasn't worth the wrecking of a tie so similar to the one that had existed between Vanessa and her uncle.

She forked delicious *pissaladiere* into her mouth and felt the pastry and anchovies dissolve on her tongue, while to her left Lucia Montez bent again to murmur something to the Don. She wore a sickle of diamonds and aquamarines at the neck of her dark evening dress, and as always the candle glow was kind to the olive skin that looked faintly sallow by daylight. Black candles and an all-white flower arrangement added to the sombre beauty of the dining-room. The rich mahogany, the window drapes of a deep ruby, the ceiling touched with old-gold, Moorish blue and ruby again, formed a perfect background for the Spaniards who dined at either side of Vanessa.

Don Rafael was always arresting in dining kit. The black and white seemed to throw into extra prominence the fierce, fine bone structure of his face. An eagle of Avila, Vanessa thought, for she had been reading a history of Spain in bed last night and the expression seemed to apply in every way to the man who had swooped upon her at Ordaz and carried her here to his eyrie.

Then, with a drawl in his voice, Ruy Alvadaas engaged Vanessa in conversation. He had emptied several glasses of wine and his usual debonair confidence was re-established. He smiled directly into her eyes, his charm switched full on. It was evidently true, he said, that the women of England were wide-minded.

'The expression is broad-minded, Señor Alvadaas,' she retorted, angered by his assumption that because she was British she approved of his rakish behaviour. 'To be open-minded is not necessarily to be lax in our views, *señor*, and girls who make fools of themselves with irresponsible men are as much in the minority in my country as elsewhere.'

'Ah, now I have angered you, Miss Carrol.' He quirked a brow, but beneath the mockery in his eyes she saw a probing sharpness. 'You no doubt long to return to your own country now there is nothing to keep you in this part of the world, is this not so?'

'Of course,' she replied. 'When the authorities have arranged matters to Don Rafael's satisfaction, then I daresay I shall return to England.'

'My good cousin takes his responsibilities very seriously, does he not?' Ruy's glance drifted briefly in Barbara's direction. The girl had evidently been waiting for him to look at her, for she broke into a smile, then quickly lowered her lashes to hide the yearning in her eyes. Vanessa had caught a glimpse of it, and her fingers clenched on her lace-edged napkin. It wasn't easy being young and being a girl, she reflected. Nature fashioned you for love, but she didn't always supply you with a built-in defence against falling for the wrong man. When that happened you had to battle against the hell of it on your own.

'You are looking very serious,' Ruy Alvadaas murmured, his wine glass full again as he lifted it to catch the candle glow in the deep red liquid. 'There are only two things that make a woman look so, having love and not having it.'

He was implying, of course, that there was green in her eye because she alone at the rosewood table was untouched by love, unwanted by himself—of no personal concern to the Don, whose profile was bronze-hammered in the candlelight, softened now and again by a smile for the woman at his side. Vanessa withdrew her glance from that haughty profile, hardly able to believe that the same man had partnered her at breakfast, his white shirt thrown open at his throat as he enthused about his work and his travels and tilted lazy glances at the lovebirds in the trees. Which was the real man? This impeccably mannered and attired *hidalgo*, or that tousled pirate who had grinned so wickedly at old Maria's revelations?

Coffee was served as usual in the *sala*, then Vanessa quietly excused herself and took a walk before going to the Don's study. The night was warm and she strolled under the clustering stars, brushing at the jasmine that creamed at either side of her as she followed the hidden tinkle of a fountain. She located it in an arbour of myrtles and sat there on a rustic seat, listening to the nightingales which, she had been told by Barbara, had been brought from Spain in the galleons of the sea-roving Rafael de Domerique who had discovered the island of Luenda and established there the gold and scarlet standard of Castile.

The glories, follies and cruelties of Spain had made the mould in which the past Domerique, and the present one, had been cast to emerge as men who were formidable and yet fascinating ...

Vanessa stiffened against the back of the garden seat; the carved wood was hard as stone yet she didn't feel any pain. All she felt was the realization that the man she had known for several years had turned into someone she had not known at all. Someone less harsh than he had always seemed, a man who had problems to battle with, who could be concerned for a couple who had needed a child to save their marriage, whose heart beat with human yearnings like any other man's.

A tremor ran from the nape of Vanessa's neck downwards, as though someone touched her, and suddenly she was running back through the jasmine tunnels in a strange panic. Her heart was drumming, the palms of her hands moist as she entered the *castillo* to the quarter-hour chime of an ormolu clock on a carved table in the hall.

The double doors of the study were opened immediately to her knock and she stepped past the Don's tall dark figure into a room that was superbly furnished. What caught her eye and held it was a softly lit Madonna and Child facing the massive desk.

'So, you appreciate my Madonna rather more than some of the canvases in the picture gallery, eh?'

Vanessa turned to look at the Don, who wore a dark velvet smoking-jacket and a sardonic smile. He had shown her round the picture gallery the other evening, where she had stood horrified before an immense *auto-da-fé* that hung there. 'What a beastly thing!' she had said. 'I'd have to throw it out.'

'Miss Carrol,' he had retorted, 'you would really have me discard a painting that is worth a great deal of money?'

'Well, at least turn it to the wall or banish it to the clutter room.' She had walked on to something less gruesome, but out of the corner of her eye she had seen him contemplating the hooded inquisitors, poor quailing victim, and the sweating chests of the torturers bronzed by the flames. With a cool deliberation he had lifted his cheroot to his lips and she had heard him laugh low in his throat, as though he found her British attitude of mind deeply amusing.

Recollection of those moments in the picture gallery were steadying, and Vanessa could clutch again at details about this man which had threatened to slip out of her grasp. Physically fascinating he might be, and concerned for the welfare of the Spanish peasants who lived on the island, but he and she were basically incapable of sharing the same sentiments. They could never be friends, she decided, as she and Jack Conroy were friends.

'I have granted your request for an interview, Miss Carrol,' his glance skimmed her face, the topaz flecks in his eyes making them unreadable. 'I venture to guess that it has something to do with our conversation earlier today?'

'Yes——'

'Please to be seated before we talk.' He took her elbow and conducted her to a cushioned settle with a tapestry frame perfect for curling into with a book. She sank back among the cushions and lifted a quick smile to his face.

He studied her, then he said: 'Are you opposed to a glass of wine during an interview?'

'Well, it isn't quite so unconventional as at breakfast,' she returned, watching as he quirked a grin and took from one of the kingwood cabinets a wine flagon and a pair of goblets. The wine creamed as it was poured, then cleared to a pale topaz as he came back to Vanessa and placed one of the goblets in her hand. He sat down facing her in a winged chair and raised his glass. '*Salud!*'

'*Salud!*' she echoed, taking a sip at her wine and finding it the potent production from his own vineyard. It prickled her palate and warmed her throat like the island sunshine at high noon, and it could be, as she already knew, equally dizzying.

As she put the almost brimming glass on a side table, she felt the Don's brilliant glance follow the action. 'We shall never make a true *señorita* of you, Miss Carrol,' he mocked. 'Shall I ring for a pitcher of orange juice?'

She shook her head, then because she was a little afraid of his observant eyes she turned and studied the great flank of books filling the space that would have held a fireplace in a European house. She saw Spanish and English titles, and upon one volume gold-leaf lettering that revealed it was a diary, that of Doña Mariana de Domerique y Granquist, mother of the man who sat regarding Vanessa with his black head cushioned against dusky red velvet, tapering fingers lightly holding the milky-blue stem of his wine glass.

'We are seated, we are alone, and I am barely bottling my patience,' he drawled. 'What have you to say to me that makes you avert your eyes, as though you fear that I shall read something in them that is not to my liking?'

Though he spoke softly, she caught a hint of menace in his voice and wondered for a panicky moment if he had noticed Barbara's manner at dinner, the looks of appeal she had kept shooting across the table, that sudden yearning smile she had given his cousin. But no, he had been too absorbed by *la viuda* to notice what was going on further down the table. Lucia had captured and held his attention.

Vanessa gathered nerve and met his narrowed eyes. She said, casually: 'I came to tell you, *señor*, that I shall be happy to accept the post you offered me.'

'Ah, I see.' His wine glass rang on the table beside his chair. 'This is interesting, that you make up your mind so soon. You were not enthusiastic when we talked this morning and I received the strong impression that you were merely polite when you said you would give the post your consideration.' Suddenly he leant forward in his chair and the light of a nearby wall-lamp shafted across his face and showed her the tension of each feature. 'What dictates your change of—heart, Miss Carrol?'

'You—said yourself, *señor*, that I'm of an independent disposition——'

'Evasive answers are irritating!' His unsparing scrutiny drove heat to her cheeks. 'You say you now want this post, yet I can tell from your eyes that you are not tranquil in your mind about it. Come, be truthful with me. Is it for your own sake, or for Barbara's, that you wish to stay on the island?'

'To stay on the island?' she repeated after him. 'I haven't any choice about that, have I?'

'It is true that the authorities have not yet secured your compensation for the loss of the plantation, but I have been thinking that if you wish desperately to return to England, then I will advance the money for you to go and to live comfortably while you train for a career.'

A blank silence followed Don Rafael's startling words, and Vanessa felt the heat fade to coldness in her cheeks. All this he could have offered a fortnight ago, yet he had chosen to insist that she remain here, under his roof, under his supervision. Now he coolly said that if she wished to go, he would provide the means, which she could pay back when, and if, she received compensation money for the razing of the plantation.

She was free to go. He had just said so.

She watched him lean to the table beside his chair and throw back the lid of a cedarwood cigar box. *'Con su permiso?'* He spoke with automatic courtesy as his long fingers selected one of the dark brown cylinders.

'Of course,' she said, listening to the faint crackle as his fingers squeezed the sheath of the Havana, watching as with unruffled calm he used a gold cigar clipper, then his lighter, finally putting back his head to savour a deep lungful of the strong smoke. His eyes in the amber wall-lighting held a subtle thoughtfulness as his cigar smoke swam up against the panelled walls, wreathing and curvetting towards the inlaid ceiling like blue question marks.

If you wish desperately to return to England, he had said.

Her mind twisted about the remark like a *corniche* that led to a deep, dark drop. She had been out in this part of the world for four years and all at once it was desperately unnerving to contemplate the pressures of life as she would find them in England. Her closest school friends were probably married, or settled in careers, and they would no longer have anything in common with someone who had lived as she had, on a coffee plantation surrounded by jungle and its primitive inhabitants.

Strange, but at the brain-numbing, heart-tearing time of her uncle's death she had thought it would be so easy to go back to England and pick up the threads she had dropped four years ago. Now, her heart sinking, she knew it would be nearly impossible. She had put down roots out here, and as is generally the case in tropical countries they had taken only too well and if she dragged them up they would not replant easily in a land less warm and vibrant.

'Have you nothing to say in answer to my proposal, Miss Carrol?'

'I don't know whether I'm coming or going, if you must know, Don Rafael,' she retorted shakily. 'One moment you imperiously say I must stay here, then you give me permission to go. You offer me a job, then presumably decide that I might not after all be capable of handling it.'

'I will admit that it seems as though I am being perverse,' he said, 'but bear with me while I explain. It was a big shock for you that your only relative should die, and I did not feel it wise at that time for you to return to England. I felt that there was no one there to give you sympathy, that your links had become broken with friends you doubtless made at school. I believed it better that you be given a little time in which to decide whether you wanted to return or to remain.' He rocked his left hand in an expressive Latin way. 'The mind is not capable of being made up when it is in turmoil, nor does the heart really know what it wants when it is in the grip of grief.'

He abruptly arose to his feet with her green eyes following him, and with a touch of masculine vehemence he thrust his cigar into a corner of his mouth and paced to the terrace doors, then back again.

'The English are more sentimental about their homeland than we Latins, but I do not think they feel the soil, the sun, the very air in their blood and being. Your good Tio Lennard was English in everything, yet England meant less to him than Ordaz. And having seen you at Ordaz, I had reason to believe that you had acquired his feeling for the scents, the sounds, the slower pace of life out here. You seemed content, but,' he shrugged his shoulders and stood looking down at her, his eyes brow-shadowed, 'you have not carried that same contentment to Luenda. You feel too much a stranger, a foreigner, a dependent. *Conforme?*'

She nodded, for it was true. She had known him since her early days at Ordaz, but still it was true. They were strangers to each other despite those four years that should have made them friends. Something immovable stood between them and the lightheartedness of friendship, which banishes all sense of obligation, was hopelessly missing.

Their eyes were locked, he seemed to her a series of cold, stern angles in the amber light that played over his swarthy face, revealing certain facets while concealing others. Hope seeped away that the man she had glimpsed briefly that morning was the real Rafael de Domerique. The real one confronted her, subtle and complex, with iron in him. Totally different from an Englishman, who would not make promises in the morning and coolly disregard them in the evening, for hadn't he said that she would enjoy the vine-growing part of the island and that one day he would take her to see it? She shivered, as though something had died to coldness inside her.

Perhaps he saw her shiver, for with a low mutter of impatience he swung to the open flank of books and plucked out the garnet red volume with his mother's name upon it. He ran his thumb over the supple Moroccan leather as though drawing from it the patience and control that did not come easily to him. 'Well, I have given you freedom of choice, Miss Carrol,' he said. 'You may depart for England as soon as you wish.'

'And what of Barbara?' she heard herself ask.

He swung to look down at her through narrowed eyelids. 'You sound concerned for the *meniña*. Why so? Have you knowledge of something that I also should know?'

'Not exactly,' Vanessa fenced, her throat so dry that she had half emptied her wine glass before she fully realized the action. Anyway, she welcomed the animation and warmth it reawakened in her. She stood up, feeling too much at a disadvantage with the Don towering over her, black-browed and suspicious. 'I'm grateful to you, Don Rafael, for offering to support me in England until I get on my feet, but I really would prefer to earn the money. I want the job you offered me—for Barbara's sake and my own.'

'A little for Barbara's sake,' he crisped, 'but much more for the independence that cannot bear to accept aid from me. *A sus ordenes, señorita. Por ahora!*'

'I beg your pardon, *señor*?' She flushed slightly, for his rapid Castilian was beyond her, though she could have sworn that a hint of a threat lay in those last two words.

'It is as you wish, Miss Carrol.' He gave her a brief, suave bow. 'Doubtless you will feel more at home with us if you have not all the time the feeling that you are accepting—charity.'

She winced at the cynical edge to his voice and bit back the retort that the night he had brought her here on his launch he had not looked exactly overjoyed at the prospect of being responsible for her. Even now she could see his dark face bent over the bunk on which she had lain weeping, the look in his eyes as she had awoken from sleep to gaze directly up at him. A look of leashed impatience mixed with a sombre resignation, as though he resented what had been thrust upon him, but had too rigid a code of honour to dismiss his unwanted responsibility by putting her on the first plane to England.

Vanessa was grateful for his hospitality, but when she took on the job of companion to Barbara there would be a change in her relationship with her host. A companion in Spanish households was not considered of much consequence and she told herself independently that she would prefer that role to her present one. Towards Barbara's *dueña* the Don need only be aloof and polite; a simulation of friendliness was not expected.

'The matter is settled, then, *señor*?' she asked coolly.

'It would seem so,' he drawled. 'Shall I acquaint Barbara of the arrangement, or do you feel that she will accept it better from you?'

'From me,' Vanessa said quickly, fearing that the revelation might lead to words between him and the girl. Barbara was in love, and in the mood to be reckless, and though Don Rafael was not a man to make scenes he might make a formidable one if he suddenly learned that her casual *novio* was none other than his rakish cousin. That blossoming affair had to be carefully nipped in the bud, otherwise it might run riot and strangle one of the nicest aspects of the Don's character—the protective, almost fatherly affection he had for his Barbarita.

He was replacing his mother's diary, then before Vanessa could murmur *buenas noches*, and escape from his presence, he had withdrawn a slimmer volume from one of the shelves and was remarking on it. 'It is a pity you cannot read Castilian,' he said, 'for I am sure you would enjoy this book. It has that fey quality which the feminine mind enjoys so much, the classic *Poema del Cid*, an entertaining mixture of legend and fact. You have heard of El Cid?'

She nodded, even as the thought flashed through her

mind that El Campeador, the famous champion of Spain when the Moors had overrun much of the country, had probably looked much like the man who stood before her, a faint smile on his arrogantly moulded mouth as he read a few lines of the poem to himself. 'What an age to have lived in,' he murmured. 'El Cid was much of a Spanish Lancelot as a knight in shining armour. He could be a tyrant as well as a daring leader, which makes an interesting combination, do you not agree?'

'Most interesting,' she echoed, feeling her heart flutter in her chest as the Don's eyes looked fully into hers between those long Spanish lashes that in no way detracted from the intense masculinity of his appearance. He smiled faintly, tossed the book to his winged chair, then with a hand shackling her left elbow he led her to the cabinet in a far corner of the room.

'Though you cannot read the poem, I can show you something you will enjoy.' His warm hand released her and she stood watching—already an obedient employee—as he opened the cabinet which held a fantastically beautiful collection of brocade and ivory fans, jewelled combs, wrought silver and gold trinkets studded with sombre stones and a glimmering array of wonderful Spanish shawls.

'These were my mother's "toys",' he said with a smile. 'I remember as a boy how she would sit and admire them, fluttering a fan as only a Spanish woman can, trying on a bracelet or a necklet, smiling up at my father with her great brown eyes and making me so envious of that look. She had many other looks for me, all of them delightful, but never that particular one, and I laugh now at my own boyish mystification and jealousy.' His long fingers took from a black velvet tray a glowing necklet of green stones strung on silver.

'These are Muzo emeralds from Colombia. The necklet is of an agreeable appearance, eh?' He glanced up from the emeralds, pooled in his palm and glowing richly, the long discarded trinket of the woman whose poised and lovely portrait hung in the *sala* upstairs. 'Would you like to try them on?' the Don enquired with a smile.

'Oh no!' Vanessa stepped away from him, startled. 'I—I couldn't do them credit.'

'Really?' He arched an amused brow and deliberately ran his glance over her. 'Is it a general habit of Englishwomen to underrate their attractions? I would say you have the eyes and skin for emeralds, or perhaps you refer to the fact that you are wearing a borrowed dress which does not particularly become you?'

She pressed her hands against the skirt of the dress, which was plum blue, a colour that clashed horribly with her green eyes and copper hair. Trust the Don to notice!

He shrugged, rearranged the necklet on its bed of velvet and casually slid the tray back into place, leaving Vanessa with the thought that he must trust his retinue of servants a great deal not to lock these valuable things in a safe. He seemed utterly certain that he had the abiding loyalty of the people who worked for him, and very likely he did have it. He was, it had to be admitted, a most uncommon man ... something almost boyish in the way he fingered the heavy silk fringe of a flame-coloured shawl.

'My mother always looked superb in this,' he smiled. 'She had magnificent poise, a trait of Castilian women.'

'Has she—been dead very long, *señor*?' Vanessa quietly asked, thinking that when his deep and vigorous voice was lowered it had a quality made strangely attractive by his alien pronunciation of English words.

'My mother is not dead, *señorita*.' He looked down at her in some surprise. 'Soon after the death of my father she retired to a Convent of Mercy in Segovia. There was much love between my parents, you see, and the world and its pleasures no longer appealed to Doña Mariana after she lost him. You are a little shocked that a woman should choose the seclusion of a convent in her widowhood? You cannot comprehend a love so devoted, so intense, that two people are truly made one by it?'

Yes, she could comprehend such a love, but she wanted to say: 'But what of you, Don Rafael? You were not yet twenty when your father died, how then could Doña

Mariana leave you to take over so many responsibilities on your own?'

He evidently guessed what was passing through her mind, for he said: 'Though the *señorito* in a Spanish home is made much of, he is automatically the head of it when his father dies. I knew of my mother's fervent wish to return to Segovia when she became widowed, and though I will admit that I wished to keep her with me on the island there was no question of doing so if her heart was not in staying. Doña Mariana was a real woman, her love was given first and last to the man to whom she was given in marriage, for it is not right that a woman should adore her children beyond the man who fathers them. A child grows gradually into an adult and wishes to go its own way, a wife and a husband should grow all the time towards each other so that with the adulthood of their children there is no gap between them. They are again as they were in the beginning. This could not be for my mother, and I had become a man. We parted. The order to which she belongs is a strict one ...'

He finished the sentence with a shrug of his shoulders, thereby telling Vanessa that he rarely saw the mother he had loved to watch among the worldly trinkets she had discarded for the austerity of convent life.

How great a love ... how stern a love had been Doña Mariana's!

A coldness ran over Vanessa's skin, and she was glad when Don Rafael closed the cabinet of fans, combs and shawls. She glanced at his profile and saw that it was tinged with a faint melancholy, perhaps that was why she did not demur when he turned to the terrace doors and indicated with a hand gesture that she precede him into the scented starglow.

This terrace was private to the study and rather like a rotunda, mosaic paved, with small seats of faience overhung by thickly hanging clusters of *dama de noche*, whose green flowers open at night to emit an intoxicating fragrance. The rotunda was encircled by a pierced balustrade that was like a band of stone crochet-work, and under her hands

Vanessa could feel the sculptured shells, cherubs and garlands.

'This is what was once called a crinoline balcony, on which the voluminous skirts of the ladies could spread out without becoming flattened.' The Don's teeth flashed whitely. 'The old conceits had a certain charm, eh?'

'Women were helpless in such finery, and men, preferring it that way, were not averse to tailoring the home to suit the clothing,' Vanessa returned, cool again after the heat of her compassion a few minutes ago. Compassion ... for the assured and sardonic *hidalgo* of Luenda! That was something she had never expected to feel in connection with such a man, and she knew as she stood beside him, listening to the faintly derisive chik-chak of lizards, watching fireflies among the tendrilled palms and camphors, that she feared the vulnerability of her mood.

Her fingers tensed on the stone shellwork as he faced round towards her and nonchalantly rested an elbow upon the balustrade. 'Even so,' he said, 'it was an age of romance such as will never be known again. Have you no secret yearning to have been a part of the gallantry, the duels, the flirtations behind a fan, which has a languge of love of its own? Do you not believe in romance, you who asserted that I would be ruthless with Barbara because she slipped out of the *castillo* in order to find it?'

'You and I—we don't believe in the same kind of romance,' Vanessa fenced. 'You like it—hedged round by restrictions.'

'In other words you think I am old-fashioned, eh?' His teeth glimmered in a narrow smile. 'What is your definition of romance? To play it like a game? Strange that the British should approach the greatest of experiences in such an off-handed way, and yet that your country should produce men who wrote of love with so much intensity. There is much imagery and vigour in our writing, but it took a countryman of yours to pen the following lines:

> *"Soul of my soul, and mine as I am thine,*
> *I cling to thee, my life, as fire to flame."'*

Had Vanessa been alone under tropical stars with any other man, and had he quoted such passionate lines to her, she would have wondered if he was in a romantic mood and leading up to an expression of his mood. But one did not think such thoughts about Rafael de Domerique. She went hot and cold at the idea, acutely aware of his gaze upon her as she followed, intently, the ghostly flight of a big moth.

'Perhaps the English express themselves better in words than in deeds,' she rejoined. 'That is, when it comes to romance.'

'What a prospect for a Latin to face, should he take for a wife one of these snow maidens,' mocked the Don. 'How quickly would his southern fire be extinguished by her northern ice. Or would he, perhaps, melt her? Ah, that is a thought! Surely even the English are capable of being melted.'

'Are you asking me, or telling me?' She was glad of the enfolding shadows, and, supposing this to be a game, was playing it in a reserved fashion.

'I am asking you,' he admitted, a tantalizing note in his voice. 'Has the amber fire of the moon and the *amour* of Señor Conroy not melted you, *señorita*?'

'That is a very personal question, *señor*.' She stiffened involuntarily by the balustrade.

'The exploring of the personalities is a most stimulating pastime,' his suavity was unimpaired. 'Spanish people are fond of indulging it.'

'I am not Spanish, *señor*!' All her British prickles were standing up at his effrontery in questioning her behaviour with Jack.

'Perhaps that is why I have a wish to delve into your personality. Come, *chica*, it is but a game.' He gave his deep-throated laugh. 'Where is your British sportsmanship?'

She had suspected from the start of this conversation that he was baiting her, and getting a private kick out of the process, and there wasn't a flicker of sportsmanship left in her as she faced his lounging figure. 'I don't care to have my private feelings dissected and cold-bloodedly discussed,' she retorted. 'It's an invasion a-and I resent it.'

'A strange remark from a woman,' there was a caustic sting in his voice. 'It is my experience that your sex likes this invasion, as you call it. It is a subtle intrusion they can allow without risking their reputations.'

'Your experiences of women seem to have been of the most cynical,' she shot back.

'Perhaps for most men that is inevitable,' he shrugged. 'Experience could not be acquired from the innocent, and in a way it is a schooling for the innocence we eventually acquire in a wife. If you have not known the devil you can never appreciate an angel.'

Really? she thought, clenching the stone balustrade. She would hardly have called Lucia Montez an angel, but men in love were notoriously blind to the faults an elegant figure and manner could conceal. And where was *la viuda's* innocence? Three years of marriage to another man had surely made inroads into that commodity.

The Don had straightened to his flagrant height beside Vanessa and what had been between them that morning was quite gone. Now he was remote again and she was perversely glad. 'An apology,' he spoke half mockingly. 'I prodded you with a question you were bound to resent, but always when we are alone you are on guard with me and it is impossible for a Spaniard to ignore a challenge. Shall we go in?'

As she walked in ahead of him, she vowed that in future she would avoid being alone with him whenever possible. He bowed her out of the double doors with impeccable courtesy. '*Buenas noches*, Miss Carol,' he said coolly.

'Goodnight, Don Rafael.' She hurried across the tiles of the hall and made her way upstairs to her room.

Concepcion, as always, had turned down the bedcovers and laid out her borrowed pyjamas along with the silk robe that was not borrowed, whose colour was always disturbingly reminiscent of the dress she had loved and worn so much at Ordaz—when she had not been a stranger, a dependant and a foreigner! She fingered the apple-green robe and resolved that with her first lot of wages she would buy some clothes of her own. A frown gathered her brows together. She and the Don had not discussed wages and she supposed that he would be generous. Not too generous, though. She didn't want more than a Spanish *duenna* would receive for her services.

When Vanessa slipped under the netting of her bed, she had achieved a '*mañana*' feeling. Let everything wait until tomorrow, the tussles and the sulks; the self-questioning and the doubts. She turned on her side with a yawn, nuzzled her cheek into her pillow and to the rockabye of cicadas drifting over her balcony she went fast to sleep.

The colours of blooms, the sea and the corals were brilliantly fresh at sun-up, dulling as the heat grew and bleached them. The distant mountains pricked the sky and a fine pink mist bled down their slopes. The warmth that lay over the infancy of the day was too lovely to be lost, and Vanessa, awakened by the sea air shafting sweet-sharp through her windows, was soon dressed and hastening downstairs. She skimmed across the hall and luckily found that the wrought-iron *cancela* of a side patio had been unlocked.

With a truant air she closed the little guardian gate behind her and passed among the massed shrubs and flower-studded trails of the patio. A smile stroked Vanessa's lips and the morning breezes lifted her hair and blew it back from her temples as she escaped the confines of the *castillo* and hurried towards the steps that led down to the lagoon beach.

The feathery coral sand was already warm, Vanessa found, when she whipped off her sandals and ran barefoot towards the *caseta* which was private to the *castillo* and used as a beach-hut. It was still so early that the lagoon lay enchanted, though out by the reef there was a white ripple of foam. Pieces of pastel coral scattered the sand like plucked and discarded flowers, while the seaward-inclining palms wore haloes of rosy gold as the mounting sun fired crests.

A paradise isle, Vanessa thought, standing there alone on

the rim of the beach, sandals in hand, her feet deep in the sand. It was as though she stood inside Rossetti's rainbow shell, everything was so peaceful right now. The sea crooned as it lapped inwards, and a few white egrets swooped with grace from their cliff perches. She drew a sigh of pleasure and continued towards the *caseta*, carefully avoiding the corals and the black sea-eggs, both of which could cause nasty festers if they opened the skin.

The *caseta* was never locked and Vanessa went inside, where gaily woven rugs covered the floor and tub chairs stood about. Over in a corner there was a small bar stocked with drinks, with an opulent chrome transistor standing on the counter. Magazines and paperbacks scattered a glass-topped table. There were boxes of cigarettes. And a closet of robes and swimsuits for guests who suddenly fancied a dip in the ocean. A couple of shower cubicles lay at the rear of this luxurious beach-hut, with dressing-rooms attached Vanessa and Barbara often used the place. Barbara had told her that when the vintage festivals began, the *castillo* would be filled with guests.

She took a leaf-green bathing suit out of the closet, along with a rubber cap, and went into the ladies' dressing-room to change. She was longing to get into the water and was scooping her hair into the white cap as she ran down the beach. She didn't notice that she passed a tall, sun-darkened figure in swimshorts with a towel thrown over a sinewy shoulder, and that he watched with decided interest as she went arm over arm through the water, her slender green-clad figure lifted now and again on the buoyant ripples near the reef. She was making for a flat black rock like a couch in the sea, to which she hauled herself, standing a moment bepearled by the water, the sun streaming off the cap and the copper strands fell to her shoulders.

Vanessa curled into a green sickle on the warm rock, an arm shielding her eyes from the sun, determined to be clam-lazy for at least a quarter of an hour. Then she would return to the *castillo*.

It was a splash and a grunt near her sea-couch that opened her eyes and shot her into a sitting position. She hardly knew what she expected to see—certainly not a tousled, lean stranger, whose sun-bleached eyebrows and cropped hair were startling against a leathery tan. He brushed her with metal-grey eyes that didn't miss a detail of her figure, turned to him in profile. He met her startled eyes and a grin slanted his mouth. He looked vigorous and yet somehow indolent, and he had a cynical type of face that obviously didn't care whether you took to it or not.

'Muy buenos dias, señorita,' he said, with a bit of a drawl but an otherwise good pronunciation. 'Su sequro servidor.'

He didn't look like anyone's obedient servant to Vanessa's way of thinking, but it was rather amusing that he should mistake her for a Spanish girl and she only wished she had enough Castilian to lead him on. *Su sequre servidor*, indeed! Who did he think he was kidding with that cynical mouth and those rather blush-making eyes?

She laced her knees with her arms as he came round and stood looking directly down at her. Her suit was still wet and it clung, and he was the type who made a girl blatantly aware of what was passing through his mind. 'Very good day to you, *señor*,' she said. 'I think I ought to warn you that this lagoon is private property.'

Up towards a bleached peak went those tangly eyebrows. 'Say, you're British!' He looked astounded, then delighted. 'Now I come to think of it I must have had my brains out for an airing, taking a gal with your copperknob for a *señorita*.'

She had to smile and evidently taking this for approval of his own blond crop, and appearance in general, he put down a square, work-hardened hand. 'Gary Elsing, very much at your service, Miss——?'

'Carrol,' she supplied, wickedly withholding her first name, though she permitted her hand to get lost and a trifle crushed in his. 'Are you a tourist, Mr Elsing?'

Her rash curiosity immediately parked him in a lounging position beside her. 'Heck, no,' he grinned. 'Is that Carol, with a single R?'

She shook her head, and with a wry quirk of a tangly brow he resumed. 'I work on the island, drilling oil for the

Tex-Rique company. Tex as in the well-known state of blue-bonnets and stetsons. Rique as in El Grande, whose lagoon we're both unlawfully using.'

'Really?' She was getting a kick out of teasing this rangy guy. 'You might be where you shouldn't be, but I happen to be—employed at the *castillo* and I have permission to be here.'

'Big surprise number two!' he whistled, his eyes roving her face and his brain obviously working overtime as he tried to figure out what sort of job she held down at the *castillo*. 'Somehow I can't see you dusting under the beds, so I guess you could be the old Doña's companion. Say,' he broke into a cheeky grin, 'El Grande hasn't gone mad and got himself a bit of distraction around his private office?'

'I'm the new companion of Don Rafael's ward.' Vanessa heard the sharp note in her voice and realized that she was ruffled by his remark and the picture it conjured up of the Don, a glint in his eye, pursuing her around that massive desk in his study. Her arms cinched her knees, she could feel herself shrinking away from the conclusion of that mental scene. It ought to have been funny, and yet ...

'The Don brought me across from Ordaz at the time of the revolt,' she said rebukingly. 'My uncle, who was like a father to me, died the same night. Don Rafael's been good to me a-and I'm grateful.'

'Of course you are, kid.' Somewhat sheepishly Gary Elsing ran a hand over his wheaten shock of hair. 'I haven't quite caught up on the island gen, you see I've been on leave and I only flew back from the States yesterday afternoon. I often filch a swim in the *hidalgo's* lagoon. He probably knows, for the servants about the place tell him everything, and you're right to bawl me out. He isn't so bad for a foreigner.'

'We're the foreigners, aren't we, Mr Elsing? The island is a Spanish protectorate.'

'Now don't split hairs—*Miss* Carrol. Look, don't you think it would be nice if we dropped the mister and miss? After all, we're a lonely pair of foreigners surrounded by Spaniards and we ought to be nice to each other.' His metal-grey eyes glinted in his craggy face. 'C'mon, Gary is short and easy to say. Try it.'

And because he reminded her a bit of Jack Conroy, a slightly older edition, scuffed at the edges, she smiled and said he could call her Vanessa. It made a break to be talking in this free and easy way with one of her own kind, for with the occupants of the *castillo* she was never quite relaxed.

'We're going to be friends,' he lazed on an elbow and let smoke drift comfortably from his nostrils. 'I feel it in my bones. How about you, Vanessa? Say, that's a nice name! Sort of exotic.'

'I've no female tricks,' she warned lightly. 'But I could do with a friend.'

'You don't need any tricks,' his smile was knowledgeable. 'So you lived at Ordaz. I heard that the trouble there had blown up into a regular shindig. What happened—or don't you care to talk about it?'

For all his cynicism there was a rugged kind of sympathy about Gary Elsing to which Vanessa couldn't help responding. She talked all of ten minutes while he listened without interruption, his bleached brows tangling together at certain points in her story. She concluded with the Don's offer of a job and her acceptance of it, but without mentioning Barbara's association with Ruy Alvadaas.

'They say,' Gary drawled, 'that the *hidalgo* of Luenda has a personal reason for everything he does. Is he—personal about you?'

'Good heavens, no!' Vanessa couldn't help laughing. 'I don't think he particularly likes me, but he was a great friend of my uncle's and being a Spaniard he feels honour bound to do what he can for me. I wanted a job and I like Barbara—also I've grown used to the tropics and the slower pace of life out here.'

'This island is quite a place, isn't it?' He stretched lazily, and Vanessa felt him surveying her through his pale lashes. 'Warm as a woman, spicy, languorous, enticing. Would you mind if I took a shine to you, Vanessa?'

'As long as it wasn't a serious one,' she rejoined, looking

down at him and certain that for all his cynical attractiveness he could not touch her heart, or her inmost self. She smiled, for she *liked* him, and that was always fatal to the expectations of a man of casual affairs.

'Haven't you a girl back in America?' she asked.

'A string of them,' he chuckled. 'There's safety in numbers when a guy does my kind of job and travels a lot, but I wasn't counting on the surprise that's been sprung on me this fatal morning. Copper hair and emerald eyes. Wow!'

'You're a flirt, Mr Elsing.'

'Grrr, I'm a wolf, honey.' He showed his good teeth in a grin as he tossed his cigarette stub into the turquoise sea surrounding their miniature island. 'Fancy the job of taming me?'

'I've got a job, thanks.' She lightly took his wrist and examined the dial of his waterproof watch. 'And it's about time I was tackling it.'

Gary was on his feet immediately, assisting Vanessa to hers. 'These Latins have got some very restrictive notions, haven't they?' he said. 'How old is Barbara del Quiros?'

'Eighteen.' Vanessa pulled on her cap.

'Bit of an overgrown baby for a nursemaid, isn't she? Or are you guarding her virtue until the Don's ready to hand her over to a guy who's already picked out for her?'

'You could say that.' Vanessa curled her toes over the smooth edge of the rock, her gaze on the golden-rose turrets of the Castillo d'Oro, gilded by the sun as she had first seen them. The fantastic, fable-like beauty of the place never failed to remind her of that morning on the launch, with the Don looking like a corsair carrying a piece of plunder to his hideaway ...

She gave a sudden shiver in the sun and dived into the sea. Gary followed and they raced each other to the beach. He picked up his towel and walked with her as far as the *caseta*, where he had left his slacks and shirt on one of the veranda chairs. 'Same time tomorrow?' he coaxed, before she went inside.

'I—don't know,' she hedged, thinking of Barbara. If her charge wanted an early swim or a ride, then it was no use promising to meet Gary. Somehow, as well, she didn't want Barbara to know that she had met this rangy American and struck up a friendship with him. 'Look, Gary,' she said, 'I can't make any promises. If I can get away on my own, I will.'

'That's good enough for me.' He grinned down at her. 'I want you to myself as well.'

She caught her breath, then laughed. 'The conceit of you men!'

'I've never yet met a woman who liked a modest man.' He touched a tendril of copper hair that had escaped the confines of her cap and lay like a flick of fire against the cream of her neck. 'So long for now, Red.'

'So long.' She opened the door of the *caseta*, turned to smile at him, then vanished inside. She found herself humming as the shower of water streamed over her, and when she was dressed and combing her hair in front of the mirror she noticed that the recent shadows haunting her eyes had lifted. She was no longer quite as alone as she had been; she now had a friend of her own sort here on the island.

She was still smiling when she reached the *castillo* and the little wrought-iron door out of which she had slipped earlier on. As she stretched a hand to the *cancela*, it swung open and she almost walked into Don Rafael.

'*Buen' dia!*' He steadied her with an alert hand, and, her smile lost, she noticed breathlessly that his light town suit made him look even swarthier than usual—or was she contrasting him with blond, light-eyed Gary Elsing?

'Have you been bathing, Miss Carrol?' he asked.

'Yes, *señor*. The water was perfect.'

'I trust you do not go far beyond the reef when you swim alone? There is an undertow of some strength just at that point.'

'Yes, I know about the undertow, *señor*, but I'm a strong swimmer.' She didn't add that she had been with the American oil-man, whose easy-going attitude towards women was unlikely to be approved of by the Don. If he knew they had met, he might start playing the heavy employer and forbid Gary the lagoon, and she wanted to repeat the snatched fun of being alone with someone so relaxed.

'Few people are stronger than the elements, Miss Carrol.' Don Rafael was gazing down at her, a sardonic smile in his eyes; they flicked her face, noting the flush in her cheeks, the clear line of her eyes in the morning light, the damp tendrils of hair that clung to her youthful temples. 'Often the more we struggle against them, the greater seems the danger. Now to your breakfast—*pronto*!'

He smiled his good-day and strode off. With a shrug she idly plucked a hibiscus bell and tucked it into her hair. What a strange, enigmatic person he could be! Now what the devil had he been getting at with that remark about the elements and struggling against them? Was it a specific warning about the undertow near the coral reef ... or had he been implying something a bit more devious?

She made her way indoors, pondering the iron and charm of the man; the maddening way he could jab, then mystify ... and almost caress at times. What had Barbara once said? That she would not like to be the woman who loved him because in his anger he could be too terrible, and in his tenderness overwhelming. Vanessa snatched the hibiscus— flower of love—from her hair and crushed it before tossing it away. She glanced back over her shoulder and saw the crushed crimson petals slowly uncurling in the sun that streamed down on to the tiles of the patio. One ... two ... tenaciously the petals seemed to stretch out and cling to life.

CHAPTER FIVE

THE afternoon sun edged through the slats of the jalousies, while the ceiling fan whirred monotonously, casting its roundabout shadow on ivory-painted walls. Outside in the grounds, there was a sleepy twittering of birds, and, feeling herself watched, Vanessa glanced up from the book on her lap and met the dark questioning of Barbara's eyes.

'You have not turned that page for so long a time,' the girl accused. 'You are just sitting there staring at it.'

'Now I'm not.' Vanessa clapped the book shut and put it aside. 'You didn't want to talk to me a while ago, but if you've now finished sulking——'

'You spoke last night with my *padrino* and you told him about Ruy and myself——'

'I keep telling you I didn't.' Vanessa crossed her ankles on a wicker footrest and leaned her head against a coral silk cushion. 'He'd have hit the ceiling and most certainly would not have gone off so calmly this morning to a hospital board-meeting.'

'You do not know him as I do,' Barbara retorted darkly. 'He awaits his moment to attack and this usually happens when one is least prepared to defend oneself. You saw how he pounced upon me on the beach yesterday morning.'

'I also saw you raise your whip to him,' Vanessa said drily. 'You were lucky he didn't ride after you and give you a paddling.'

'Have I not told you, Vanessa—he has the iron control.' Barbara gave a wild little laugh and jumped to her feet for a prowl round this comfortable pretty den attached to her bedroom.

Following lunch, and looking very much as though she had a grievance to air, Barbara had near enough ordered Vanessa to come to her room. Good idea, Vanessa thought. They would be alone and she could get the girl's slant on having an English *dueña* for a change. But Barbara, having found out that Vanessa had talked alone with the Don last night, had got it into her head that the English girl had split on her. That was how little she knew about British prudence!

Young, bewildered and love-ridden, that was what Vanessa was thinking as she watched Barbara. The coin bracelet on the fine-turned wrist kept up a persistent jangling as the pointed fingernails flicked against matador pants. The girl distrusted everyone around her—excluding darling Ruy, of course—because she instinctively distrusted her own emotions and the danger they might be leading her into. She heaved a sigh and bent to a cigarette container shaped like a gondola. As she put back the lid an Italian tune tinkled out, and Vanessa wondered if the 'toy' had been brought back from Venice when the *hidalgo* had visited there in order to see its frescoes and canal palaces.

'You think I shoot the moon because I am crazy for Ruy?' Barbara tapped a corktip on a fingernail and met Vanessa's clear green glance. 'You are warm-coloured, you should have emotions to match, yet you regard me like—like an English schoolmarm. You English, do you distrust everything which has not the British lion on it?'

Vanessa had to laugh, for there was something irresistible about the girl, even when she was being perverse. 'You wouldn't meet Ruy so secretively if you felt confident that your guardian would approve of the—friendship. Nor would you be so huffy with me in case I've told him about those meetings, which I haven't.'

'Why do you not like Ruy?' Barbara sullenly demanded. 'What do you know of him—or any other man? You said you had never had a *novio*, and it occurs to me now that you are envious of what Ruy feels for me.'

'If you mean that *I'd* like to be made love to in dark corners, then you're very much mistaken,' Vanessa retorted.

'Perhaps you are frightened of being made love to at all.' Barbara puffed at her cigarette and struck a pose which she obviously fancied was very sophisticated, one knee slightly bent, a hand in the sliver of leather around her waist, eyelids half lowered. 'Is it not a fact that the English are very reserved? One wonders how such a nation continues its species.'

'I assure you we haven't yet carried everything to the automation stage.' Vanessa spoke flippantly enough, but she felt a dart of disappointment, and a sense of defeat, that fundamental differences should exist between herself and the people she planned to live among for a while. She watched the hypnotic whirling of the fan and wondered if it might be best if she returned to England. Her eyelids suddenly stung and she felt the wetness of tears as she blinked. The truth was—and it hurt—she didn't seem to belong here, or there.

'Vanessa...' all at once Barbara abandoned her defiance and sat down on the footrest, an arm hooked over Vanessa's legs, 'I make you look *triste* and I do not mean to do that after all you have been through. But you think like my darling, devilish *padrino*, that I am impetuous with my emotions. Is it not? You think I throw them away on Ruy, that I am a child who cannot know what love is. But I do know!'

Vanessa tucked a strand of Barbara's hair around a pink shell of an ear, to which was attached a small gold hoop. 'It's terribly easy, Babs,' she said, 'to mistake infatuation for love. And, charm apart, Señor Alvadaas is a very good-looking man——'

'He has such eyes, eh?' Barbara kissed her fingertips with Latin extravagance. 'They carry laughter in them, just like stars reflecting in the depth of wells. Ah, I know what you are thinking, of the *muchas novias* there have been before me, and that he is not of strong character like the *compadre*. But to love is to accept the worst before the best and then the two together. *Por cierto!* If I know this, Vanessa, then how can I be still a child?'

The moment was a delicate one, but Vanessa decided to be forthright in her reply. 'I can't help wondering, Barbara, if you would be encouraging Ruy Alvadaas if he were not good-looking—with the laughing eyes. He's an attractive, practised charmer, but surely in your heart you want more than that from a man?'

'I know what I do not want,' Barbara's mouth set in mutinous lines, 'and that is to be persuaded into marriage with someone I hardly know. I cannot bear the thought of it—you are safe from such a tradition, Vanessa, but Don Rafael has complete control of my life and he will do what *he* thinks best for me.' She grimaced at her cigarette. 'Best for me! It would be better if he let me marry Ruy—oh, I know what you think, that Ruy would want marriage with me only for the money I am to inherit. *Oiga!* We could buy a *ganaderia* in Spain and breed bulls. Ruy would like that, to be a *ganaderos*.'

'It all sounds very romantic,' Vanessa smiled drily, 'but I'm sure Don Rafael would never force you into a marriage with anyone against your will. He's very fond of you, *chica*.'

'*Chica*, you say? So I *am* a child to be humoured.' All the same Barbara smiled grudgingly and dug the toe of her ballet-type slipper into the carpet. 'The trouble is . . . I like to be kissed by Ruy. Is this not love, when the senses respond and seem on fire?'

'A while ago you said I couldn't know these things on account of being a cold Britisher.' Vanessa laughed. 'The truth is, my dear, you're warm-hearted and awake to the fact that you want to be loved. It's what is called being in love with love.'

'And you, too, have known this?' Barbara demanded, dark eyes intrigued.

'I—suppose I have.' Vanessa recalled the few kisses she allowed under the moon at Ordaz, and the exciting world of the senses she had glimpsed while held in a pair of male arms. It had given her a heady feeling of exhilaration to realize that when she chose she could enter this world and be lost in it . . . enraptured by it. But with the right man! And she felt she would know him the moment he kissed her, for his kisses wouldn't merely hint at what could be, they would show her.

'You are the deep one, I think.' Barbara was looking at her with her dark head cocked on one side in that attractively impudent way of hers. 'How could you look like a Velazquez model and not have the emotions to match? Come, *cara mia*, what is his name?'

'Burlington Bertie!' Vanessa teased, jumping up with a

laugh. She walked over to the partly closed jalousies, then turned and stood framed by the green slats that let in slim bars of gold. 'I've a bit of news for you, Babs. Don Rafael has asked me to be your *dueña*.'

'What do you say?' Barbara stubbed her cigarette and came over to clasp Vanessa's hands. 'Is it true?'

Vanessa nodded. 'Do you like the idea?'

'So,' Barbara gave a laugh, 'you convinced him that you should be employed by him? *Esta bien*, I like you for my new gaoler.'

'Well, that's a nice thing to call me,' Vanessa protested. 'I prefer to call myself your companion, someone you can confide in and go places with.'

'And not find the dark corners in which to canoodle with the so-charming Ruy, eh?' Barbara held her shrewd young head on one side like a bright jay. She studied Vanessa for a long moment, then in her ingenuous way she said: 'With your beautiful hair and your pale throat that curves and pools, you must be most attractive in the eyes of men—ah, such a delightful blush! The *compadre* should see it!'

'I doubt whether he'd be particularly impressed,' Vanessa rejoined, exasperated by her tendency to blush—like a schoolgirl!

'He is *muy macho*—but then you do not like him, eh–?' Barbara gave a mischievous chuckle. 'I feel it is dangerous to dislike a man so much. Dislike is related to hatred, and hatred they say is love turned inside out.'

Love in reverse, Vanessa mentally corrected, a moment before it forcibly struck home to her that upon several occasions she had violently disliked Don Rafael. She said hastily: 'Shall we go and amuse ourselves with the puppets? I'm just beginning to get the hang of moving them properly.'

The puppets Vanessa spoke about had belonged to an uncle of Don Rafael's. He had built a miniature stage and fashioned with great artistry the characters for several costume dramas. Vanessa had taken a fancy to the hobby and she and Barbara often amused themselves with the delightful wooden puppets whose costumes were of real velvet, brocade and lace. Carlitos, the Don's secretary, was an enthusiast and he had already taught Barbara how to manipulate the strings. Vanessa, who had agile, slender hands, was rapidly acquiring the trick, and the two girls planned to give a real show one evening.

'To the puppets,' Barbara agreed, dark eyes still twinkling. '*Pronto!*'

The following week was a quiet one, for Lucia Montez had been invited to spend time with friends further inland and Don Rafael went with her. On business, he said, but when Lucia and he drove off in his car Barbara put into words what was going through Vanessa's mind, that he would be combining quite a bit of pleasure with his so-called business.

On the Tuesday following his departure, as Vanessa and her charge strolled up from the beach after their morning dip, there was a noticeable return of alertness in the demeanour of the servants. The somewhat lax atmosphere that had persisted for a week had rolled away like a heaviness out of the air, and the reason was made abundantly clear to Vanessa as she followed Barbara through a patio archway into the hall. The master of the *castillo* had returned and he was standing by a table where calling-cards were placed on a salver.

He swung round at the sound of girlish chatter, and into a characteristic peak went his left eyebrow as he flicked a glance from one girl to the other. Fresh-looking from their swim, they also presented quite a contrast in colouring standing, startled, as they did beneath the sculptured archway with its glowing frieze of *azulejos*.

'You are back, *padrino*,' Barbara exclaimed, adding saucily: 'You have done good business?'

'I cannot say at this stage, *picara*,' he drawled, twin glimmers of humour in those wincingly penetrating eyes of his. 'One sows a seed with the hope of success, but only time will reveal a flower or a weed. And how do you progress with your new *dueña, queridisma*?'

'We are *simpatica*, eh, Vanessa?' Barbara cocked a merry

glance at the other girl, then as though impelled by irresistible affection for her godfather, she suddenly ran to him, reached for his shoulders and pressed a tawny cheek to his swarthy one. 'We all miss you, *padrino*, though you have your searching eyes in every corner of the *castillo* when you are here.'

'You *all* miss me, eh?' He was gazing ironically at Vanessa as he spoke. 'I wonder?'

'Lucia has returned with you?' Barbara asked.

'No. Her friends wished for her company a little longer and I was persuaded by them to return alone.' He passed an arm about Barbara's waist and drew her to his side so that he could directly address Vanessa. 'I think, Miss Carrol, that it is time your wardrobe was replenished, therefore if the pair of you will change out of beach pants into respectable skirts, I will drive you into town for a shopping spree.'

Barbara gave an exclamation of delight. Vanessa also caught her breath, but for a different reason. She had not yet been paid a *peseta* of her wages and hadn't the face to mention the fact. 'Don Rafael,' she blurted, 'my shopping can be done at any odd time——'

She got no further, for his deep voice cut across hers in so decisive a manner that she was left gaping. 'You will please not to argue over the matter, Miss Carrol. Señora Montez, and also other smart women of my acquaintance, buy their clothing at a salon which has my full approval. I will drive you there and you will provide yourself—no expense spared—with a full and suitable wardrobe.'

'Suitable to a *duenna*?' The words were out before she could stop them. His eyes went narrow—chilled jet with fire in it!

'You are well aware that I do not regard you entirely in the light of an employee,' he gritted. 'As a fairly frequent visitor to your home at Ordaz I naturally noticed that you wore attractive dresses. I am not quite of stone, Miss Carrol, with no understanding of what it means to a young woman to lose everything. Most certainly clothes cannot recompense you for the great personal loss of the man who was like a father to you, but you have the feminine heart—I think—

and assuredly the courage to begin life anew. And it begins today, with no more arguments.'

Abruptly his eyes softened and filled with mocking amusement. 'Was there ever so much independence in one small *muchacha*? *Ay Dios mio*, I think not!'

Barbara, standing there encircled by his arm, was eyeing the two combatants in a very interested fashion. '*La paloma y el leopardo*, how they fight,' she murmured impudently. 'One could sell tickets for this *corrida* and make a profit.'

Vanessa, not looking exactly dove-like with her fiery hair framing green eyes and flushed cheeks, was certainly of the opinion that there was something of the leopard about Don Rafael as he put back his black head and laughed at his goddaughter's wisecrack. Lithe in superb steel-grey suiting, no bulging of muscle or jutting of over-large bones, yet with a kind of simmering power in his lean body that suggested indefatigable vitality. In repose, she had noticed, his body still simmered with activity. There was always something long, smooth and menacing about his way of walking. He could purr and he could rend.

Leopardo, eh? And it would seem that this particular morning he had Vanessa Carrol marked down as a victim of his menacing charm. Helplessly, she watched a slow smile slash creases at either side of his mouth as he shot a glance at the gold watch strapped about his left wrist. 'I give both of you ten minutes in which to change. Now up to your rooms, *pronto*!'

As though we're children, Vanessa thought, and wished she dared take her time up the stairs. But Barbara caught at her hand and made her run all the way. In her room, as she changed into one of the day dresses that were fine on Barbara but far from flattering on herself, she was aware of a queer breathlessness. It wasn't merely that race up the stairs which had caused it, nor the blaze of annoyance she had lit in the Don's eyes with that crack about buying clothes suitable for a *dueña*. No, it was more like excitement. And why not? She was female, she liked good clothes, and she was about to shop for outfits, *carte blanche*, at probably the most exclusive salon on the island.

She ran a comb through her hair, then meeting her own eyes in the mirror she bit down on the nerve that quivered in her lower lip. 'You had no need to snap at the man,' she reprimanded her rather guilty reflection. 'No wonder he isn't all that keen on you as a person, he's beginning to think you a disagreeable little shrew.'

Shrew? It was a thought terrible enough to alarm any girl, and one Vanessa had well in mind when she returned downstairs along with Barbara.

They made their way out to the forecourt, where Don Rafael awaited them beside a sleek black convertible with a silver replica of a Jaguar poised on the gleaming bonnet. He handed the two girls into the back with an attentiveness and courtesy so entirely Latin that Vanessa had to admit to herself that it was no wonder Spanish women of the upper classes kept up the pretence of being helpless and fragile. 'Th-thank you,' she said, still with that strange breathlessness as her employer's lean brown hand released her wrist and she sank into the soft embrace of wine-coloured upholstery.

'You wish the top of the car left open, Miss Carrol?' he asked.

'Yes—please. It's such a marvellous morning.'

'You like the wind through your hair, eh?' His eyes flicked the sun-burnished swathe that danced lightly on her slim shoulders, then he turned his attention to Barbara, and a minute or so later he was behind the wheel and they were rolling along under the exotic flamboyant trees, which were interspersed with plumy palms, jacarandas with huge violet bells and ferny leaves and statuettes swathed in cascades of wistaria. The scents mingled richly in the sun-laden air, and Vanessa saw dragonflies fluttering gauzily among the trees, humming-birds like big whirling moths and black-speckled yellow birds that whistled with a poignant sweetness as they winged among the flames of the flamboyants.

Her breath caught suddenly. There was in the island air this morning an insidious magic that quickened the blood and raced the pulses. It was almost electrical, so that as she pressed her sandalled feet into the pile carpeting of the car sparks seemed to tingle all the way up from her toes—a sheer awareness of being alive and young and healthy.

Seated as she was on the right, at the back of the car, she was able to study, if she so wished, the profile and well-barbered hairline of the man at the wheel. The sun lit his forehead, nose and chin every now and again, intensifying his bronze-coin look, and Vanessa was acutely aware that the antagonism she had felt, on and off for four years, was no longer as potent as it had been. She was able to enjoy the beauty of Luenda, and this tingling awareness of being alive, because of Rafael de Domerique. Her heart gave a queer little lurch. As though drowning, every aspect of that last evening at Ordaz floated in front of her eyes. She seemed to feel his hands again, when he had yanked her away from the wall just outside her uncle's study, and the rush of his breath in her hair when he had warned that the drums were beating louder and they must make a bolt for safety. He would, had she fought him then, toted her over his shoulder!

A smile quivered on her mouth. Had she ever really believed that she hated him? Infuriating, arrogant, bossy. He was all three at times, but there were other aspects to his character she had never really let herself get to know. What had Barbara once said, that there was an angel and a devil in Spanish men? In most men, probably, but in this one to a more marked degree. Maybe because of his upbringing and his status as overlord of Luenda.

If he had a 'monarch of all I survey' outlook on life, it had to be accepted as part of the man. The arrogance was offset by a great deal of charm, and if there was iron in him, there was also, she now suspected, a well of tenderness beneath it. The woman he married would have a devil to deal with at times, but she would no doubt find a lot of compensation in his arms, and in his generosity.

Abruptly startled by the train her thoughts had taken, Vanessa switched to another tack, that of listening to him rather than thinking about him as he told Barbara about his recent trip inland with Lucia, and the various clubs and theatres they had visited in the evenings, accompanied by her friends.

'Soon now, I suppose, we can expect an announcement of your betrothal to Lucia?' Barbara said, with a conspiratorial sideglance at Vanessa. 'Yet you surprise me, *padrino mio*, that you wish to take for *your* wife a woman who has belonged already to someone else.'

'Really, *pequeña*?' he drawled over his shoulder. 'Do you consider that you know me so well?'

'Of course I do, at least as well as you permit anyone to know you.' The girl leant forward and touched the palm of her hand to the side of his neck for a fleeting moment, an affectionate gesture that slanted smile-lines at the side of the eye Vanessa could see.

'Come, *padrino*,' Barbara coaxed, 'have you marriage on your mind?'

'And if I have, *picara mia*, it is none of your business until I am prepared to discuss it with the woman in question.' Though he spoke gently enough, there was a firm note in his voice that made his goddaughter shrug her shoulders and lean back again beside Vanessa. She wrinkled her nose at Vanessa, as if to say silently that you could go just so far with the *compadre*, and that he never hesitated to put you in your place if he considered you were overstepping the mark with him. Vanessa couldn't check a little grin, though she too was curious to know when the announcement of his engagement was likely to be made. She had little doubt that the woman in question—Lucia—was waiting anxiously for him to propose.

Love, she reflected, at once wild and innocent, pathetic and passionate, wanted and yet unwanted. She wondered a little at her own sure knowledge when she had not yet come into personal conflict with the emotion. 'The sweet swindles of passion.' She had read the quote in a book belonging to her uncle, and he had said that it was the nostalgic witticism of an old man and that a young girl must not believe that it was true.

Sitting here in Rafael de Domerique's car, and cut off for ever from the gentle influence of her uncle, she found herself wondering what she would do when Jack Conroy came into her life again. She had a feeling he would, some time, somewhere, when today was almost forgotten by her and she was no longer employed by the Domeriques at the Castillo d'Oro. Lucia would not always want her around, and there seemed little doubt that Don Rafael had marriage plans for Barbara. Vanessa studied her folded hands in her lap as though they were strange and interesting. Alone again, as she must be alone some time, would she be swindled into thinking that what she felt for Jack was love, and would she in the end dismiss her well-kept dream of finding someone of whom she could say, 'Soul of my soul, and mine as I am thine?'

Don Rafael had quoted those burning lines as though he really believed them, which seemed to indicate that he had in Lucia Montez someone to whom he could cling 'as fire to flame.'

The car had left behind the golden dust of rustic roads, the small coppery *burros* pulling high-sided carts, and the sleepy stone and thatched houses set in an olive-yard or a small field of crops. They were now passing picturesque Spanish houses nearer to the town, and heading into a medieval atmosphere that chased like a sudden thrill through Vanessa's blood. Despite the cars, a few modern blocks of offices and the plate-glass of smart shops under awnings, a strong sense of past history still lingered here. Narrow streets meandered into gay little *plazas,* and from the wrought-iron balconies geranium petals floated to the cobbles over which the car wheels bumped as they entered the shopping centre.

Here they became wedged in a snarl-up of traffic, with horns tooting and vociferations in Spanish milling about them. A policeman in a white helmet and white gloves was doing his agitated best to unravel the tangle, and with a smile of amusement in his eyes, Don Rafael turned to say to Vanessa: 'Over to your right, Miss Carrol, you might be interested in an ancestor of mine. It was he who discovered this island, and had the *castillo* built so that he could survey his domain ... like an eagle from his eyrie.'

Vanessa turned her gaze to the direction he indicated,

taking in her mind's eye his deeply ironical smile. Darn the man, he seemed to know exactly how she regarded him!

'What a fierce person *that* Rafael must have been!' Barbara remarked, studying with Vanessa the armoured conquistador in stone who dominated the town square. His jutting nose and eagle-like eyes had been handed down to the present Rafael, along with his lithe, arrogant posture.

'Are you thinking that I resemble my fierce ancestor?' a voice drawled amusedly to the left of Vanessa.

'There's a decided resemblance,' she retorted. 'I can just see you roving the high seas and plundering the golden hoards of Brazil and Peru.'

'El Conquistador has an interesting history—one could envy him,' the Don laughed softly. 'He married a Cornish girl who was snatched from her home by Moorish corsairs and carried to Tangiers to be sold as a slave or a concubine. Don Rafael's galleons were in harbour and it is recorded that he bid a fantastic price for the girl, against one of the most powerful Emirs. Just imagine it, that fair, lovely English girl set up for auction in front of a crowd of corsairs, barbaric Moors and Spanish soldiers. Her terror must have been indescribable, no?'

'Yes!' Vanessa exclaimed. 'Poor thing, was she forced into marriage with your—with Don Rafael?'

'Would you not say that marriage with him was a better proposition than—something else with a black-skinned Emir?' Smile creases slashed the lean dark face of the man half-turned to Vanessa. 'From all accounts—it is again a pity that you cannot read Castilian—the founder of Luenda and his English wife were extremely happy together. Love works in mysterious ways, does it not?'

With a deep-throated laugh the Don swung round to the wheel and not many minutes later the car was braking in the Plaza de España, in front of a large, discreet-looking salon with tubbed plants at its entrance and a uniformed porter to open the glass doors for customers and keep an eye on the various opulent-looking cars parked in the kerb.

Don Rafael escorted the two girls into the salon, and there he left them in charge of the manageress. He would return for them in two hours, he said. Then looking directly down at Vanessa he added, a decided glint in his eye: 'Not clothing suitable for a *dueña,* you understand. And nothing in plum blue! *Hagame el favor?*'

'Very well, *señor,* nothing in plum blue.' She gave him a slight smile. 'And thank you.'

'*De nada.*' He snapped his fingers. '*A los uno, meniñas.*'

With a gracious nod of his head at the salon manageress he turned on his heel and strode out into the *plaza,* having reiterated that he would return for the girls at one o'clock.

Though this was an island salon, it was certainly switched in on the latest fashion trends. The severely coiffured manageress said with deference, for the young *inglesa* was of the household of the *señor hidalgo,* that the Señorita Vanessa had the most *difficile* colouring, but all the same she managed to come up with a selection of dresses and suits which might 'go' with Vanessa's vibrant hair and eyes. A svelte model by the name of Rozana came swishing through ruby curtains, showing off a raw-silk suit in champagne pink; a white silk-rib dress with a slender bronze belt and matching shoes; a leaf-green fabric coolie suit with a figured shantung blouse. Then there was a play-suit in cream with copper and tangerine flowers sprawling over it and love-letter pockets at the hips. Vanessa was uncertain about this, thinking it a little young. Barbara, who was thoroughly enjoying herself, said laughingly: 'The *compadre* has given his orders and you had better abide by them. You are to look gay, not sombre—and surely you cannot resist those cute little pockets?'

A trifle too cute in Vanessa's opinion, but what she couldn't resist, and agreed to try on, was an evening dress in cream honeycomb lace over apple-green silk. With it went strap sandals in green kid; they had very high heels that gave her almost a model-like poise when she appeared from the dressing cubicle clad in the dress. Her shoulders curved out of the lace with a delicate suggestion of a flush under her pale skin, it clung at bosom and waist, then flared and rustled from the hips downward. She stared at her reflection in the long triple-mirrors. It was a special-occasion dress, entirely unsuitable for a *dueña*. A smile—almost of regret— touched her mouth.

'I don't think Don Rafael meant me to go this far, Barbara,' she said. 'It's gorgeous, but when would I ever wear it?'

'At the *castillo* ball to celebrate the vintage, of course. You will steal all the limelight,' Barbara added gleefully, 'and make Lucia jealous.'

'If I do that,' Vanessa said drily, 'I'll soon be out of a job. No, *señora*,' she added to the manageress, 'I won't take this dress. It's lovely, but what I want are plainer, darker dresses for dining in.'

'Vanessa, you must have it,' Barbara insisted.

'I think not, *chica*.' Vanessa rustled away to take it off, stifling a regret that she hadn't money of her own with which to buy the rustling, flattering dream. It tugged at all the femininity in her, but she hadn't an obstinate set to her chin for nothing and off came the dress, to be handed to an assistant and carried away to await some other lucky purchaser.

She badly needed undergarments and after selecting several sets of pastel lingerie, along with lightweight girdles and bras, Vanessa changed into the white silk-rib sheath with the bronze-toned accessories. She had an idea Don Rafael might take Barbara and herself to lunch, and it would hardly please him to see her clad in a borrowed dress when she had just spent quite a bit of his money on brand new outfits. The sleek lines of the white sheath somehow called for up-swathed hair, and when she returned to the showroom she looked cool and poised. Very much the English Miss, Barbara asserted.

The girl seemed a trifle uncertain of this new Vanessa; this slender stranger in the high heels, whose well-fitting ribbed silk hinted at a slim but delectable figure. On the way downstairs to the vestibule she kept casting sideglances at Vanessa, and in the end she said: 'You look chic, *cara mia*, but I prefer you when you have the copper hair let down.'

'I prefer myself that way, my pet,' Vanessa smiled, 'but Don Rafael is now my employer and I shall feel more comfortable, meeting him on formal ground.'

'I wonder if it could be that you are a little bit afraid of him?' Barbara mused, looking intrigued by the idea.

'Oh, what nonsense!' Vanessa laughed—but for a moment, frighteningly, her breath had felt cut off, as though by a pressure against her windpipe. 'The ideas you get into that head of yours! Why on earth should I be afraid of Don Rafael?'

'Perhaps because you are English and he is a Spaniard, and he has not the outlook of your own easy-going countrymen. Always he is the master. Never *la que lleva los pantalones* for him!'

'If I get your meaning correctly, Barbara, and I think I do, it isn't my wish to wear the trousers with any man— least of all with a man such as Don Rafael!'

They had reached the vestibule and Vanessa had spoken rather louder than she intended. Colour stormed her cheeks as she met the suave, interested gaze of the man in question. He had just stepped between the glass doors and it was obvious from the way he was looking at her that he had caught part of her remark. The Don, however, was always the embodiment of courtesy and if he was curious to know what she had meant by those last few words—least of all with a man such as Don Rafael—he concealed it behind a bland smile.

'The replenishing of the wardrobe is concluded?' he asked, brushing her ensemble with his eyes.

'Yes, *señor*.' She felt discomfited, and somehow she wanted him to know that the first part of her remark had been quite innocuous, but instead she had to let herself be ushered with Barbara to his parked car and handed into it. Her purchases would be delivered by van.

'You must both be feeling hungry,' he said, 'so we go to lunch at the Skylight Room. You have not been there, Miss Carrol. I think you will like its atmosphere.'

The restaurant occupied the top floor of a smart tourist hotel and Vanessa got the Don's meaning about liking its atmosphere the moment they walked into the dining-room and were escorted by the maitre d'hotel to a table by the window. There were quite a few Europeans sitting at the tables. At the sound of English voices, and a smattering of American, Vanessa glanced round with an involuntary smile...

And looked straight into a pair of metal-grey eyes under a blond crop. Gary Elsing! He winked one of those impudent eyes, and then slid his glance to Don Rafael, measuring the tall, lithe figure as it settled into a chair beside Vanessa's. The Don, always alert, caught the American's glance upon him. He inclined his dark head, then before Vanessa could wipe away her own smile of recognition at the rangy Texan with the lopsided grin, the Don had swung his gaze to her and impaled her upon it. His eyes narrowed.

'You are acquainted with Señor Elsing?' he demanded.

Swiftly resenting the brusque note in his voice that commanded a truthful reply, she tilted her chin and admitted that Gary had struck up an acquaintance with her on the beach one morning. 'He's very friendly, it would have been boorish of me, *señor*, to ignore him.' She met those narrowed jetty eyes with their inner fires. 'What should I have done as a member of your household, referred him to you for an introduction to—to a mere *dueña*?'

They were at it again, she thought, seeing the muscles tauten at the corners of his mouth.

'You are welcome to make friends with whom you wish, Miss Carrol,' he said. 'Señor Elsing bears a distinct resemblance to the young Conroy—is it not so?'

Barbara, an elbow propped on the table, small white teeth nibbling at a stick of celery, was shooting interested glances from her godfather to Vanessa. 'Conroy,' she murmured. 'Is he the one whose kisses you have enjoyed, Vanessa?'

There comes a moment to most people when it would be distinctly good of the floor to open and swallow them. The floor, however, stayed firm under Vanessa's feet, and, already annoyed by that contemptuous inflection of the Don's whenever he spoke of Jack, she said sharply to Barbara:

'That was told to you in strict confidence. If I had thought for one moment you would tell anyone else——' Heat broke in a sudden wave over Vanessa's body that it had to be Don Rafael to whom Barbara had let out that piece of girlish indiscretion. She felt the blood storm her cheeks, while small hammers seemed to beat at her temples. The extent of her agitation was made worse by dark, alert eyes scanning the blush as it travelled all the way to her hairline.

'Come, Miss Carrol,' the Don examined a fork, then laid it down again, 'you must not feel distressed because Barbara has revealed your secret to me. You forget that I have seen you seeking the moonlight in the company of the young man.'

He spoke drawlingly, mocking the romance she might well have found with Jack. How dared he? Who did he think he was to—to look down his nose at the kisses and feelings of others? Was his own romance so very elevated? A sort of made-in-heaven affair? Not likely! It was no more than the coming together of an ambitious widow and a man in his middle thirties who chose sophistication in preference to innocence. No doubt because it would bore him to have eager hands ruffling his well-groomed hair, and adoring but uncertain kisses tattooing his cheek with lipstick.

The man was inhuman! Vanessa flicked her table napkin and spread it on her lap as the waiter placed a platter of *entradas* on the table. Fat green olives stuffed with anchovy. Curls of smoked ham. Small pickled cucumbers, and tiny rolled fishes.

Feeling sure she would choke on an appetizer, she found herself, nevertheless, with an olive on a tiny coloured stick. She chewed the olive and tried to win back some of the cool nonchalance she had felt back at the salon. She even glanced in Gary's direction and gave him a smile when—oh, how she envied him so much natural nonchalance—he raised his wine glass to her. He was lunching with an older, heavily built man who might also have been in the oil-business.

Barbara's healthy young appetite was unaffected by those currents of tension which she had, without malice, exposed and set humming in the air between Vanessa and the Don. She tucked into her food and chatted away, while it was with a real effort that Vanessa made inroads into the *gambas* in a spicy sauce; white slivers of some delectable bird cooked with rice in saffron, mushrooms and various other vegetables.

Don Rafael made conversation, purely out of politeness, she knew, for she had seen him animated across a table and carried away by enthusiasm. This aloof individual with the faintly mocking eyes bore hardly any resemblance to the wind-ruffled corsair who—it sometimes seemed in a dream—had breakfasted with her in a garden lost in time and the scents of the sea and sun-intoxicated flowers ...

During the course of lunch, quite a few glances were directed at the Don's party from nearby diners. It didn't need the smooth, deferential attention of the waiters to inform onlookers that someone of local importance was lunching at the Skylight Room. All that was needed was one look at the Don's forceful blade of a profile, and the assured poise with which he wore his superbly tailored suit. Vanessa and Barbara also underwent scrutiny, for as always they were a foil to each other, one a tawny brunette, the other cream and copper with green eyes that caught the light when she moved her head.

Their final course came to the table, a cherry and icecream dessert with a brandy sauce which their waiter ignited. The flaming sauce was poured over the cherry confection, which felt hot and cold together in the mouth.

Vanessa caught the Don's eye as she ate her sweet. He smiled, abruptly, hot and cold as the cherries and cream slipping over her tongue. 'The white dress is charming, Miss Carrol,' he said, adding with a sardonic glint in his eye: 'I hope you did as I specified and purchased garments for all occasions. Soon we will be having the vintage and there will be guests at the *castillo*. I will expect you to mix with women who take notice of each other's gowns. It is their way, you understand. Spanish women are extremely feminine, inclined to vanity, and one of their keenest occupations is an interest in their own appearance and that of other women.'

He played with the long stem of his wine glass. 'You selected evening dresses, *señorita*?'

Whenever he addressed her in the Spanish way, she found herself instinctively responding, with a touch of humour. '*Tres, señor*. I really am grateful for all your generosity, but——'

'I must one day allow you to repay me,' he mockingly finished for her. 'So be it! You owe me repayment for a few dresses, a post and a roof over your head. The bill should be quite a formidable one, but I promise I shall one day present it to you.'

His smile was odd as he spoke, he seemed amused and at the same time irritated to the edge of sarcasm. He leaned back in his chair and inclined his head to an elegant, dark-haired *señora* lunching a few tables away. She flashed him the vivacious, appreciative smile of the very feminine Spanish woman, and Vanessa, taking a quick look at him under her lashes, surprised an expression in his eyes that could only be called one of hungry impatience.

The smart, attractive, man-conscious *señora* presumably reminded him of Lucia Montez. Had he held her in his arms last night and urgently whispered that she must return soon to the *castillo*? Had he yet told her that he intended to install her there as his exclusive possession? Had he said it in words, or had his kisses been enough to convey his intention?

Vanessa, dabbing at her lips with her table napkin, found herself looking at the Don's lips. Boldly cut, something ruthless about them, and yet she had noticed that when he smiled they had a tender quirk. The complex nature of the man lay in that cruel-kind mouth. It revealed that he would make a passionate and exciting lover, that his self-will would often exert itself, but that he had humour enough to be got round if the woman knew how to go about this ticklish task. And Lucia, who was Spanish to her fingertips, no doubt knew the secret of winding a masterful Spaniard about her little finger...

At this point in her reflections, Vanessa gave a start as someone lightly pressed a hand down on her shoulder, while a gay, drawling voice said above her head: 'I'd like to take Miss Carrol out one evening, Don Rafael. Would it be okay?'

'But of course, my friend.' The Don flicked a cool, faintly speculative glance from the Texan's sun-bitten face to Vanessa's startled one. She hadn't expected Gary to carry his fire into the Don's camp, as it were, and she listened dumb-founded as he went on to ask what specific evening she had free.

'Miss Carrol is at liberty to choose her own evening,' her employer replied, in a voice that was smooth as steel. 'No doubt she will appreciate your company, *amigo*, after several weeks of being exclusively in the company of—foreigners, shall I say?' A suave lift of a black brow, flecked-jet eyes flicking again from Gary to Vanessa. 'There is little doubt that the temperament of the North American is closely allied to that of the English. You agree, Señor Elsing?'

'Wholeheartedly.' Gary chuckled, unruffled by the Don's cool and tantalizing manner even if Vanessa wasn't. His carefree eyes met hers and he said, gay and sure of himself: 'If Saturday is okay with you, Vanessa, I'll call for you around seven-thirty and we'll have ourselves an enchanted evening.'

'A-all right, Gary,' she heard herself say, too swept along by his ebullience to be really sure whether she wanted to go out with him or not. It was true she had enjoyed his company the other morning, but she didn't want to be rushed by him. He was a virile and attractive man, for one thing. And for another—well, she was ever conscious that a woman facing possible loneliness was a vulnerable one, and ripe to make emotional mistakes...

'Until Saturday, honey.' He squeezed her shoulder, grinned at Barbara—a very interested observer—and said to the Don: '*Mil gracias, señor,* for permission to come courting.'

The Don smiled, cool and aloof, then he said: 'Do not

forget, *amigo*, that my household is a Spanish one in all respects and that I shall expect the *señorita* back under my roof by ten o'clock.'

'What?' Gary hooted a laugh, and then looked uncertain. 'You must be kidding!'

'If you mean am I joking—I assure you I am not, Señor Elsing.'

'But I can't promise to break up our party that early——'

'I think you had better,' Don Rafael interposed crisply. 'Miss Carrol is in my care while she remains on the island, and from seven-thirty until ten o'clock represents quite a pleasant length of time for the enjoyment of a woman's company.'

'It's darned Victorian, if you want my opinion, Don Rafael!' Gary spoke with exasperation. 'Vanessa is an English girl. She isn't accustomed to having her life controlled. Ten o'clock, by heck! The evening's only just beginning—come on, have a heart, *señor*!'

An ice-cool smile flickered the Don's lips. 'Believe it or not, Señor Elsing, I have a heart and I understand your feelings only too well. Your luncheon companion appears to be getting restless, let me add.'

Gary shot a look over his shoulder, then angrily brushing his surrealist tie into his jacket, he said to Vanessa: 'You've really got yourself into something, haven't you? I'll have to see what I can do about that—*hasta pronto*, Honey!'

He swung away and rejoined his friend. A few minutes later the two rugged figures had strolled out of the restaurant, and Vanessa was gazing across at the man who could, it seemed, literally take over your life and run it. His shoulders lifted slightly as he caught her glance, he flicked cheroot ash into a tray near his lean brown hand and was so illimitably sure of himself. A feudal autocrat, whose forebears had charged his blood with their ruthless arrogance.

Her eyes flashed emerald sparks into his dark ones. 'I'm not a child, Don Rafael,' she said. 'I can take care of myself.'

'You say that with a touch of defiance, Miss Carrol, and you make me wonder if you really believe it,' he rejoined.

'Oh, you're impossible at times!' He had touched a nerve, for it was only too true that with a man like Gary —whose fair, grey-eyed, rather gay look made him a slightly older edition of Jack Conroy—she might find herself being taken in by feelings of the moment. Feelings that swindled her into thinking she had found love and security. It could so easily happen, with the moon in the sky, and the spicy scents of the island drugging her to a sweet lethargy that stole away all resistance...

Something touched her and she jerked back to an awareness of the restaurant and her two companions. Lean fingers lay dark over her left wrist, upturned on the table in a kind of lost, almost poignant appeal.

She gave a little shudder as the Don said to her, crisply: 'Trifling with the affections is a pastime I do not advocate, and Señor Elsing seems to me a man who has often played such a game. You will recall that when I first brought you to Luenda, I said I would put myself in the place of your good uncle and provide the guidance he could no longer give you. I am a man of my word!' As though to underline this declaration, he now held her wrist immovable on the table, while his brilliant eyes, lit deep down by glimmers of sheer gold, were delving into hers and imposing his arrogant will upon her. She struggled to withdraw her gaze and her wrist, but both were securely held. Her breath came in little, unknowing pants between her lips. She hated him... because he was so horribly right about Gary... and because at his touch something was zig-zagging through her bones which left her shocked and trembling.

'I—I'll have Gary for a friend if I want him,' she fought back. 'There's nothing you can do about it.'

'On the contrary, Miss Carrol, there is always something I can do about occurrences on this island.' His fingers tightened, painfully. 'Señor Elsing is employed here, is he not?'

Her breath caught in her throat. No, she couldn't believe that he'd actually deprive Gary of his job... but the wild look she flashed over his dark, autocratic face was sufficient to put her wise.

In order to get his own way, the *hidalgo* of Luenda could be utterly ruthless. She saw it in his eyes, felt it in his grip, knew it in the pounding of her heart. As her lips moved in silent protestation, his wore a smile of deadly intention.

CHAPTER SIX

It was Friday night, and Vanessa lay under the tent of netting over her bed, listening to the cicadas and tree-frogs, the faint rattling of palm fronds and now and then the weird rising pipe of a night bird.

She might have been back at Ordaz, for the murmurous nocturnal noises on the island were much the same. Ordaz, where she had been happy and free. Sighing on the thought, she turned over and tried again to woo the sleep that had been so elusive these past few nights. She plumped her pillow, concentrated on the tick-tock of the clock on her beside table, but the peace of sleep continued to elude her.

Darn it! She slipped out from under the netting, stepped into her mules and draped round her shoulders the dressing-robe that, along with her other purchases, had arrived from the salon a few days ago. She walked over to the open doors of her balcony and stepped out under the stars. They clustered in swathes above her, while far below the sea glistened as though scattered with mother-of-pearl. The haunting cry of a peacock somehow intensified the midnight blues that were gripping Vanessa.

She was aware of an ache that stole out from her heart and spread right through her body as she gazed in the direction in which Ordaz lay. Why was she looking in that direction? For what was she searching? The kindly uncle she had lost for ever—or the elusive promise of something more that had haunted, like an uncertain sunbeam, the picnics, the tennis bouts, the foxtrots and discussions she had enjoyed with that gay-hearted rover, Jack Conroy? Where was he now? Not, she thought, at the hotel in Chile where she had always written to him, but deep in the heart of a green and jungly forest in search of diamonds or emeralds.

A smile wavered on her lips, then drifted away again, and, irresistibly as sharp pins to steel shears, her thoughts were drawn back to the man who had brought her to

Luenda.

Ever since that lunch at the Skylight Room she had been a tensed-up bundle of nerves, and she hated the feeling. As though her fighting spirit had been temporarily crushed by the man who used his masterful charm, his vitality and power to such overwhelming effect that people submitted to his will despite themselves.

'He has most power who has power over himself.' Those lines had been running through her mind for days, and there was a moistness in the palms of her hands as they clenched the wrought grille around her balcony. Bars of iron holding her a prisoner in a tower of her own making! To be fair, the *hidalgo* had offered to pay her passage to England, but what had she done? Gone all British and proud, and asserted that she would sooner earn the fare home, and money enough to keep her while she undertook a secretarial course. She had given him authority over her as an employer, and now she was realizing the position she was in.

No money as yet but the wages she earned. Affection for Barbara making daily inroads into her independence. And, behind it all, an almost panicky reluctance to pull her roots out of the soil of the tropics. Four years ago she had successfully transplanted out here ... she felt that something vital within her would wither and die if she left the sun and the sea, and the spell of star-laden nights with the musical insistence of the cicadas throbbing in time with her quick-beating heart ...

How quickly it was beating, high in her throat like a bird trying to get out. Almost making the escape as below her in one of the patios she watched again what could have been the moving spark of a firefly. But it wasn't! Now her eyes had grown used to the darkness she realized that she had been following the slow rise and fall of the lighted end of a cigar.

A tall figure was standing alone down there, cloaked and masked in the midnight shadows, enjoying a solitary smoke within the castellated wall of his medieval domain. Don Rafael de Domerique, whose eyes had flashed with such devilry when he had talked of his ancestor, El Conquistador, who had bought himself an English bride with plundered gold.

Was it really possible, Vanessa wondered, that the girl had cared for such a man? Or credible that tenderness had lain in his fierce heart, waiting to be lavished on the girl who had been torn from her home and carried in a pirate ship to the slave market at Tangiers? It was a barbaric story and exactly the kind to appeal to the man who had related it. There could be no pity in him for the woman who had been at the mercy of the swarthy, unscrupulous sea-rover from whom he had sprung ... not only to resemble El Conquistador physically, but doubtless in more basic ways ...

At this point, Vanessa suddenly backed away from the wrought grille. There was a crash behind her as her impulsive movement swept to destruction a forgotten tumbler that had been standing on the balcony table. The noise made by the breaking glass couldn't fail to be heard down in the patio where the Don stood smoking, and Vanessa could have kicked herself for her clumsiness. Now he knew that she had been standing up here, sharing with him the pulsing beauty of the night.

She stood a moment in a tense, almost trapped attitude, then clutching her robe around her flimsy nightdress she hurried into her bedroom. Safely obscured once more beneath the netting of her bed, she felt a tremor take possession of her from her toes to her eartips. It clutched at the nape of her neck like—like lean fingers, while she seemed to see again a swarthy face above hers, and feel the rocking motion of the bottomless ocean ... love is beautiful and cruel ... and deep as the sea, a voice crooned. *O mar e lindo.*

She slept, and awoke with the feeling that she had dreamed strange things that skipped away and would not be recaptured in the prosaic daylight streaming across her balcony into her room. A silver teaset stood on her bedside table, catching the sun and blinking as she poured a cup of tea and added two cubes of sugar, then a swirl of cream from the little silver pitcher. She sipped lazily at the delicious brew, her gaze upon the reflection that a large wall mirror gave back to her. Copper hair ruffled above drowsy silver-green eyes, the lacy straps of her nightdress half off her rounded shoulders and showing the pale skin that eluded the sun's rays. The pink pillow behind her was a foil for her hair and eyes, while the airy clouds of netting were like pale green billows of spindrift thrown up about her slim figure in the regal bed.

The princess and the pea, she thought, and saw her reflected lips twist in a reminiscent smile as she took a biscuit off a leaf-shaped dish and bit into it. Mmmm, coconut with a thin, sweet layer of icing. Each morning a different sort of biscuit was brought with her tea, and always on Saturdays it was these delectable coconut fingers ...

Of course, she sat up sharply, today was Saturday, and that evening she had her controversial date with Gary Elsing!

A current of excitement ran through her veins, chased by an apprehension that seemed to tighten strings under her rib-cage. Gary was going to kick against bringing her home at ten o'clock, but she knew—with a sense of fatalism experienced before at the *castillo*—that there was no defying the mastery of its *hidalgo*. The man got his own way not only because the habit of dominance was bred into the hard bones and core of him, but because there was usually a logical reason for his rulings that made them a medicine you accepted, crossly aware that it was for your own good despite the bitterness involved in swallowing it.

Gary, in his eyes, was another Jack Conroy, and though her uncle would have resigned himself to the inevitable had her association with Jack developed into an engagement, Don Rafael was decidedly not the resigning sort. Things went *his* way, or else.

Vanessa licked icing off her fingers and slid out of bed. It was infuriating to have to give in to the man, but she couldn't risk losing Gary his job for the sake of defying her 'guardian'. Her overlord was a better term. How well it suited him. 'You will replenish your wardrobe, Miss Carrol.'

'You may have whoever you wish for a friend, Miss Carrol.' Smooth emphasis on the 'friend'. What had he in mind, she wondered, a slightly hysterical little laugh breaking from her—a plan to provide *her* with a suitable husband? She wouldn't put it past him!

She opened the big mahogany wardrobe that held her new dresses. Concepcion had hung them for her when they had arrived from the salon and she had not looked all that closely at them until now. She slid the hangers along the rail, enjoying the feel of chiffon as she examined the smart black number with the see-through lantern sleeves, stroking the fine nap of the moss-green velvet—then stiffening as her eyes settled on a glimmering lace and silk dress that she had last seen being carried off by one of the salon assistants to await another buyer.

She took hold of the hanger and lifted the dress out of the wardrobe. The honeycomb lace over apple-green silk was unmistakable, but she had told the manageress not to include it in her order! She could feel her heart thumping, strangely disturbed that she should find herself in possession of something she had wanted with all her feminine heart, yet which she had rejected because—because it would have meant taking it from Rafael de Domerique.

Now here she stood holding it, feeling it, listening to the rustle of it—for her hand was shaking. She felt certain the manageress of the shop would not have sent the dress with the others unless specifically told to do so, therefore Barbara must have told the Don about it, and he—who liked nothing better than exerting his authority over the independent English Miss—had telephoned the salon and had the dress replaced on her order. Cold with anger, Vanessa replaced it in the cavernous wardrobe, right at the back. She wouldn't wear it! Let it rot first!

She slammed the doors on the dresses, and the subtle perfume of the sachets that hung among them, no longer in the mood to decide on what to wear for her date with Gary. There was a shine of tears in the corners of her eyes as she gazed at her mutinous reflection in the gilt-edged mirror filling the wall panel between the wardrobes. She could no longer feel amused, in an exasperated way, by the lordly creature who had taken over the management of her life, even to the extent of invading the privacy of her secret yearnings and forcing upon her something she could have loved—and now hated.

His arrogance was beyond toleration, and grown impatient with looking at her simmering mutiny that yet could not break out into open revolt—must she face, as well, the mortification of knowing she feared him?—she hurried into her bathroom and turned on the shower in the self-contained cubicle with glazed walls. She lifted her face to the tingle of cold water and when it had washed away the last of her angry tears, she felt more in the mood to face her odd, disturbing life at the Castillo d'Oro.

The bells of the *castillo*'s private chapel were fluid and musical on the morning air, while the attractive bell-tower of the small white building showed above the trees of the breakfast patio. This meal was always a leisurely affair, with quite a selection of foods wheeled out on a trolley by one of the white-jacketed servants.

Upon coming through the cedarwood archway, over which clambered a riot of pink and wine clove carnations, Vanessa was startled to see the Don seated at the circular table under the crimson and gold blaze of the tulip tree. Usually he was off about the affairs of the estate, or his various other concerns, before Vanessa and Barbara came down to breakfast. But today, perhaps because it was the start of the weekend and he felt lazy, he was still at the table with a newspaper propped up in front of him and wearing a spiced-wine shirt with short sleeves. The wine colour against his swarthy skin, the glint of his teeth in a brief smile as he glanced up, gave him a devastating corsair attraction that Vanessa was conscious of despite a heart full of resentment.

He loomed to his feet as she approached the table and drew out for her one of the wrought-iron chairs cushioned in a jewel colour. '*Muy buenos dias, señorita.*' He flicked a look over the sleeveless leaf-green fabric coolie dress she was wearing, the green-heeled sandals, an inexpensive shell necklace she had let Barbara buy her the other day, and a dash of coral lipstick. 'You slept well last night?' Adding with a quick smile: *'Hablo castellano!'*

She knew her Spanish to be improving and obligingly replied in his tongue: *'Muy bien, gracias, señor,'* stiffening as his hard brown arm brushed hers, an involuntary contact caused by the swoop of his palm upon a fairly large spider that had just dropped to the lace tablecloth from the swooping branches of the tree above them. He took a couple of paces to a magnolia hedge and released his captive among the silky platters. As he returned to his seat, a hint of mischief glimmered in his dark eyes.

'It is becoming a habit for me to rescue you from these various *bêtes noirs*,' he drawled.

As always she suspected a double meaning behind his words, but she summoned an answering smile, albeit a constrained one, as she slipped the silver ring off her table napkin and laid the fine, monogrammed linen across her lap. She hoped to goodness Barbara wasn't going to be much longer coming down to breakfast. Sharing the meal, *tête-à-tête*, with Don Rafael was not going to be easy in her present mood.

'I grew used to spiders at Ordaz,' she replied. 'I don't like them, but they don't send me screaming for help to the nearest, more courageous male.'

'Because you are an English girl, of course, and must keep the firm upper lip,' he mocked, turning to the trolley that stood between them. 'Will you take *cafe con leche*, or dare I hope that you have acquired the Spanish fondness for breakfast chocolate?'

She was immediately tempted to ask for coffee, but her mind was changed by the taunting awareness in his eyes. 'Go on,' they gibed, 'say you like very little that is Spanish, least of all myself, the embodiment of the cruelties, courtesies and creeds that make up the Spanish character!' They looked right through her, those shrewd, mocking, brilliant eyes, and it was as though she had been dispossessed of her secret self. They knew about her fear of him, her dislike of him ... and because of Barbara's prattle they knew that she wasn't always the cool and reserved English Miss. They knew she had been kissed and that she had quite liked the experience and glimpsed beyond it a warm and promising land of love.

'I'll have chocolate, *señor*,' she said, and saw his thin upper lip quirk at the edge as he poured her a cup of hot chocolate and a small glass of the iced milk that was drunk in alternate sips with it. It was redolent of cinnamon as he handed her the cup. She took a *churro*, a crisp fritter, and dipped it in the thick chocolate. The two together were delicious, and it was maddening that appetite should be stronger than her principles and rob her of the satisfaction of rejecting something he strongly liked. She knew he often indulged in the cinnamon drink, for on more than one occasion she had noticed a servant carrying a tray to his study on which it steamed in a jug, or stood iced in silver-lined pewter.

He was a strange mixture, she reflected, her nostrils quivering as the aromatic steam rose out of her own cup. Had anyone ever really got near to knowing him? Had his beautiful mother, now shut away from the world in a Segovian convent? Or that regal old lady, Doña Manuela? Did he reveal a totally different side to the people he loved... especially to Lucia Montez?

He was now lifting the glittering domes that covered various dishes on the trolley. 'You will have a little fish, or perhaps an omelette?' he enquired, the courteous host, but with a glint in his eye that denoted an enjoyment of the charged atmosphere between them.

It could have been simmering temper that was putting an edge on her appetite, for the omelettes looked and smelt mouth-watering as he lifted the dome over the chafing-dish in which they lay neatly folded and crisply golden. She couldn't resist one.

'*Su servidora.*' He seemed ironically disposed to wait on her, and over came her plate with the glistening, mushroom-and-tomato-packed omelette. He, too, had one, and as they reached in unison for the salt, the silver minaret toppled over and a trail of white grains scattered out.

'*Mala suerte!*' he exclaimed, and Spanish to his smallest bones and therefore superstitious, he quickly tossed three pinches of the spilled salt over his shoulder. 'Who is the clumsy one, *señorita*, you or I?'

The wincing penetration of his eyes met hers, and she knew he had heard the tumbler fall and break on her balcony last night. 'Do I make you nervous?' he drawled, accepting the salt sifter after she had used it. He jabbed his fork into a saffron-tinted mound of macaroni and expertly rolled and carried it to his mouth. He peaked an enquiring eyebrow at Vanessa as he chewed. 'It is difficult to comprehend why you should feel nervous of me when we have been acquainted for several years.'

'You were my uncle's friend, *señor*,' she replied, feeling a faint heat in her cheeks and bending her head to butter a twist of home-baked bread. 'To you I have always been rather flighty, a-and flirty, it would seem. Actually I'm neither, but it's disconcerting to be thought what you are not.'

'A sentiment I thoroughly endorse.' The drawl in his voice was even more pronounced. 'Perhaps we have misjudged each other, and that would make for antagonism, would it not? Where understanding is sparse, sympathy is always difficult to establish.'

'I quite agree,' she said. 'Very probably you expect me to feel and react like a Spanish girl, and it tries your patience that I'm unable to.'

'In Señor Elsing's words, you are an English girl and unused to having your life controlled, eh? Come, would you say that I make of Barbarita a prisoner, much as she is fond of calling herself a fair captive in the tower? Am I really such a dragon, Miss Carrol?' A smile sparked those topaz glints in his eyes. 'I invite you to be entirely candid.'

'Well, you breathed quite a lot of fire at the idea of Gary Elsing dating me,' she rejoined. 'I assure you I have no intention of eloping with the man, attractive as he is.'

'Ah, but you consider him to be attractive,' the Don quickly took her up. 'Does not love begin in the eye?'

'Love!' she exclaimed, breaking into a laugh. 'Do you think I'm ripe to—to fall in love with the first man on the island who strikes up a flirtation with me? Lord, do you think I'm that *young*?'

'You have still to mature emotionally.' He pushed aside his empty plate and his long fingers deliberated over a platter of delicately flushed peaches, dark rich grapes and the lovebird green of papaya. He chose grapes and she watched his white teeth crushing them. The man was lazily deliberate in his movements, as darkly striking as a pagan prince out of mythology—Pluto who also stole a bride and took her to his kingdom in the nether regions!

Vanessa gave herself a shake, for it seemed that with this man she was invariably led into fantastic conjectures about *his* approach to love.

'You have enjoyed your omelette?' he enquired.

'It was light as a bird's flight,' she smiled, schooling her curious thoughts and helping herself to a papaya. Despite the many black seeds of this fruit, she liked its refreshing tang.

'That lightness is acquired from the olive oil,' he told her. 'There are various Spanish sayings with regard to the oil of the olive, which we regard as extremely precious. Have you heard the one which likens a wife to the smooth suavity of the oil, and a husband to the tempestuous warmth of wine? The comparisons are very Spanish, no?'

'Yes,' she laughed, for it seemed to her that Spanish women had to be pretty even-balanced and bland to cope with the masculine superiority of their men, their emotionalism, hauteur and fiery tempers. Then added to it these men were often far handsomer than their women, therefore the feminine tendency to jealousy would have to be well in subjection to a loving maternalism if friction was to be kept at a minimum in a Latin household. A handsome man did as a handsome man wanted, whether in a Latin land or elsewhere!

'You have the talking eyes, Miss Carrol,' the Don said drily. 'The Spanish woman is undergoing your mental sympathy, eh? Yet, as I have indicated before, she is cherished by her husband often to an extent undreamed of in your country. At heart the Spaniard is a primitive, and his wife his possession. *His*, you understand. She knows it, even when he strays, for men are not angels and real women would not have them so. Of course,' a droll shrug of the shoulders that stretched their hard strength under the fine fabric of the spiced-wine shirt, 'I do not expect the cool English to understand this, or to sympathize with it, but you have my assurance that there is a fire in Latin love which burns out all the angers and troubles which cannot help but arise in the close marital association.'

'I'm sure all you say is applicable to the Latin temperament, Don Rafael.' Vanessa, wiping her fingers on her table napkin, was aware that they were shaking. Barbara had presumably overslept this morning, and if she abruptly made an excuse to leave the table, the Don would be bound to assume that she was running away from this incredibly intimate conversation they had drifted into. Would she be running away? Her eyes dwelt wide and startled on his dark face, then pulling herself together, she said lightly:

'I used to think that the Latin approach to love was an extremely romantic one, but it would seem from what you say that you approach it without high-flown sentiments.'

'On the contrary,' he rejoined with a smile. 'The Spanish language of love is probably the most exciting in the world. What I think you refer to is that we are not squeamish about discussing the more earthy aspects of romance, whereas in England you probably edge round them. Physical love has a strange beauty—ah, do I shock you?'

An uncontrollable wave of colour had drowned her throat, earlobes and cheeks. Why, she wondered swiftly, was he speaking to her like this? Had he shocked her? No, for she was not a prude, but never before had she heard him speak his thoughts so openly in such a warmly pitched voice ... the voice of a man in love contemplating the joys of possession that lay in store for him.

Love, he was saying, was a passionate involvement with a woman that could be strangely beautiful.

In as natural a voice as she could summon, Vanessa said: 'I'm not shocked, *señor*, just too English I suppose to be able to confess as openly as you that love is more a—a physical emotion than a spiritual one.'

'It is a primeval chemistry.' His smile was one of sardonic indulgence towards her youthful confusion. 'The body's awareness that it must have love is swifter than the mind to accept the inevitable. That is why mistakes can so often be made, and why it is a custom of my country to guide a girl in her choice of a lifetime partner. The young can be blinded by their self-seeking for love and so throw away their hearts on the first man who embraces them and reveals why nature made them soft-skinned and without the male angularity. It is a woman's true power, the power of the body and the only one she should exercise, but a girl blinded by the discovery of her power— which can overthrow the strongest man—has a curious tendency to incline towards the feckless, even the weak in character, as though her blossoming maternal instincts are involved as well and she is unable to distinguish between being a lover and a mother—do I make myself clear, *señorita*?'

Oh yes, he made himself as clear as daylight! Vanessa was now sitting up like a leaf-green ramrod in her chair, the sunlight burnishing her hair to flame about the creamy pallor of her neck. 'The lecture is a personal one, isn't it?' she flashed. 'You're warning me not to let my maternal instincts go astray when—and if—Gary Elsing takes me in his arms. I had no idea I looked so love-starved!'

'Many are starved of love,' he drawled, 'but most women mix their wisdom with a liberal dash of foolishness, and it could be, at this point in your life, that you are feeling insecure and your feeling may latch itself to the young Americano in the guise of—love.'

'But I'm already in love!' Vanessa heard the words before she fully realized she had spoken them. And as the tide will be driven relentlessly to the beach regardless of its own inclinations, other words came tumbling with a wayward will of their own. 'You are forgetting Jack Conroy, *señor*. Didn't my uncle tell you that I was writing to Jack and seeing quite a lot of him whenever he came to Ordaz? Uncle Len knew I had not shown much interest in other male visitors to the plantation, but when Jack came it was different. You saw this for yourself, didn't you? How we felt about each other?'

With a detachment that was chilling, even faintly contemptuous, the Don sat looking across at her. 'I saw a girl with a rather feckless boy,' he retorted, 'but if you want to believe it was love then go ahead and do so. It will, in the circumstances, perhaps stop you from making a fool of yourself with Señor Elsing.'

'How dare you!' Vanessa jumped to her feet, her nerves leaping with the palm-tingling anger this man alone could arouse in her. 'You imagine that because you're the *hidalgo* of Luenda you can say and do exactly what you like, regardless of the feelings of others. You're the most arrogant, self-willed man I've ever had the misfortune to meet!'

He, too, got to his feet and a couple of strides had brought him round to her. She felt his fingers close hard as steel over her shoulders, and looked into eyes that were storm-dark and flickering with electricity. 'And you, Miss Vanessa Carrol, are the most quick-tempered female I have ever had the misfortune to meet. You must learn to control such wildfire emotions, they are not becoming and reveal your immaturity.'

'I'm sorry I can't oblige your superior instincts by being a placid *señorita*, bedazzled by your masterful looks, your *castillo* and your wealth,' she shot back, feeling the race and thud of her heart as his fingers slowly tightened over her shoulders. 'I have none of the qualities you admire. I'm well aware of it, and I couldn't care less.'

'That latter statement is usually made by the childish and stubborn, and often means the reverse of what it implies. Do you want me to say that I admire your hair and eyes ... your skin?' His lips smiled thinly as his glance slid down over the pallor of her throat revealed by the square neckline of her dress. 'Does it displease you that I have never invited you into the moonlight, and kissed you?'

She gazed back at him, rendered speechless by the idea of feeling his ruthless lips on hers. A kiss from Rafael de Domerique! Surely there would be hell in it ... and enough heaven, a mocking voice seemed to whisper in her ear, to torment a woman through all her life with another man!

'Come, Miss Carrol, you are not as a rule lost for words with which to express your independent thoughts.' His smile was caustic, and tinged with an indefinable quality. 'You look at me as though kissing were a pastime I had never indulged, or enjoyed. Am I made of stone in your estimation? Have I no human longings, like other men?'

She felt the warm, checked violence of his hands, while he was close enough for her to have counted the fine lines beside his eyes. The throb of a nerve near his mouth chained her gaze and made her more aware of his human vulnerability than anything he had said. The courteous, self-disciplined *hidalgo* was partially unmasked as a human being; a full-blooded and passionate man who *had* kissed a woman in the moonlight and whispered the sweet, absurd nothings the moon beguiles out of lovers.

She could feel her eyes widening and locking with his. 'I—I don't think of you as made of stone,' she protested. 'You saved my life at Ordaz, hardly the action of a man without any feelings. Then again it's no secret that you and——' there she broke off, catching her breath as she realized that she was trespassing into private territory.

'You were saying?' he encouraged smoothly, a glint of devilry in his eyes that told her he well knew the substance of her unfinished sentence. 'It is no secret that I have marriage on my mind, eh?'

She nodded.

'And how does it strike you, *la romantica*, this question of marriage?' And gently, incredibly, he touched her hair as once before on his launch he had touched it, stroking back a wave from eyes that held all the stresses of youth—youth blundering in search of itself and making mistakes that produced at times an intolerable sense of inadequacy. 'Despite this nonsense you have talked about *loving* the young Conroy, love unbidden should hold more magic for such as you, *pequeña*.'

'For me, but not for you,' she heard herself reply, dazedly, for his flash of tenderness had struck through her bones that zig-zag of bitter-sweet pain she had felt the other day when he had touched her. 'Love unbidden, *señor*, is too much in opposition to your custom of selected wives and husbands.'

'What I believe, *señorita*, and what I might practise is as much a thing of chance as whether or not a moth will be burned or left unscathed by the flame it must try itself in. You look at me and see only the overlord of a Caribbean island, yet I am a mere man like any other and I, too, must face the flames of love. If I am burned, I shall feel as much pain as the next man.'

'I don't think you'll be burned,' Vanessa said with certainty, for she had seen the smiling admiration and assurance in the candlelit eyes of Lucia Montez, and it seemed that love unbidden had come to him, after all. The elegant *señora* was a widow, and as Barbara had said, the *hidalgo* did not strike one as a man who would deliberately choose for his wife a woman who had belonged already to someone else. But love was no respecter of anyone's fundamental beliefs and desires. It marched into the most barricaded heart, took possession of the fortress and from then on issued the orders which the blood and nerves leapt to obey.

Vanessa's nerves were leaping with the desire for freedom from the touch of the Don's lean, steely fingers, and as though her desire communicated itself he released her and turned to fold his newspaper. He shook the little handbell that stood on the table, and Vanessa realized that he was summoning a servant to clear the table and remove the breakfast trolley.

'Barbara *is* late coming down this morning,' she said, to fill the silence that suddenly brooded over the patio. Even the bright little birds had ceased to chatter and sing in the trees, and when Vanessa took a look at the sky she saw that it had dulled to a slate-grey that presaged rain.

'Ah, I should have informed you,' the Don swung to look at her, 'Barbara was unwell in the night. Something she had eaten, I think. Concepcion attended her and now she sleeps. The child over-excites herself and occasionally suffers these bilious attacks. She will be herself again in a few hours, so there is no need to feel anxious, Miss Carrol.'

'Oh, I am sorry she isn't well!' Vanessa exclaimed, recalling that Barbara had looked rather flushed when they had gone up to bed last night. She had put the flush down to the game of cards the girl had been playing with Ruy Alvadaas. He had teased her a lot, and with the Don in the same room it had probably struck Barbara as deliciously dangerous to flirt with Ruy right under her guardian's haughty nose.

'Miss Carrol——'

Her gaze dragged from the billow of clove carnations that drenched the air with their poignant scent. 'Yes, *señor*?'

'I am not blind, you know.'

'I—I don't follow you,' she faltered.

'The fever of calf love seems to have hit the island, and Barbara also imagines she has met her fate, is it not so? In the shape of my cousin?'

Vanessa flushed at the sardonic amusement in his eyes, then felt herself lose colour. He knew about Barbara and his cousin!

'I had thought that she might have struck up an acquaintance with a local *muchacho*, but you have been so inordinately anxious, *señorita*, to be in the company of my goddaughter when she is with Ruy, that I naturally drew the correct assumption,' he shrugged and spread his hands expressively, 'that it was he, not a local boy, who was engaging her young emotions.'

'*Señor*, I—I don't know what to say.' Vanessa knew it was useless to deny Barbara's infatuation for Ruy. 'I can only assure you that he merely flirts with her. I'm sure his intentions go no further than that.'

'All the same I am going to arrange that he returns to Spain. You will not speak of this to the *chica*.'

'Of course not!'

A white-jacketed servant was now approaching across the patio, and the Don lightly took her elbow and when they had entered the hall, he said: 'Barbara is sleeping and you are at a loose end. Would you therefore be as good as to go to the apartment of my grandmother for an hour or so? She would appreciate your company, and was saying to me only last night that she has not had a real opportunity to get to know you.'

Vanessa always found Doña Manuela a trifle awesome, and the Don broke into his quick, charming smile as her glance lifted in some doubt to his dark face. 'Madrecita has only this outward look of hauteur. You will find that underneath it she is very human and appreciates fully a feminine gossip. Tell her about the new dresses you have bought.'

Which suggestion couldn't help but switch Vanessa's mind to the resentment she had felt earlier on, in the privacy of the bedroom he had somehow invaded when she had discovered the apple-green evening dress in her wardrobe.

Her expression wasn't all that guarded in that moment and the Don's alert eyes were quick to notice the annoyance that stiffened her features. With his warm fingers suddenly locking her wrist, he crisped: 'Is there nothing I can do that pleases you? Would you really have me believe that you prefer to wear garments that do not become you, rather than a dress such as the one you are wearing at the moment? That cool shade of green is most attractive and blends perfectly with your hair the *color de fuego*.' He broke into his deep-throated laugh. 'Is it the spirited hair that gives you the quick temper?'

The man was exasperating, and also curiously disarming when he chose, and as Vanessa met his quizzical eyes she found herself breaking into a reluctant smile. 'My mother was Irish, *señor*. Perhaps that accounts for—for the red hair and the temper.'

'Also for the small lilt in the voice, eh? Children have a tendency to imitate such things. *Sua madre* died when you were a schoolgirl, I believe?'

Vanessa gave a pained little nod. 'My parents were on their way to a Christmas party at my boarding school. It had been snowing hard the day before, and their car skidded as it was crossing a bridge. Th-they were both killed instantly.'

'Poor little one, that must have been a great shock for you.' The Don's eyes were suddenly a deep, gentle brown. 'Since the death, also, of your good uncle, I think you have erected a barrier against a further invasion of love—and I do not refer to this emotion you profess to feel for the young Conroy. Now let me escort you to the apartment of my grandmother.'

As they crossed the sumptuous hall with its splendid tiling, lace-like carving on panelling and furniture, and the fierce realism of niched statues, Vanessa was pondering the Spanish insistence on love. Did the Latin male consider it was all women were born for, to feel and give love; to devote all their life and energy to it? She was half inclined to argue the point with him, but a swift glance at his profile showed her that he had fallen into one of those private reveries that threw his eyes into the shadow of drawn brows and intensified somehow the formidable cut of nose, mouth and chin.

They mounted side by side the double staircase, so grand and impressive with its jewel-toned *azulejos* set into the facings of the wide steps, and the wrought-iron sweep of its balustrade. The kind of staircase which would frame perfectly a beautiful woman clad in a gown of shimmering silk, a fan moving languorously in her hand, and a jewelled Spanish comb holding fine lace over upswept hair.

Doña Manuela's apartment was situated on the first gallery, and this would be the first time Vanessa had entered the *sala* of the old *señora*. Don Rafael swept open the double doors of the small lobby—a veritable flower bower, with a sunken fish-pond in the centre of it, with a delightful fountain in the shape of a boy on a dolphin—and as Vanessa gave a murmur of delight and went to the edge of the fish-pond to peer at the enchanting occupants, not unlike feathers plucked out of a peacock's tail, a black-gowned woman came through the brocaded archway of the *sala*.

This was Luiza, the old *señora*'s maid and companion, and it was apparent from what she said after greeting them that Don Rafael had already arranged for Vanessa to keep

Doña Manuela company for an hour or so. *La huespeda*, the lady guest, was expected. Would she and the *señor hidalgo* please enter th*e sala*. All very formal, and quickening those troublesome nerves about the vicinity of Vanessa's heart. It went thump as she stepped through the archway ahead of the Don, into a large room that was supremely Spanish in embellishment and furnishing. Against the warm brilliance of mahogany walls hung richly coloured portraits of the long line of Domeriques, male and female, each clad in the garb of the century in which they had lived; each possessed of that autocracy of feature, pride of bearing and simmering passion deep in the fine eyes which is so essentially Spanish.

Wrought sconces, inlaid tables, carved footstools and touches of ruby in cushions, the shimmering shawl thrown over a couch, and the tapestry seats of upright chairs, produced together an old-fashioned harmony that blended with the aromatic incense stealing out from a brass censer.

Vánessa took quick stock of the room as one takes a deep breath before facing up to something unnerving—in this instance the proud little ramrod seated in a tapestry chair with her tiny, elegantly shod feet disposed on a footstool. The tightly drawn ivory skin over fine bones was minutely lined under an application of face-powder. Jetty eyes, with the somewhat hooded lids that gave these people their rather formidable look, gazed unwaveringly at Vanessa. The silvery white hair was covered by a mantilla of fine black lace arranged over a *peineta*, the carved tortoiseshell comb which adds height and dignity to the Spanish female figure. A point-lace shawl was draped round the dignified shoulders, lorgnettes hung against the black silk dress on a gold chain. Jewels glinted in the lobes of ears that might have been carved from small pieces of ivory, the small folded hands were agleam with big-stoned diamond and ruby rings.

'*Beso las manos, abuelita.*' Don Rafael took the tiny hands of his 'little grandmother' and warmly kissed them. Her ruby-tipped fingers affectionately tapped his dark cheek, while a lively eye still dwelt upon Vanessa over the broadness of her grandson's shoulder. A resemblance between them was still traceable; she, too, had an indomitable chin, an obstinate set to the mouth, a firmly set belief that the codes of Spain—old Spain—were unsurpassed in honour and chivalry.

Vanessa knew that the elderly members of a Spanish family were looked after and cherished as a matter of honour, as well as love, while it was obvious in this instance that for Doña Manuela the sun shone out of her grandson.

'*Bienvenida*, Miss Carrol,' she graciously inclined her patrician head. 'Please to take a seat—the one facing me, that is right!'

The old *señora* spoke emphatically rather than sharply, and her chiselled nostrils flickered with a hint of amusement as her grandson gave her a faint frown. 'What is it, *amado mio*, do you think I frighten the young *inglesa* you have added to the formidable list of your concerns?' The gold-rimmed lorgnettes were lifted to the bird-like eyes and Vanessa, now seated in an amber velvet chair, was scrutinized from her fine-boned ankles to the nervously clenched hands in her leaf-green lap.

'Do I frighten you, my child?' There was a caustic note in the emphatic voice, then before giving Vanessa a chance to fabricate a reply, she added: 'My sight is no longer quite so sharp and I must resort to these *impertinentes*. *La muchacha esta bella*, Rafael. Is it not so?'

Confusion stormed colour into Vanessa's cheeks as Don Rafael gave her a lazily interested look. 'English girls are often beautiful, Madrecita,' he said with a smile. 'Was not that at the root of your concern when I visited Miss Carrol's country a few years ago? Did you not say that I was to remember that I owed my allegiance to Spain, in all matters?'

'Yes, I recall that I said words to that effect, Rafael.' Jewelled fingers tapped the lorgnettes against a powdered cheek. 'Now you are older, I realize that my insistences were as bells chiming in the wind. I need not have been concerned that you would take a bride without due thought— I am now concerned because you seem to have given the matter too much thought and have reached the age of thirty-five without making me a great-grandmother.'

'Like all women, Madrecita, you want everything to go your way,' he laughed.

'You have been *soltero* a trifle too long,' she rejoined tartly. 'I cannot dandle a baby on my knee when I am in my box.'

A sensible point of view, Vanessa reflected, inordinately glad that the old *señora*'s interest had shifted from her to the Don. Somehow, though, she could not picture the elegant Lucia dandling a baby on *her* knee.

'You are giving the matter a little thought, Rafael,' his grandmother persisted.

'Naturally, my persistent *abuelita*. I promise to do my duty and not let the Domerique name sink into oblivion.' He broke into the rather wicked grin that made his teeth flash against his swarthy skin. 'Of course, there is the chance that I might father a brood of girls.'

'*Ay Dios mio*, spare me the thought!' One of the tiny ivory hands leapt to touch a cross of pearls that hung against the black silk of her dress. 'No, you will have a son —the strong and imperious Domerique men always father a son, but make it soon, Rafael *mio*.'

'You talk as though you are fading away, Madrecita.' He shook an affectionate, mocking head at her. 'You have many years ahead of you in which to enjoy your own life and the prattle of my offspring. And now,' he shot a glance at the crocodile-strapped watch about his wrist, 'I must be off about my business.'

'When you take a wife, you will perhaps be less concerned with the *viñedo*, the oil gushers and the boards of management on which you sit,' his grandmother snapped. 'I am informed that you pass siesta in your study, dictating correspondence to Carlitos?'

'I have too much energy to waste it beneath the netting of my bed.' His rich laughter rang out at the idea.

'That is *now*.' Suddenly all the provocation and the femininity of the Spanish woman was showing in the smile which Doña Manuela gave her grandson. 'The story will be a different one, and your energy channelled elsewhere during siesta when the netting and the bed are shared.'

'You are a rather wicked old lady.' The Don quirked a brow and brushed a kiss across her veined temple. 'Do not impart any of your *avant-garde* ideas to Miss Carrol, who has, I assure you, plenty of her own without needing a fresh supply.'

'Be off with you, *guapo*! And if I feel like telling the Señorita Carrol what a trouble and a nuisance the male animal can be, and how to tame him—to a certain extent— then I shall do so.'

'Such a pity, then, that I cannot stay for such an enlightening conversation.' His smile included Vanessa. 'You are about to learn some fascinating secrets, Miss Carrol, for in her day this grandmother of mine has been a much admired beauty.'

Then, after helping himself to a piece of nut-studded jelly out of a little silver shell held by a porcelain cherub, he sauntered from the *sala*.

'We shall now have a cup of tea, Miss Carrol.' Doña Manuela shook a little brass bell and when Luiza came into the room, she ordered a pot of tea and some cakes. During the interval before the arrival of refreshments, Doña Manuela asked questions about England, and then with an unsuspected gentleness led Vanessa to talk about her uncle and the plantation. 'These things should not be bottled up,' she said. 'Time brings to most of us bouquets of joy, and packages of grief. But it is all life and we are enriched by it, or we should be. You had several years of great contentment with your uncle, did you not?'

'They were wonderful years,' Vanessa replied, her young face tinged by the bitter-sweetness of remembering good times that were now irrevocably part of the past. 'Uncle Lennard was a fine man. I was lucky to be able to live with him and know him.'

'My grandson had a great respect and fondness for him —ah, here comes our tea. I, too, am an addict for the beverage, though when Rafael joins me for a game of chess he declines my delicious Souchong for coffee or wine.'

Vanessa smiled at the remark, and noticed on a small side table a set of ivory chessmen of exquisite workmanship. The game was half played, with a black knight held in check by a white queen. Vanessa wondered who was held in check, the *señora* or her grandson.

'The game should go to me,' Doña Manuela spoke in a droll tone, 'though Rafael has a deadly kind of patience for so energetic a man. He sometimes makes moves which are grossly reckless, then again he will bide his time and take his poor old grandmother completely for a ride.' The jetty eyes twinkled with sudden mischief over the fluted silver teapot she was wielding. 'I learn the slang from Barbarita. She is a puss, that child. You find her at all troublesome, Miss Carrol?'

'Not in the least, Doña Manuela. I like her very much— thank you.' Vanessa accepted one of the bone-china cups in which the fragrant tea glimmered as dark as the eyes watching her across the silver teatray. There was a jug of cream on the tray, but Vanessa knew that the delicate smoky flavour of Souchong was impaired if you added anything but lemon. Doña Manuela gave a nod of satisfaction when Vanessa dropped a slice of lemon into her tulip-dark tea. The elderly eyes met the young ones, and both women suddenly exchanged one of those quietly warm smiles that indicate a wish for understanding and friendship.

'We should have exchanged gossip over a teatray long before this,' Doña Manuela said. 'Two women, a teapot and a man to talk about, have within their grasp one of those bouquets of joy I have mentioned. You agree?'

'Oh—yes, *señora*.' Vanessa took a quick sip at her tea. A man to talk about! Presumably that dark-browed autocrat who had sauntered from the room ten minutes ago!

CHAPTER SEVEN

A SILVER basket of cakes had been brought in with tea, little pastry horns filled with whipped cream and small boats of jam set with grapes or apricots.

'I have the sweet tooth, like my Rafael,' Doña Manuela smiled, as she forked pastry into her mouth. 'Are you not going to join me—or do you have to watch the figure?'

'I've not long had breakfast, Doña Manuela, but luckily I don't put on all that much weight,' Vanessa smiled.

'It was never a problem of mine, but many of my countrywomen have this problem. As girls they are often incredibly lovely, but with the years, and the *chiquititos*, they become more and more well padded. Our men,' that almost youthful, provocative gleam came into the *señora*'s eyes, 'retain the lean figure well into maturity—the obstinate, self-willed, handsome brutes!'

Vanessa laughed, more at home with her hostess than she could have believed possible. Her look of hauteur was indeed on the surface only, beneath it lay a warmth and a humanity that had not been revealed before in Vanessa's presence.

'You find Latin men of an agreeable appearance, my child?' she enquired.

'They have fine features,' Vanessa agreed, 'but I must admit that I find them intimidating in comparison to Englishmen.'

'You refer specifically to my grandson, I think.' Doña Manuela dabbed at her lips with a lace napkin, her lively eyes upon Vanessa's face. 'He is a strong and emotional man, and it will take a woman of very warm and understanding heart to give him complete happiness. My son Juan was of a similar temperament, but he was fortunate enough to find a woman who understood all his moods—they were extremely happy together, those two, and this I would like for Rafael.'

The old *señora* sat lost in thought for several moments, then she said: 'Tell me, Miss Carrol, what sort of opinion have you formed of the Señora Montez?'

Vanessa felt her pulses skip a beat at this unexpected question, for Lucia was the woman Don Rafael evidently meant to marry, and for the English *dueña* to pass her opinion on his choice seemed little short of impertinent. Barbara wasn't wholeheartedly keen on the elegant widow, but Vanessa was always tactful when their conversations included her—she wouldn't care to have her private opinion of Lucia launched into the conversation as Barbara had launched that confidence about Jack Conroy and his few casual kisses.

'Come, *señorita*,' Doña Manuela tapped her knee with the ivory handle of her fan, 'you may speak freely to me. I have long since reached the age of discretion and another's opinion of this young widow would be welcome. You see, Rafael is Spanish to the core of him, therefore his wife must be a woman all through. Not merely feminine, but unselfish, warm-hearted and vibrantly in tune with the warm, elemental man Rafael assuredly is beneath his air of stern responsibility. Señora Montez might make the perfect hostess, for she has charm, graciousness and is most elegant, but the best kind of marriage is established behind the scenes, not at the dining table or in the drawing-room, and I continually ask myself whether Lucia has the temperament to strike sparks from the stone in Rafael's nature——'

'Ah, yes, I know there is also stone in him,' his grandmother opened her fan and fluttered it, 'that is why I want him to marry the right woman. If he does not do so, neither he nor his wife will reap the happiness I know he is capable of giving. So tell me frankly, do my grandson and this woman strike you as suited to each other?'

'Yes, th-they seem suited to me,' Vanessa faltered.

'But do you like her, do you feel that she is warm at heart?'

'One can't always judge from appearances, Doña Manuela. But surely a man must know whether he is choosing a—a warm woman or a cold one?'

'I wish I could agree with you, my child, but men are not as good at reading the female of the species as they suppose. A woman of purpose, with her eye on a wealthy and personable husband, can pretend to be several things in opposition to her real nature in order to obtain her ambition.' The ivory sticks of the fan snapped together. 'If Lucia Montez is an actress, and if she has fooled Rafael—*Dios mio*, he is only human!—then their marriage will take place. He is now in the middle thirties. He is aware that he should marry, and it could very well be that he has fallen in love. *Quién sabe?* Sometimes, just of late, it has seemed to me that he wears the somewhat distracted look of a man *enamorado*. He falls into reveries. He is restless and paces the patios at night. Yes, it could be that this woman his invaded his heart—and only saints and devils can live alone. An old proverb but a true one.'

Doña Manuela smiled, shrugged her shoulders, then said: 'You are a good child to listen so patiently to an old woman's ramblings. The question of my grandson's happiness cannot be of deep interest to you, eh?'

The lively, jetty eyes had a disconcerting directness. They seemed, like the grandson's, to probe and search for truths beyond the mere politeness of social repartee. It had occurred to Vanessa that her job at the *castillo* would be terminated when Lucia took over as *prima mia*, but she hadn't given the Don's marital happiness any concrete thought. He wasn't a boy, expecting heady intoxication from his marriage. He must know what he was doing—yet, fleetingly, there darted through Vanessa's mind a picture of a smiling corsair in a garden above the sea. Was that a man who asked only elegance and sophistication of the woman he married?

'I respect Don Rafael, and owe him my life,' Vanessa replied.

'And beyond that there is no personal feeling?'

'There couldn't be, for either of us!' Vanessa's green eyes widened at the incredible idea.

'You are very emphatic,' Doña Manuela laughed. 'Attraction between a man and a woman is rarely impossible, why then do you feel that my grandson could never have looked at you with eyes other than those of a guardian and an employer?'

'I—I don't know.' Vanessa found it impossible to meet Doña Manuela's probing eyes and she stared instead at a spray of white oleanders arranged in a silver vase. She was confused, and prickly with inner vexation that she should feel so. Why didn't she laugh off the idea of being looked at, as a woman, by the Don? Dismiss it with a flippant quip, as she had at breakfast when he had suggested that she was attracted to Gary Elsing?

'Forgive me, I embarrass you.' A small ivory hand pressed her knee. 'The English are not accustomed to bringing their inner selves into the open, is it not so?'

'W-we are inclined to be reserved.' Vanessa clutched at this spar and felt herself drawn out of the deeps where unimaginable things lay hidden.

'And yet in England girls are permitted far more freedom than they are in my country,' the *señora* mused. 'This is paradoxical, no? You fence round the emotions, we put a barrier of convention around the container of them—the girl. Does not the freedom between the young people in England make for romantic involvements and troubles?'

'To a certain extent, I suppose,' Vanessa agreed. 'But I often think that girls who are restricted in their contacts with boys are much more likely to become obsessed with the sex thing.'

'You no doubt have Barbara in mind when you say this. Rafael was telling me last night that the young *mini* has developed some sort of feeling for Ruy. That will be dealt with! Ruy is extremely charming, but Rafael would never permit an alliance between those two. That young man has been—how do you say it, a rake?—but this would not be a drawback if he were fundamentally stable enough to settle down at running a business and being a husband. Ruy is not stable, unfortunately. There is in his blood from his father's side a strain of wildness, and Rafael, who takes his godparenthood very seriously, is too fond of Barbara to see her made as unhappy as Ruy's mother was made by her husband. A girl is at her most appealing when she hovers between innocence and realization, and I think it was very sensible of Rafael to employ you as Barbara's *dueña*, and most kind of you to accept the post.'

'I enjoy being with Barbara.' This was the truth and it showed in the brightness of Vanessa's silvery-green eyes. They caught the light as she put back her copper head in the way she had when she was stating something about which she had no uncertainty at all. It was an attractive gesture, though she was quite unaware of the fact. 'Babs is amusing and rather—well, like a young sister. Having a sister was something I always missed, though being at boarding school made up for the loss to a certain extent.'

'Ah, so you consider there should be more than one child in a family? That is good! You are of a progressive turn of mind, yet you do not overdo the modernity.' The *señora* leant forward with a smile and tapped her jewelled fingers against Vanessa's smooth, curved cheek. 'I like you, my child, and I am going to call you by your so pretty name. Van-essa. Your parents gave you a name with an endearment on the end of it, do you know that? It suits you.'

Vanessa's cheeks were petalled with a pink that gradually deepened as the handsome old *señora* continued to gaze at her, taking in her features and her hair. 'You have excellent bones, Van-essa,' she said. 'They are a sign of breeding, passion and wilfulness. That is a good combination in a woman, for there is no virtue in being docile. A man needs electricity in the air—it keeps him on his toes. You have a male friend here on the island, I am told. A young *Americano* from the oil fields.'

It seemed, despite the fact that Doña Manuela kept to her own apartment a great deal, that she was well up on the *castillo* gossip, which Luiza no doubt collected and imparted to her mistress. Or—a rather heart-jarring thought—had Don Rafael mentioned Gary Elsing to his grandmother? Had they discussed the advisability of allowing the friendship as they had sat over their game of chess?

The vital-witted *señora* must have guessed something of

what was passing through Vanessa's mind, for she said: 'You must not think that we disapprove of your friends, Van-essa. It is just that you have not long passed through the *valle de lagrimas* and we have a concern for you in case, in your state of feeling you have no one of your own, you make the unwise—marriage. Is it not a fact that *Americanos* have a liking for the union of marriage because their laws permit of its easy untying?'

'But Gary and I—why, we've only just got acquainted. There's no question of—of marriage,' Vanessa protested.

'All the same, my child, you must feel very alone now that your only relative is dead, and there is no worse feeling in the world, for many women, than the one of feeling adrift without a tie either of the blood or the emotions. We here at the *castillo* realize your predicament, and if Rafael seems stern with you over the matter of the *Americano*, it is only because of his regard for you as the niece of his good friend, and as a person——

'Ah, again you look at me with doubt in your eyes! Whatever has Rafael said or done to make you feel he is antagonistic towards you?'

'Antagonism is a mutual thing——'

'You dislike my Rafael?' Doña Manuela bristled at the idea of anyone harbouring anything but adoration for her beloved grandson. 'Come, you play with me, Van-essa. It is not dislike you feel, but mere aggravation because you are of an independent nature and he is the masterful Spaniard.'

Yes, Vanessa thought, he aggravated with his high and mighty air of always knowing what was best for her, but that didn't entirely account for what had flared between them at times—like scorched brush bursting into flame and running wild and searing within seconds of its involuntary combustion. Some violent emotion had shimmered in the air between them, dragging them to the very edge of something almost alluring in its rage and its danger. It had to be antagonism! No two people could face each other as tensely as a pair of tigers and kid themselves they could ever be real friends. If you were a man, friendship with him was possible, but he was too overbearing towards women to rouse anything but their most basic instincts—the urge to fight with him, as in her case. Or the desire to conquer him, as in Lucia's.

'My child,' Doña Manuela was looking at her in a faintly amused way, 'to allow your feathers to be ruffled by Rafael is to encourage him to go to extremes. He has a devilish sense of humour, you know.'

'But it doesn't always feel like a—a game,' Vanessa rejoined, with exasperation.

'Is it entirely unenjoyable, *pequeña*?' The *señora's* jetty eyes twinkled with sudden merriment. 'I recall that as a girl I enjoyed nothing better than a verbal sparring with one of my countrymen. It is true the Spanish woman is a born seductress and that a flirtation with a man, conducted as it is between the bars of the *rejas*, encourages daring exchanges. But surely the English woman likes also this subtle by-play of the sexes? There is an element of delicious provocation attaching to it, do you not think?'

'I agree that Spanish men are provoking,' Vanessa ruefully laughed. 'Were you a great flirt, Doña Manuela?'

'I was the despair of my various *dueñas*, then Rafael's grandfather came along, and I really had to show him that he wasn't the cock of the walk. I sometimes had three suitors at a time at the *rejas* of my window.'

'Wasn't your marriage arranged?' Vanessa enquired, intrigued by the picture of this regal old lady as a raven-haired *señorita*, flirting shamelessly with young gallants, being wooed by the guitar strings, the red rose and the outrageous flattery of Spanish courtship.

'Don Rafael Luez, who eventually became my husband, was one of the suitors my father had in mind for me to choose from.' Doña Manuela gave a reminiscent chuckle. 'A cock often pecks the hen who pleases him the most, and when Rafael refused to bow down to me as the others did and even had the audacity to order me about, I knew he was the man I would marry. We say in Spain that a woman should love her husband as a friend and fear him as an enemy ... it is a good creed to live by when one marries a Domerique.'

Vanessa could well believe it, then with the handle of her fan Doña Manuela pointed to one of the full-length portraits hanging on the wall of the *sala*. 'There is a strong resemblance between my husband and my grandson, do you not think so? Rafael, my grandson, is somewhat broader in the shoulders, no doubt owing to his years at a modern college and his liking for field sports, but his eyes flash with the same hidden fires. There is corsair blood in the Domeriques. Did you know this, Van-essa?'

'Your grandson told me—he seemed rather proud of the fact,' Vanessa added, a smile edging her lips.

Doña Manuela chuckled. 'Each time he looks in a mirror he must see his forebears gazing back at him. My child, I have some quaint old jewellery from those days which I would like to show you. Will you be so kind as to open that cabinet over there and hand me that old jewel box?'

The box was of dull and battered silver, but Vanessa felt a thrill tingle her fingertips as she took hold of it, for she guessed that long ago it had travelled the piratical Caribbean in the sea-chest of El Conquistador.

'*Gracias.*' Doña Manuela took the box and turned the key in its lock. Vanessa knelt on one of the tapestry stools, exclaiming over the pirate hoard of trinkets. Rings and brooches set with enormous stones of sombre hues. Pendant earrings, heavy necklets and jewelled collars. Vanessa excitedly wondered if these had been worn by El Conquistador's English bride. Had his swordsman's hands hung these necklaces around her slender neck and attached the heavy pendants to her small ear-lobes? Had he then stood back to admire with flashing, possessive eyes the gleam of plundered gems against the pale skin of the wife he had bought by auction?

Vanessa was lost for breathless moments in her mental picture of a girl, perhaps with fear in her heart, fingering the gems she didn't dare refuse from the swashbuckler in whose keeping she found herself...

'Of what are you thinking, my child?' Doña Manuela asked softly.

'Of the girl who married the first Don Rafael.' Vanessa spoke with an equal softness, as though reluctant to break the spell these tarnished old trinkets had somehow woven around her.

'So Rafael has told you that famous story, eh?' The *señora*'s twinkling eyes held Vanessa's green ones. 'Did it shock you?'

'When I first heard it,' Vanessa admitted. 'But your grandson said—they loved each other.'

'Does this seem incredible to you, my dear, that a woman could come to love the Spanish corsair who, you know, risked his life in order to spare her the ordeal of a far more terrible fate? After he had acquired the girl, his galleon only just managed to slip out of harbour before Moorish vessels were sent in pursuit of him. She sailed two years with him, until he discovered the island of Luenda where they settled down to govern it and to raise a family.'

'It's certainly a romantic story,' Vanessa smiled.

'And it must be understood that El Conquistador was a product of his time,' Doña Manuela added. 'A ruthless man, perhaps, but he had courage—and he married the girl! It was inevitable that she should love him, for most women, even these days, have a primitive side to them which can best be satisfied by an aggressive man. I speak of the truly feminine woman, you understand. Her nature demands dominance, though she will often fight her own impulses. She is like a tigress who resents—yet loves—her tamer. This mastery, believe me, has thrilled women through all the ages.'

Vanessa supposed it had, for even she at times had been shaken by the glint of mastery in Don Rafael's eyes. 'What's this, Doña Manuela?' Her delving fingers had brought out of the old silver casket a square, tooled leather case.

'It is an album of photographs!' Doña Manuela took it eagerly. 'So this is where it was hiding, and I had my poor Luiza hunting high and low for it the other day! See,' the elderly fingers unlatched it and pulled it open, to reveal about a foot of family snapshots. Vanessa peered at them with the *señora*, and when told that a grinning imp in a sailor suit was Don Rafael as a boy, she couldn't help exclaiming: 'Why, he has curly hair! What a delightful little boy he looks!'

'*Carai*, he was a rogue!' Doña Manuela chuckled at the surprised delight in Vanessa's voice. 'He was up to all the mischief imaginable, but most of all he liked sailing his dinghy and fishing for squid with the Indians. He would come home from those expeditions as ink-black as they. I hoped there would be brothers and sisters to keep him company, but Mariana, my daughter-in-law, was not able to have any more children after Rafael's difficult birth. It was fortunate that he was a son. It is said that while Luenda has a Domerique at its helm there will not be these uprisings and troubles that abound on the mainland. You know, my child, how high a price the innocent pay so that unscrupulous men can satisfy their lust for power.

'My Rafael has power, but he does not misuse it. The years have bred out of the Domeriques their *conquistador* instincts and a strong sense of responsibility and obligation have taken their place. Rafael is a good *compadre*. The islanders respect him for a strong man and a just one. One might also say that he has their love as well as their loyalty.'

The old lady smiled proudly. 'What a *fiesta* they will make when Rafael takes a bride—ah, if only—but then, if this widow is the woman he wants and he feels a happiness with her, I must not cry for the moon. She has intelligence, and perhaps he feels the need of a woman of intellect. I am old-fashioned and sentimental, and I cling to the belief that what should come first in a wife is a loving warmth, impetuosity, a desire for children——'

She shrugged and closed up the album of snapshots and set it aside on the table at her elbow. She smiled down for a long moment at Vanessa's upraised young face, then searched in the jewel box and took out of it a carved bracelet of lime-clear jade and a matching pair of carved jade eardrops. She held one of the eardrops against the small lobe of Vanessa's right ear.

'Not every woman can wear jade, but you have the colouring for it and I think it is a pity to let the set remain unused in an old box when it can decorate a vibrant young woman. Give me your wrist, child!' Doña Manuela ordered.

Vanessa merely gazed back at her, astounded.

'Come, your wrist.' One of the *señora*'s wiry hands closed on Vanessa's wrist and a moment later the jade bracelet had been pushed over her knuckles and was gleaming against the pale skin of her arm. 'There, how do you like it?'

'Doña Manuela, I can't possibly accept jewellery like this!' Vanessa gazed, stunned, at the carved facets of the bracelet. 'It belongs in your family—why, whatever would your grandson have to say?'

'It is no concern of his if I give away some of these trinkets,' the *señora* chuckled. 'They have a certain historic value, but they are in no way as grand as the heirloom pieces that will eventually deck his bride. Come, *chica*, allow me to clip these drops to the lobes of your ears—ah, most attractive! They pick up the green in your eyes. You must—I insist—wear them this evening for your outing with Señor Elsing.'

'You're kind to let me wear them, Doña Manuela——'

'I am giving them to you, my child. They are pleasing on you, and I am sure the woman to whom they originally belonged would be delighted that they enhance again the good looks of an English girl.'

'They—belonged to the bride of El Conquistador?' Vanessa caught her breath and fingered the bracelet in an awed fashion. 'Doña Manuela, I don't know what to say. I-I'll treasure the set—if you are sure Don Rafael won't mind me having it. I mean, I'm only an employee here——'

'You are a little more than that, Van-essa.' The *señora* patted the smooth young cheek that held the warmth of a sudden flush. 'I promise you Rafael will not mind that you wear the jade set—why should he, when for his own *amiga* there is much more splendid jewellery?'

Doña Manuela shrugged, frowned and fell into an abstraction that Vanessa hesitated to break. The wrinkled eyelids brooded over the jetty eyes for several minutes, then they lifted and with a suddenly tired air the old *señora* said she would now like to rest. 'I have enjoyed our talk, *pequeña*,' she added. 'You must come again and gossip with me over a cup of tea—now, please, would you tell Luiza to come to me.'

Vanessa again thanked the old lady for the jade set, then after informing Luiza that she was wanted, she made her way to Barbara's room to see if her charge was feeling better. Barbara was awake, but lying listlessly against her pillows and looking sorry for herself. Vanessa encouraged her to get up and they sat out on the balcony, where the sunshine was fitful and that promise of rain still loomed in the sky.

'It will be a pity if it rains,' Barbara said languidly. 'It will spoil your date with the attractive American with the lopsided grin.'

'Oh, I shan't let a drop of rain spoil my evening.' As Vanessa took a look at the sky, she felt the jade eardrops swing against her cheeks. She put up a hand to touch one of them, and she smiled a little. It had been a pleasant surprise to find Doña Manuela such a warm and understanding person, for upon the few occasions when she had joined the family gatherings there had been a reserve about her which had led Vanessa to think her a cold, haughty matriarch. She hadn't been either of those things this morning.

Vanessa, intrigued, let her mind revert to those gatherings in the main *sala*. A few neighbouring friends had been present at them, but Vanessa felt sure Doña Manuela was not the sort to dislike company at the *castillo*—was it therefore possible that she had deep misgivings about her grandson's association with Lucia Montez? To such an extent that her natural warmth was chilled whenever she was obliged to watch her beloved Rafael enjoying the company of *la viuda*?

Obviously she wanted for him a glowing young *señorita*, whose heart had not known any man's invasion but his.

Lucia could give him sophistication, but she couldn't give him innocence, and Doña Manuela's love demanded perfection for her grandson.

Perfection was an impossible dream, Vanessa reflected. She had harboured such a dream herself...

'A *peseta* for them.' Barbara clinked the glass stirrer against the side of the lime-juice pitcher on the balcony table, jerking Vanessa back to the present. 'Does the rugged oil man engage your thoughts, *cara mia*?'

'No, I was thinking about my chat this morning with Doña Manuela.' Vanessa absently plucked a nearby geranium flower and at once the scarlet petals spattered the skirt of her dress. She gathered them up, one by one, her sensitive mouth expressing regret at her thoughtless action. Human beings, it seemed, were driven to spoil things and then to feel regret when it was too late!

'I see.' Barbara was gazing across at her with curious eyes. 'Did I figure in your discussion with Madrecita?'

'Only in general terms.' Vanessa managed a casual smile, and wondered how Barbara would take it when Ruy was packed off to Spain. 'Doña Manuela was kind enough to give me these eardrops and matching bracelet. I—I felt rather awkward about accepting them, but she insisted and it would have seemed ungracious not to take them. They're rather attractive, don't you think?'

'They are not very up to date in style,' Barbara wrinkled her nose as she tried on the bracelet and held out her tawny arm to get the effect. 'Green is not my colour, but it suits you, Vanessa.'

'Are you hinting that I'm not exactly a modern miss?' Vanessa quipped, taking her bracelet and giving it a polish with her handkerchief. Already the jade set had come to mean something to her—a mysterious kind of link with that other English girl who had been brought to the island by a swarthy corsair.

'You are a Velazquez, I have told you before. A throwback to other days—like that devilish man who has control of my life!' Barbara brooded on this, her sullen underlip spoiling the coin-modelling of her profile. 'Did you see him looking at Ruy and myself last night? He suspects something—and I no longer care that he does! It is best that these things should be out in the open.'

'You were rather asking for those black looks last night,' Vanessa remarked. 'You say you don't care what he guesses, and you want a showdown, but all the time you're pepped up by defiance. You know that in this matter he's in the right, but you'll let a petty infatuation for Ruy Alvadaas drive you to a fight with your godfather. Be sensible, Babs. You don't want a man who's fundamentally unstable.'

Even as Vanessa spoke, she realized that in different words she was repeating what Don Rafael had said himself at breakfast, that the young, awakening woman has a tendency to incline towards the weak and feckless, as though her maternal instincts were overriding her other emotions ... which were not unlike crocuses in spring, blindly thrusting their green tips towards the warmth of the sun.

'What kind of man must I like?' Barbara flashed. 'One who is chosen for me? I will not be forced into marriage with a man I do not know. Ah yes, smile and shake your head as though it is not possible! You cool, composed English! You cannot know how love can grab the heart in a fist and——'

'Now stop working yourself up,' Vanessa said firmly. 'You'll give yourself another bilious attack.'

'Do not give me orders!' Barbara jumped swiftly to her feet, her raven hair swinging loosely about her shoulders, her young bosom heaving stormily under the white halter top she wore with pirate pants. 'You are only the English Miss here—remember it and keep your unwanted opinions to yourself!'

With this the girl flounced into her den and straight through into her bedroom, slamming the door after her. Vanessa sat biting her lip for a couple of minutes, then she got to her feet and deciding to let Barbara simmer down in her own time, she let herself out of the den and went along the corridor to her suite. It was almost lunchtime and though her appetite had lost its edge, she had better have a wash and put in an appearance at the lunch table. Don Rafael would be sending up a servant, otherwise, to enquire after her.

There were several business associates of the Don's to lunch, and Señora Montez still being absent, and Barbara shut in her bedroom with a fit of the sulks, Vanessa was the only feminine member of the luncheon party.

It had started to rain, great drops spattering the *piazza* beyond the long glass doors of the dining-room. The drenched roses and other flowers wafted their scent into the room, and Vanessa, accustomed from her days at the plantation to meals eaten in the company of several men, was tolerably at ease with the Don's guests. Men of aloof Spanish charm, with deep bass voices, whose remarks to her had to be translated into English by their host. Every now and again Vanessa perceived an amused twitch to his bold eyebrows, and she wondered whether some of his friends' remarks underwent censorship in translation. She spooned her crab-stuffed avocado and wished she was able to follow the rapid Castilian that accompanied the expressive hand gestures of her companions.

After a dessert of sweet wild strawberries with grated nuts and cream, coffee was brought to the table accompanied by a liqueur brandy. Vanessa tipped hers into her coffee so she could drink it quickly and then leave the men to talk. The Don was looking expansive and she guessed she had laughed in all the right places and helped mellow his associates into the mood for a conference. Her guess was correct, for he escorted her to the door and smilingly murmured: 'You are an acquisition to a business luncheon, Miss Carrol. These hard-headed men were balking a certain scheme of mine, now I think they are in the mood to be won over.'

'I wish you luck, *señor*.' She met his smile in a conspiratorial fashion, certain that his scheme involved the welfare of the islanders.

He gave her a formal bow, but the brilliance of his eyes held hers for a long moment before she turned to hurry away. The rain had stopped and the afternoon heat had been soothed down to a benign warmth. Vanessa decided to stroll as far as the lagoon, her transient mood of gaiety petering out and leaving her slightly melancholy as she recalled her tiff with Barbara. The girl would take some living with when Ruy made his departure, and Vanessa didn't doubt that the Don meant to send him packing. No doubt with money enough to keep him away from the *castillo* for several months.

She sighed as she ran down the cliff steps to the lagoon. Great silvery breakers were surging inland, and she stood alone on the beach for quite a while watching them. Their tireless energy was fascinating; with the regularity of strong heartbeats they boomed over the tideway coral and came lashing to the pale sands, scattering spindrift against Vanessa's legs and the skirt of her dress.

She eventually realized that was getting spattered, and she turned and made her way to the beach house. She settled into a cane lounger on the veranda and lay listening to the breakers, and the birds that twittered and sang in the casuarinas and palms that grew quite close to the *caseta*.

'Wake-up-pretty. Wake-up-pretty,' one of the parrot birds seemed to pipe, causing her to smile and reflect that the mind played odd tricks. On the train to London, the day she had left her school to fly out to her uncle, the wheels had cheerfully told her that there was no-going-back.

No going back, her destination eagerly anticipated because there had been nothing more to keep her in England. No actual sense of being desperately alone, for she had someone awaiting her at the end of her long journey. No uneasy ache deep inside her, as now, for which she couldn't fully account.

She snoozed on the veranda for well over an hour, then some sixth sense jerked her awake and compelled her to reach hurriedly for a magazine off the table beside her. She flipped it open and didn't notice, until the dark invader of her solitude had mounted the *caseta* steps in lithe strides and was standing tall by her chair, that she was gawping at the print upside down. 'Do you find the stories more interesting that way round?' Don Rafael mockingly enquired.

'Why, how stupid of me!' She reversed the magazine and suffered the mortification of his amused eyes upon her blush as he sat down in a chair beside her. He comfortably crossed his knees, showing an inch or two of black sock below a grey tapered trouser leg. He fired a cheroot and Vanessa felt him taking in her ruffled hair, and the innocent bareness of her neck curving away into the green sheath of her dress. Her heart jarred under her ribs at his frank scrutiny. He was a Latin, and she knew from the way those other Spaniards had looked at her at lunchtime that they had been intrigued by the paleness of her English skin. But it was curiously more unnerving to have this man looking at her in—in such a male way.

'You were taking your siesta, no?' He sat back, peaceably enveloped in cheroot smoke. 'Then you sensed that someone was approaching—it was I, and so you were confused.'

His voice sank down meaningly on that tail-end remark, as though he well knew that no one but he had the power to plunder her composure so completely. Her fingers clenched on the bulky magazine and she felt like aiming it at his disturbing head. A rather unreasonable urge, for he had every right to come and enjoy a smoke on the veranda of his own beach house. *She* was the intruder.

'Did your business talk reach a satisfactory conclusion, *señor*?' she asked politely.

He inclined his head, which had a dark vibrancy as it caught the brilliant rays of the sun, dipping gradually to the sea and turning it to an expanse of liquid pewter. Then he said: 'Once or twice at luncheon, when you thought yourself unobserved, I noticed that you looked a little unhappy. Yes, I saw this, though you smiled and charmed my associates. When the heart is troubled the eyes reveal it. The eyes of a woman more so than those of a man, whose entire emotional equipment is less sensitive—which is not to say less intense. A woman carries her emotions into everything, she cannot help it.' He flicked ash to the mosaic paving of the veranda. 'Are you troubled in your heart, Vanessa?'

Once or twice before he had addressed her by her first name, and then, as now, she had been teased by an almost tender inflection in his voice, a velvety bearing down on those last four letters of her name. She tensed, there beside him, and told herself that he did it to tilt at her composure. He knew he had charm. How could he help but know it, when so many other women had angled for his favours? Did it pique him that she remained impervious to his Latin profile and his startling stripping away of the veils that concealed the female mystique?

'Cannot you talk to me as you would—an uncle?' The face he turned towards her was quite unsmiling, while his eyelids had so narrowed that his eyes seemed like flickering points of fire between the dense lashes.

'You aren't my uncle,' she retorted.

'No, that is very true.' He sank back with his head pillowed against a ruby cushion. Cheroot smoke drifted from the quirked edge of his mouth. 'I am not your uncle. I would not care to be.'

'Why, because you know I wouldn't take kindly to Spanish restrictions?' She brushed a film of sea salt from her left leg. 'You think I've been terribly spoiled by Uncle Lennard, don't you, *señor*? I—I suppose when we care for someone we are inclined to spoil them and let them have more of their own way than is really good for them. But it's human nature.'

'I am not disputing the foibles of human nature, least of all where the heart is involved.' He puffed smoke and it drifted across to tickle her nostrils. 'What is troubling your heart, *señorita*?' A tinge of mockery there, as though he knew that his use of her name wasn't welcome. 'Has your air of melancholy something to do with Barbarita?'

So the line he had dropped into her tranquillity *was* hooked; he was determined to drag something out of her. Darned man, couldn't he be content to busy himself with his various sociological and money-spinning concerns? Why did he have to come poking into her blue mood?

'Barbara knows you've guessed about her friendship with Señor Alvadaas,' Vanessa shrugged. 'She's frightened of you——'

'When the moon falls out of the sky!' He snapped his fingers in ironic negation. 'She is feeling her female wings and fluttering rather dangerously round a flame that could burn her. She will not be burned if I can prevent it, and if she must suffer a little in her adolescent feelings she will in the end realize that it is better to have the wing-tips scorched rather than seared right off.'

He was right, of course! He always was! And frowning at the sea, Vanessa fiercely told herself that she would enjoy, just once, seeing him shaken out of his superior imperturbability and wincing from a thrust through his armoured guard. A little explosion of bright birds, disturbed by something and obeying group hysteria, rose like a shaft of flowers out of the nearby trees. The flutter of their wings made Vanessa jump a little, and at once lean, warm fingers were gripping her wrist and the man beside her, in a rough tone of voice she had never heard from him before, was saying: 'Why is it that you find my company so disturbing, Miss Carrol? When we are with other people you are quite relaxed, but directly we find ourselves alone together you are tensing yourself for battle with me. I grow rather impatient of your attitude.'

'I'm sorry,' she said stiffly, 'but it's hardly my fault alone that we generate a mutual antagonism. Such feelings are beyond control——'

'Not only they, Miss Carroll!' His fingers tightened to crushing point about her wrist and his eyes blazed into hers. 'I am warning you not to arouse the devil in me— you would not enjoy the experience, I promise you.'

'*I*—arouse the devil in you?' she blazed back. 'I must take your overbearing dictums lying down, like everyone else who works for you, or who lives under your dominion. Your threats with regard to my friends are not supposed to make my blood boil, I'm supposed to regard them as the accepted thing while I remain under your supervision.

While I'm doing that, everything in the garden is blooming——'

'So that is it?' His voice had gone dangerously quiet. 'I decree that you follow a rule other female members of my family are expected to follow—that of not being out past a respectable hour with a man with his *soltero*—and you hold it as a grudge.'

'That isn't true,' she rejoined with feeling. 'You insinuated that Gary's job on the island would be endangered if I chose to let him disregard your—your Spanish protocol. I don't expect to do just what I like when Barbara is not allowed to, but I object strongly to threats aimed at my friends!'

'You think this man Elsing wants you for a mere friend?' The Don looked scornful. 'Do not tell me the English believe in that amusing adage about platonic friendship being possible between a normally endowed man and an attractive woman? *Por Dios!* We of Spanish blood might cling to customs which you consider antiquated, but we at least do not insult the male virility by suggesting that a man can be alone with a woman and remain unmoved by the enticements of her skin, her form, often her smile. Perhaps you are, as yet, too innocent to fully appreciate that woman is far more sensual than man by reason of her shape, that is why we Spaniards lay down rules governing the courtship. We do this to protect the man as well as the girl. Friendship, you say? You are fooling yourself, Miss Carrol!'

'Being a woman also automatically labels me a featherhead in your Spanish estimation, doesn't it?' she said cuttingly. 'Gary is at least one of my own kind, not a feudal overlord who likes everyone bowing and scraping to him——'

'*Qué barbaridad*, how dare you speak to me in that way!' Glittering fury leapt in the Don's eyes, and viciously flicking his cheroot from him, he gripped both of Vanessa's wrists and jerked her painfully towards him. She had shaken him out of his imperturbability with a vengeance and found herself face to face with a man who looked furiously capable of breaking every bone in her shrinking body.

'Often before you have made it hard for me to like you,'

he took a breath, as though fury was almost choking him, 'now you go almost too far with this thing you say to me. So this man Elsing is one of your own sort, eh? You like the man who plays at love as though it were only a game?'

'L-let me go——' Vanessa's heart was pounding, for just as lightning will fuse metal and make it dangerous to touch, so did it frighten her, and hurt, to be near this simmering man with his bruising hands. 'Y-you're breaking my wrists, y-you bully——'

'I am in the mood to cause you a little anguish.' He was close, and raking her with ruthless eyes. 'What shall I do? We are quite alone—I could prove your accusation and have you on your knees, grovelling if not bowing and scraping. After all,' a flare of utter devilishness lit his eyes, 'I am the descendant of notorious sea-rovers, men who took their pleasures as they came. Heredity cannot be ignored, eh? These instincts must stalk through my blood, like a jaguar waiting to spring.'

Helplessly magnetized, Vanessa gazed back at him, feeling the frantic clamour of her pulses as his hands pushed upwards to her shoulders. He laughed low in his throat, then holding her shoulders he gave her a shake. 'You are quite safe, my little English Miss, despite the traits of heredity I cannot always control. You are as safe as Barbara would be, so you can stop looking as though you are about to be ravished by the Spanish tyrant.'

Temper had given way to the usual irony in his eyes, and taking hold of her wrists he examined the marks his fingers had left on them. 'Woman is as elemental as the sea, and at times equally terrible in her power,' he murmured. 'Man resorts to brute force in order to subdue her subtle cruelty, for he is constantly aware of the forces which can overcome his strength and drown his will to a mere incoherent murmur in the silken hollow of a fragile white shoulder. Be wise in your power, *pequeña*. It can bring you happiness or despair.'

In the sudden strange calm that usually follows a storm, Vanessa was wearily glad to be submissive before something rather big in this man. She was ashamed of the things she had said. They made of her a lesser person than she had thought herself. Her green eyes met the compelling, flame-lit jet of the Don's. 'I'm sorry, Don Rafael,' she said. 'I had no right to talk to you in such terms.'

He shrugged and gave her wrists their release. 'You resent that I behave like a Spanish guardian rather than an English one. But then I am Spanish, and my intentions are well-meaning.'

As they made their way back to the *castillo*, the sky was tinged with delicate flushes of coral and lavender. The suggestion of melancholy left by the rain added to the westering beauty of the sun, and there on the cliffs Vanessa and her companion paused side by side to watch the going down of the sun behind the mountains. Quite suddenly—just as someone close to death arouses to life in those final moments —the last of the day was drenched in superb colour, then slowly it all died and the hushed, violet dusk of the 'little twilight' was upon them.

'*Qué gloria!*' Don Rafael murmured.

Vanessa glanced at him, unaware that the lovely melancholy of the sky painted her face and revealed delicate facets of beauty at which his eyes narrowed as he looked at her. He had assumed a quality strongly medieval as the dusk cloaked him in darker garb and shadowed the alert glitter of his eyes. A god in the twilight, Vanessa found herself thinking.

'You admire this view, do you not?' he said. 'Often I have seen you standing here on this spot, gazing raptly towards the sea and the mountains.'

Her heart gave an odd little thump inside her as he said that, for upon the occasions when she had stood alone here she had not been aware of his observation.

'From my private part of the *castillo* I can see this entire coastline,' he revealed. 'For what do you search so wistfully? Can you not accept that your girlhood days at Ordaz are over?'

'It's natural to cling to good memories,' she sighed.

'Store them away like jewels, *pequeña*. Others even richer should take their place for you.' A sudden smile softened his voice. 'Did not old Maria assure you that happy events lie in store for you? One of them must be love, but be sure it is the genuine emotion and not your human need to *belong* which turns you to one or other of the men in your life.'

He meant Jack or Gary; one or the other was destined to be her lover, her fate, her bringer of happiness or despair. Her pulses didn't quicken, for her bewildered heart seemed to be sagging like a weight in her breast.

'What is love?' she heard herself ask, and knew that only in the cloaking dusk could she have voiced such a question to the man beside her.

'Love is like an uncut diamond, Vanessa,' he replied, his voice as velvety as the shadows enclosing them. 'One false stroke and it can shatter into fragments and all that remains is a scatter of teardrops. Love is a chill and shaky hand, a hot cheek and eyes that like the bee know exactly which part of the flower to settle on—the lips. Love is many things, *chica*, but most of all it is a gift, and when we give it we must be certain that its value will be truly appreciated.'

They walked on to the *castillo*, and Vanessa knew that only a man in love could have talked of the emotion in such warm and knowledgeable terms. Did Lucia Montez appreciate fully the intensity of devotion this man would give— and expect to receive?

Up in her bedroom Vanessa prepared for her date with Gary. She dressed in a short evening dress of bronze silk which flared into chiffon frills just below her knees, then she clipped on her jade eardrops and as she slid the matching bracelet over her wrist she noticed a faint discoloration of the skin. She touched the bruise and recalled the Don's glittering anger with her on the veranda of the beach house. Anger that had melted into those moments of half-melancholy tenderness on the cliffs.

She gave a little shiver and evaded her eyes in the mirror of the dressing table. In an automatic way she picked up a perfume container and sprayed the subtle, delicate fragrance on to her hair and the bare upper skin of her shoulders. As she breathed the fragrance that was like no other she wondered if it had been specially blended for the Don's mother. A supposition that seemed likely in view of the fact that this suite of rooms had been hers.

Vanessa adjusted her silk stole, clicked off the light and hurried out to the corridor. She paused when she reached the door of Barbara's room, then tapped on it and went in. The girl was sprawled on her bed with a record-player thumping out music beside her. She didn't take a bit of notice of Vanessa but went on clicking her fingers to the flamenco dance rhythm.

'Are the sulks likely to go on for long?' Vanessa had to raise her voice above the music. 'It isn't my fault your guardian has guessed you've been conducting a mild flirtation with his cousin—Babs, turn that thing off and let us talk sensibly!'

'If you do not like the music, then you are not obliged to stay and listen to it,' Barbara rejoined, half closing her eyes in a way that made Vanessa feel like shaking her. She took quick steps to the record-player and switched it off herself. The silence that fell was pregnant with her irritation and Barbara's finger-clicking. Click-click, her gaze fixed on the ceiling, one orange-clad knee upraised.

'If you expect to be treated like an adult, then you had better start behaving like one.' Vanessa's voice shook slightly, though she strove to control it.

'And if you expect to remain here as an employee, then you had better start behaving like one.' Barbara swivelled her lithe young body and glared at Vanessa. 'It is your place to stay in the background, not to poke your nose into *whatever* is between Ruy and me.'

'Barbara, I don't like to see you unhappy——'

'Don't you?' The girl fell back into a sprawling position and crooked an arm over her eyes. But Vanessa had glimpsed their misery and defiance, and painfully clenching her bottom lip between her teeth she wondered whether the term 'mild flirtation' was the right one when applied to Barbara's association with the rakish Ruy Alvadaas....

CHAPTER EIGHT

'MISS PRIM,' Barbara was laughing raggedly, 'what are you thinking—that Ruy has seduced me? I wish he had, then Don Rafael would have to give his consent to our marriage. But instead he will send Ruy away, I know it. Vanessa,' Barbara slid off the bed and grabbed the other girl's hands, evening purse as well, 'you must talk to the *compadre*. He might listen to you——'

'Your godfather listen to *me*!' The idea was laughable, but Barbara's miserable young feelings were not to be laughed at. 'Babs, I'm afraid he thinks of me as a flighty teenager like yourself, and anything I said—well, he'd shrug it off with one of those aloof smiles that put up a barrier far more effectively than the most cutting rejoinder. There's also the question of Ruy's instability. Don Rafael was fond of Ruy's mother and she was made too unhappy by his father for the Don to let you run the same risk of a repeated unhappiness——'

'But if two people love each other, what else is important?' Barbara insisted. 'If Don Rafael sends Ruy away, then I shall follow him. I—I mean it!'

'That's wild talk, and you must stop it, Babs——'

'*Madre mia*,' Barbara sighed extravagantly, 'you just do not understand! That is because your heart has never been touched by a man—it cannot have been, otherwise you would realize that I would sooner be unhappy with Ruy than miserable without him, and you would agree to try a little persuasion on Don Rafael. He is but a man!'

'Babs——'

'Please, *cara mia*.' Tears wavered in the girl's dark eyes.

Vanessa gave a sigh. She supposed she could but try to make him realize that some sort of genuine feeling did seem to exist between his ward and his cousin. Perhaps, as a man in love himself, he might be susceptible to persuasion. 'We can't discuss this any more right now,' she said to Barbara, 'but I-I'll see what I can do.'

'*Cara mia*, you are a poppet, and I have been so wretched!' A vigorous pair of arms hugged Vanessa's slim figure, while a tearful kiss landed on her cheek. 'Forgive me for my meanness to you today?'

'Of course, you baby.' Vanessa didn't know whether to smile or weep, for somehow she didn't hold out much hope that Don Rafael would lend a sympathetic ear to her plea on behalf of his ward. He was, as his grandmother had pointed out, a Spaniard all the way through and firmly convinced that he knew what was best for his womenfolk. In this case Vanessa was inclined to be on his side, but there was no getting away from the fact that Barbara was being made genuinely wretched by the thought of being separated from Ruy.

'Get to bed early and have a good night's rest,' she urged the girl. 'I've got to be off now.'

'Have a good time.' Barbara smiled wistfully. 'He seems quite nice, this grey-eyed American. You like him?'

'Yes, I like him. *Buenas noches*, my dear.'

'*Buenas noches, cara mia.*'

Outside in the corridor, as Vanessa closed the door of Barbara's room, she felt a tight band around her throat and realized how emotionally involved she had become with the unusual occupants of the Castillo d'Oro. She made her way downstairs, and saw Gary awaiting her in the hall, rangy and fair in a crisp white tuxedo over tapering evening trousers. He stood in conversation with the master of the *castillo*, who turned smartly about as Gary's glance flashed eagerly to the staircase down which Vanessa was hurrying. The chiffon frills of her dress flounced above her slender legs, jade green as her eyes bobbed on her earlobes and the light of the Moorish hall lamps caught the shining copper of her shoulder-length hair.

Gary strode to the foot of the stairs, his eyes agleam as they rested on the fine-boned charm of her face. 'Hey, girl!' He caught at her free hand. 'You look terrific!'

'Thank you.' Though it was at Gary she smiled, she was overwhelmingly aware of the man who stood a few paces away regarding them. The compulsion to look back at him was too much for her, and her breath caught in her throat as the Don's dark eyes swept from her earlobes to her bronze-coloured evening shoes. If he recognized the jade, it didn't show in his eyes. They remained cool and impersonal as he escorted Gary and herself to the door.

He wished them a pleasant evening, watched them to Gary's car and politely waved his cigar as the vehicle shot away down the avenue of rustling trees.

'*Qué hombre!*' Gary exclaimed. 'Toledo steel sheathed in black velvet! I bet you're glad to get away from him for a while, aren't you, honey?'

'Yes, he can be a bit overpowering,' she admitted.

'Anyway,' Gary shot a smile at her, 'we've been reprieved from that darned ten o'clock restriction. He said I could bring you home at eleven, so I guess he has his human moments.'

'Yes, now and again,' she murmured, remembering the Don beside her on the cliffs in the velvety dusk, telling her that love was a chill hand, a warm cheek ... a gift that one should give with due care.

Her cold fingers crept over the beaded silk of her evening purse, and her cheeks grew so intolerably warm that she was thankful for the shielding dimness of the car. By the time they reached the restaurant where they were dining, she was quite composed again, outwardly.

The evening that followed was an enjoyable one, for Gary had the American gift for easy conversation. He liked talking about himself, and Vanessa was in the mood to listen rather than to contribute anything but her presence, which her companion obviously found easy on the eyes.

They dined at a place called the Hibiscus Patio where tables were set among fronded trees that rustled in the flower-scented, star-spattered night. Strolling guitarists strummed music appropriate to the atmosphere, and a waiter was soon hovering at their table. Gary ordered a rum and vermouth. 'Carta Blanca rum,' he specified, in the voice of a sophisticate who knew what he liked to drink. Vanessa decided on a Virgin Mary, a tomato cocktail minus the vodka.

'A Virgin Mary!' Gary sat laughing at her as the waiter hurried away through the hibiscus garden. 'They seem to have you well trained up at that fantastic Spanish castle. Girl, it's a good job I came along to remedy things—and I intend to!'

'Gosh, another masterful male,' she laughed, gazing across the table and finding the oil-man ruggedly attractive in his dining kit. The gleam of his tropical jacket and taslon shirt was clean and masculine against his sun-bitten skin, metal-grey eyes and oblique, white grin. 'What is it about me that makes men think I need taking in hand?'

'I know where I'd like to take you,' Gary drawled, deliberately adding: 'Our drilling outfit moves on to Chile in about a month's time, so why don't you pack your gear and trek along with me?'

Chile! That part of his remark really caught her attention and made her sit up. 'Does my suggestion appeal to you, honey?' Gary leant eagerly across the table. 'Or are you bristling because you're getting me all wrong? It's true my motives aren't exactly geared to a brother–sister relationship, but I have married friends in Chile who will put you up while we go through the hand-holding, candy-giving, kiss-and-go part of the business. For my part——'

'Gary, you're racing ahead on a lot of hot air,' she protested. 'I haven't said I'll come—and as for anything else —Really! Do you propose to every girl you've known only a few days?'

'Heck, no! But I've always known that I've been shopping around for a gal who looks like a Lenci doll come to life. You've gorgeous colouring, Vanessa, and a wow of a figure. I just can't let you waste your potential playing *dueña* to the ward of a Spanish Don. The guy saved your life, but that doesn't give him exclusive rights to what you do with it.' Gary's large hand captured hers and held it. 'There's a rumour going around that the *hidalgo* has a marrying gleam in his eye and that a certain attractive widow has put it there. It's dollars to doughnuts, honey, that she isn't going to want a young, sugar-'n-spice governess cluttering up her domain. She'll want to share it exclusively with that virile spouse of hers. Do I make my point?'

Only too stabbingly, Vanessa thought, pulling her hand free of his as the waiter arrived with their drinks. They consulted the menu and agreed on scampi as a starter, with a white Riesling wine, and garlic bread, Gary added. As a follow-up filet mignon with a *sauce bordelaise* looked good, with artichokes and other trimmings. Then they were alone again in their secluded part of the patio and Gary was raising his glass to Vanessa.

'*Vive la différence*, as the French say.' His eyes held hers, wickedly twinkling, as he took a deep swig at his drink.

'One certainly can't accuse you of being conventional,' Vanessa rejoined. 'Cheers!'

'Are you conventional?' He quirked a tangly brow. 'I suspect that you're trying to kid me, you are, but like me you've a dash of the old Irish in ye.'

'How did you know that?' she demanded.

'Come off it, Red! Eyes like green gems dropped in snow, hair with the devil gleaming in it! Was it in your mother's side?'

She nodded and cradled her tomato cocktail. 'Heredity's a funny thing, isn't it?' she murmured. 'Neither of my parents had red hair or a temper, but I've got both.'

'Good, I like a gal who likes a fight. What I don't go for is positive knowledge in a woman, but some fire, decorativeness and a response to my nonsense is fine. You qualify all along the line, honey.'

'I'm flattered, but what makes you so sure *you* qualify as far as I'm concerned?' she bounced back at him.

'Ouch, don't damage my reputation as a Casanova,' he laughed. 'What's wrong with me, then? I've been told that I'm a huggable sympathetic guy and it's also been whispered in my ear that I make a gal feel like one. But I'm forgetting, you haven't been that close yet, have you? We'll decidedly have to do something about that.'

'Really?' Her eyes clashed with his laughing ones. 'I'd heard that Americans were fast workers, but you must hold the record.'

'I meant,' his voice went all innocent, 'that after we've had dinner we could go on to the Skylight Room and dance.'

'I like to dance,' she admitted, cautiously.

'Then it's settled—ah, here comes our chow!'

All through their meal Gary talked about his admittedly interesting self. The places where he had wild-catted for oil, his two years on a Texas ranch, the time a Mexican farmer had almost made a shotgun bridegroom of him. 'You've got to watch these people with Spanish blood,' he said meaningly. 'They've got some funny notions when it comes to love and marriage.'

'You mean they take it seriously,' Vanessa rejoined, giving him a quizzical look over her baked bananas and coconut cream. 'It is a serious business, not a game.'

'Sure, real love's a serious business,' he agreed. 'But working your way towards it's kind of like a game, a mighty pleasant one in which no one has to get hurt. I've never hurt a girl, Red. D'you believe that?'

His eyes had actually gone serious, and after a moment Vanessa nodded. 'I suppose I do. At least I believe that you've probably never meant to hurt any of the girls you've been involved with, but the trouble is, women are more deeply involved with the processes of life and few of them can play at love and remain unhurt.'

'I'm not asking you go play at it, honey.' His voice had deepened. 'I want to fall deep in it with you, have it way over my head.'

Which all sounded very breathless and heady, and amused Vanessa rather than impressed her. Gary knew little about love, she reflected, despite his boasted experience. You didn't talk about it for a start ... it was a kind of secret, precious thing, and you were afraid all the time of exposing your heart and what another person had gone and done to it ...

There in her thoughts she broke off sharply, for how did she know all this unless ...

'Love,' Gary mused, gazing into his tiny glass of curaçao, 'should be an ocean-deep thing, don't you agree?'

'Yes.' Vanessa heard the breathlessness in her voice, for she knew exactly what she wanted love to be. A warm, emotional need; an absorbing, humorous companionship; a close knitting of her life with the man's as the years went by. How she wanted all this, but her mind, her heart, her entire being, shied away from any more self-probing and like someone who had been running, she stammered at Gary: 'I—if we're going on to the Skylight Room, hadn't we better be making a move?'

'Sure.' He finished his liqueur and watched her do the same, then in an almost feverishly exhilarated mood she went with him to the Skylight Room, which catered for European tourists and therefore had a modern dance orchestra and a smooth, romantically lit floor. Vanessa was a naturally good dancer, her partner a practised one, and it was almost like being in Jack's arms again if she closed her eyes. She pictured her uncle smiling by the gramophone, cigar smoke drifting about his grey head. Someone else stood by the veranda doors, watching with a cold detachment as Jack suddenly gathered her closer to him and went into a daring routine that she followed without a falter ...

She gave a sudden shiver, as though a ghost had brushed her, and screened what might be showing in her eyes by gazing fixedly at Gary's crisp white shoulder. The music eventually pulsed to a climax, they executed a final flourish and he released her out of his arms with a sigh. They went to the halfmoon bar, where Vanessa had a pineapple drink and Gary yet another rum and vermouth. It didn't show in his voice that he had been drinking pretty steadily, but Vanessa noticed that the lines around his eyes seemed deeper etched. The eyes themselves looked more reckless.

The orchestra struck up a foxtrot and this time when they danced, Gary's hand was hard against her waist and she could feel his breath fanning her neck. 'I go for that perfume you're wearing,' he murmured. 'I thought I knew all the blends, but this one eludes me. What's it called?'

'I don't know,' his accelerated breathing and the strong grip of his arms were beginning to alarm her more than a little. 'I—I think it must have been specially blended for

Don Rafael's mother. I occupy the suite of rooms she used to have, and I make use of the perfume instead of letting it go stale.'

'It doesn't smell very motherly to me,' he murmured in her ear. 'Having fun, sweetheart?'

'Mmm, best time I've had for—for weeks.'

'Best time for me, too. Nothing to beat it when a guy has his arms full of a gal with copper hair, jade eyes and a delectable aroma—shall we go out on the terrace?'

'No.'

'Say, you've got the shakes.' He laughed, wafting a tang of rum to her nostrils. 'Come off it, Red. I know all about girls—I know they have exotic blue thoughts as well as guys——'

'I—I think we ought to be going home, Gary——'

'You little nettle, what you on the fret about, that darned Spanish employer of yours? Like I told you, dollars to doughnuts you'll be out of that job when he gets married, so your best bet is to come to Chile with me. Honestly, I have friends there who you can stay with. I'm not suggesting anything that isn't above board.'

Chile! Where Jack had his headquarters when he wasn't traipsing about in the jungle. Jack ... surely the only real friend she had ...

'Say you'll come to Chile and I'll be a good boy and run you home after this dance,' Gary wheedled.

'All right,' she heard herself say, 'I'll come to Chile—but only on the understanding that it's as a friend. No strings, Gary. No tying me to promises I might not be able to keep.'

'Okay, no strings.' Gary held her slightly away from him and his oblique grin was crooking his mouth. 'I wonder what the *hidalgo* will say? Will he try to stop you?

'He'll probably try,' defiance lit her eyes, 'but as you said, he has no exclusive rights to my life and what I do with it. He was my uncle's friend and he felt duty bound at the time of the Ordaz revolt to come and help me get away. H-he was furious with me for staying until the situation had grown really dangerous. Gary,' her fingers clenched his sleeve, 'I want to get away from the *castillo*. I-I'd have gone before, but it would have meant placing myself deeper still in his debt...'

'He's got plenty stashed in his sock, honey,' Gary broke in, laughing at her scruples. 'He's the richest guy on the island.'

'That isn't the point,' she argued. 'He's a generous man, but when you feel that someone is being generous out of a—a mere sense of obligation—well, it makes you hate taking anything from them. I know all this sounds involved and odd, but he's the kind of person who convulates a situation and winds it up to a kind of nerve-racking tenseness. That's the only way I can describe it. That feeling is always there between us—as though if the tension snapped——'

She broke off to catch her breath, then gave a rather shaky little laugh. 'I'm working for him to buy back my independence. H-he kind of plundered it from me the night he whipped me away from Ordaz and took me to the *castillo*.'

'Anyway, he saved your life, honey, even if he only did it out of a sense of duty instead of a feeling that your type of girl is kinda rare these days and should be preserved.'

'You make me feel like a museum relic,' she laughed wryly.

'Aw, you know what I mean all right.' His cheek pressed her hair and his hand moved caressingly against her waist. 'It isn't often these days that a guy finds himself a gal with principles as well as S.A.'

His closeness was disturbing, but not in a way that affected her senses. It was her principles that were giving her trouble, for how could she tell him that another man was her reason for wanting to go to Chile? Of course, she could fly out there on her own! Her wages would pay for her air ticket and there might be a European woman there needing a nurse for her children. Yes, perhaps it might be wiser in the long run for her to go alone...

The music came to an end and as they walked off the floor towards the cloakroom, Gary slicked back his hair with a hand that shook slightly. Vanessa noticed and wondered if he was sober enough to drive. The trouble was, his car was an American one and she had started driving lessons only a short while before the abrupt termination of her life at Ordaz. In these circumstances she didn't like to suggest taking the wheel. Anyway, he was probably used to driving with quite a few drinks under his belt.

As he adjusted her stole, his hands were hot against the bare skin of her shoulders and she could hear the heavy way he was breathing. Panic quivered inside her and she hastened ahead of him to where his car was parked. He caught up with her as she reached it and swung her to face him. The moon had risen and was glowing through a drift of cloud, showing the pallor of Vanessa's face and the reckless glimmer of laughter in Gary's eyes. 'Passion is fed by resistance, honey,' he murmured. 'Say, the moonlight in your eyes makes them look silvery.'

'L-let me go, Gary,' she said sharply. 'It's late and——'

The rest of what she had to say was lost under his mouth as he caught her close and held her firmly, insistently while he tried to draw a response from her lips. When he finally let her go, her mouth felt bruised. His had thinned into a cynical line.

'What with you?' he demanded explosively. 'Are you cold or are you sacred?'

'I'm old-fashioned, perhaps,' she retorted, 'and being pounced on in car parks is not my idea of fun. I've quite enjoyed this evening—why did you have to go and spoil it?'

'Spoil it?' He flung open the car door beside her. 'Most girls expect to repay a guy with a kiss or two, but I guess all that Spanish gallantry you've been receiving up at the *castillo* has gone to your head. Chile looks like it's going to be chilly this season!'

Vanessa slid into the car and gave a jump as the door slammed. A moment later Gary was seated beside her and crashing the starter lever forward. The engine kicked, gravel spat and they backed out sharply on to the road and shot away along tarmac that glistened from yet another spat of rain while they had been dancing. The Chevrolet packed quite a lot of power under its hood and Vanessa's hands tightened over her bag as the needle on the speedometer moved past seventy towards eighty.

'Am I going too fast for you?' Gary enquired insolently. 'You're so eager to get home on the dot that I'm obliging you.'

She held on to her temper, just about, and draged her gaze from the luminous speedometer. She glanced out of the window and saw that they were travelling rapidly along the gorge road that wound upwards to the *castillo*. Soon she would be home!

Home? How strange to be thinking of the place in that term when she planned to leave it! She hadn't changed her mind about going to the city where Jack was bound to turn up some time or other, her only change of plan lay in her decision to go alone ...

At this point the car suddenly jarred and slid on a patch of mud, throwing Vanessa forward and jerking a cry from her. 'For heaven's sake slow down, Gary!' she said. 'This road is a narrow one and there are several tricky bends.'

'I've ne-negotiated bends that would raise your hair,' he rejoined, his speech more noticeably slurred. 'This itty-bitty island is nothing compared to where I come from—easy does it, Gary m'boy, or you won't get Cinderella home before the clock strikes the fatal hour——'

'Let me drive, Gary,' Vanessa broke in. 'This is madness——'

'Temper, temper!' One of his hands came off the wheel and patted her knee—and it was in that instant that the car struck another patch of mud and lurched into a skid. Gary wrenched on the wheel, but his drink-hazed mind had reacted seconds too late and the front wheels were over the edge of the road and the heavy rear end of the car was rising up to topple them into a somersault. As Vanessa was pitched headlong against something that jutted, she heard a name break from her in a scream, then pain gushed and dropped her into an illimitable darkness. She fell through it like the Lenci doll she had been called and lay unmoving in a swirl of chiffon.

The shifting moonlight played over the wreckage of the car, while the car horn wailed under the slumped figure of Gary Elsing...

Thump, thump, thump...

Oh, those drums, why didn't they stop! Why did they go on and on? Uncle Len had been so good to these people... they couldn't mean to harm him, or herself!

There was a sickly-sweet smell, like crushed jungle flowers, and a hand to which she clung as the thumping went on and on and it seemed as though the seething darkness all around would never lift—then, abruptly, there was a stab of light and she moaned at the pain that shot through her head.

'She is arousing, *señor*,' said a voice.

The voice was unfamiliar and she thought it belonged to a woman. *Señor*? Coming out of her uncle's study with a gun in his hand—so tall and dark! So angry with her!

She made the effort to open her eyes, shuddering at the light and the thumping right inside her head. 'Vanessa,' a man's dark face came slowly into focus above her, 'do you know me?'

Yes, of course. He came often to see Uncle Len—had something happened to her uncle?

'Has he been hurt?' She struggled to sit up, and at once gentle but compelling hands were on her shoulders and she was eased back against her pillows. 'Oh, please, I—I must go to him——'

'I think she is concerned for the young man,' he spoke over his shoulder, 'but thank God she has come at last out of that deathly, concussed sleep.'

There was another face, older, seamed and kindly, and above it a winged white headdress like a halo. Vanessa stared at this kindly apparition—why, she was a nun!

'Would you like a little chicken soup, my child?' The nun sat down in a chair beside the bed and the spout of a drinking cup was inserted gently between Vanessa's lips. She gulped at the liquid and saw the white halo incline towards the tall, dark figure at the other side of the bed. 'The child is hungry, *señor*. A good sign. Soon now we will have her well and strong again.'

He replied in Spanish, and Vanessa, still only half aware of being back among the living, turned her dark-circled eyes towards him, unaware that his lips tightened because her face looked even more peaky by reason of the bandage swathing her head. She was aware enough to know that she had been ill—or hurt. She tried to remember what had happened, but the effort made her head feel muzzy and inclined to go to sleep again.

'Your head is hurting you, my child?' The nun touched a cool hand to her forehead. 'You must not worry—all is well. Ah, that is right, close your eyes and sleep. When you wake up you will be feeling much better.'

Vanessa's strength seeped back in the next few days, and along with it remembrance of what had really happened. Sister Ysabel, her nurse, told her that Gary had received lacerations and a couple of broken ribs when the Chevrolet had plunged down an embankment not far from the *castillo*. Several of the Don's tenants had hurried to the scene when they had heard in the night the wailing of the car horn; the Don had been informed and soon an ambulance had arrived to rush Gary and herself to the hospital. Vanessa had been found to be suffering mainly from a severe concussion, caused by the blow she had received when she had been pitched against the car door, which had opened and thrown her out.

She was no longer at the hospital, for only this morning an ambulance had brought her home to the *castillo*. Sister Ysabel had come with her, to stay a week or so until Vanessa was back on her feet.

'So many flowers,' Sister Ysabel smiled, gazing around at the vivid blooms that were arranged in vases on every flat surface. 'It is more cheerful for you here than at the hospital, eh?'

Vanessa nodded, for she was still feeling touched by the

thoughtfulness which had provided the flowers, the beribboned basket of fruit and the delectable casket of fondants that she had already delved into. There were English novels as well, and a big bottle of eau-de-cologne from Barbara—for her poor head!

Barbara had been in to see her, but Sister Ysabel had quickly noticed that the girl's chatter was inclined to tire Vanessa, so she had shooed her away. Vanessa had lain weakly laughing against her banked pink pillows, her head no longer bandaged and her hair carefully brushed over the healing scar that ran from her left temple into her scalp. Sister Ysabel, in her rustling black habit and winged head-dress, had looked rather comical shooing from the room a pony-tailed, pirate-trousered rebel. 'You are a tyrant,' Barbara had called back over a tawny shoulder under a halter-strap. 'This place is filled with tyrants!'

A bit ominous, Vanessa reflected. It looked as though Don Rafael was still determined to separate his ward from his unreliable cousin. Poor kid! Vanessa took a chocolate and lay nibbling it as her nurse rustled away to her own room for a while. The jalousies were partly closed and the big bedroom was restful and redolent of the flowers filling it. Vanessa, who had never been ill before, was inclined to fret about her listlessness, but somewhere at the back of her mind there lay a fugitive relief that she didn't have to face, as yet, a parting from Barbara. Or the shattering business of telling Don Rafael she was going to Chile.

She stretched a hand to the magnolias on her bedside table. Their fragrance was rich and dizzying, their sensuous luxury almost like a caress of pleasure running down over her body, so that she wanted to scoop up the flowers like handfuls of water and bathe herself in them. Lordy, the fancies that one had following an illness! She gave a little shiver and saw the skin of her arms go goosey. She was emotionally undermined, that was the trouble, and still slightly off her head from that bang on it ...

'Oh, please come in,' she called out, as fingers tapped on her door.

The Don entered, swarthily distinctive in an impeccable

beige suit; his superbly knotted brown tie was speared by a sword-pin, and his hair was at its raven smoothest. He came to the side of her bed and, aloofly polite, he took her right hand and she felt the warm brush of his lips along her fingertips. 'You begin to look very much improved in health, *pequeña*,' he smiled. 'May I sit just here?'

He patted the Spanish throwover, and even as she nodded she was nervously wondering what he had come to talk about. He sat down beside her and she felt his dark gaze on her champagne-pink bedjacket with the soft white fur running round its neckline. A half dozen in assorted pastel colours had been delivered at the hospital the day following the car accident, and though, when her faculties had begun operating again, she had wished he wouldn't give her such things—after all, he was soon to marry another woman, and bedjackets were rather intimate items of wearing apparel—she had known no way to refuse his gift without appearing ungracious.

'Do I disturb your siesta?' he asked, looking quizzical.

'No,' her fingers curled together. 'I was just wondering what you have come to talk to me about.'

'I may only wish to ask how you are feeling, unless you consider that I should make such enquiries of Sister Ysabel?'

Vanessa met his eyes and saw ironic glints in them. A wary little smile touched her lips as she admitted to herself that there was pleasure in looking at someone so striking and vital. He made her feel that extra bit fragile, but somehow that was always his effect on a woman, to throw into relief her femininity and basic response to a dominant personality. It was infuriating, of course, to be so female as to derive pleasure out of submittance to a male, but she was too weak right now to put up any fight against her own treacherous instincts. For once she just let herself enjoy looking at those well-carried shoulders, that proud Spanish head, the firm lips that probably sent sparks up and down the spine of Lucia Montez when he held her in his arms and kissed her.

'The injury to the head was *muy malo*, no?' With lean

fingers he carefully touched the scar that would mar her temple for a while. 'Naturally I have a concern for you which cannot be wholly satisfied by mere enquiries of a nurse. She can tell me that you progress physically towards a return of health, but she cannot know what effect it has on you inwardly, this accident—this delay of your plans.'

Something winged under her rib-cage and placed a dart of apprehension in her heart. Her plans! He knew, then, that she had decided to leave the *castillo*? But how—had she talked while she had been unconscious?

'Surely you realize that I have spoken with Señor Elsing since the accident?' He spoke drily, but with a hint of hardness in his voice. 'He told me that plans had been made between you to go to Chile. Is this not so?'

'I—I had decided to go there,' she admitted, glancing away from him and deeply reluctant to discuss that trip to Chile.

'Come,' he put a hand against her cheek, his thumb under her chin, 'stop gritting your teeth in that way.'

'You'll try to stop me from going,' she said, and she was trembling under the touch of his hand. 'Don't you see, I must build a life of my own and there—there's no future for me here.'

'And in Chile there is a future?' he crisped, gently but firmly forcing up her chin so that she was compelled to look directly into his eyes. 'You plan to marry this reckless young man who drove his car off the road and almost killed you? There you lay in the wreckage, with a face like milk and the blood of a fearful cut seeping through your hair. It was a sight I will not forget for a long while—he was groaning and coming to himself, and it was obvious he had been drinking.' The Don's eyes glittered, those topaz flecks in them looking for all the world likes points of flame. 'You would have me believe that you love such a man?'

'No, I don't love him——'

'The good Cristo be praised! But all the same you make plans to accompany him to Chile?'

She shook her head. 'I said at first I'd go with him, b-but

later on I changed my mind——'

'He gave you cause to change you mind?' The question leapt at her. 'He took a liberty of some sort?'

'He kissed me—*señor*, you're hurting me!'

His fingers slowly relaxed, slid down to her shoulder then away. 'Forgive me, *guapissima*. There has been much anger in me towards this man since the accident and I forget myself. So he kissed you? You did not like this?'

'No, I didn't like it.' She gave Don Rafael an exasperated look. 'Must I go through this—this inquisition just because I mean to go to Chile? I'm not going with Gary——'

'Then of course you are going because the young Conroy often stays there?'

'How did you know that?' she gasped.

'You forget that I was the confidant of your good uncle. It was he who told me that you wrote letters to Conroy at a hotel in Santiago. So,' the Don rose to his feet and, towering beside the bed, he gazed down dark and inquisitorial upon the fragile picture she made there against banked pillows, flounces of netting echoing the green of her eyes, 'you are driven by a need for this young man's arms and you tremble with fear in case I stand in the way of your desire? Am I such a cast-iron tyrant in your estimation?'

'No, you aren't completely cast in iron.' She smiled faintly, straight into those deep-set eyes that she had seen laughing gently at a baby, and glowing in the sunset light when he had talked wth a sure knowledge of love. 'Mothers spoil their sons and give in to them, and every woman afterwards is expected to.'

'My mind is relieved that I am but a spoilt boy and not too much a tyrant.' His lips smiled, but she noticed that his eyes remained coolly detached, without a ray of amusement in them. 'It is also a fact that a man ceases to argue with a woman once her mind is made up. If you wish so much to go to the young Conroy, then of course you must go. I had hoped that you would forget him, but if you are unable to,' his shoulders lifted the smooth beige suiting, his hand moved in one of those expressive Latin gestures, 'then you have a love for him which I have no right to stop you from enjoying.'

'*Señor*, you don't quite understand—Jack and I are just good friends!' she protested.

'How discreet and British!' Again that humourless smile touched his lips. 'Do not the English always say that, while meaning something totally opposite? Please to relax, *pequeña*. I have probed enough into your heart, and it is one relief that you are not going to Chile to be with that Elsing man. I admit that I should have kept you a prisoner here rather than see you exposed to any more of his recklessness.'

As he spoke he paced over to the dressing table—supple as a leopard, Vanessa found herself thinking—and stood tinkering with the crystal toilet set. She watched him take the glass stiletto out of one of the perfume flagons and hold it to his nostrils. A bar of sunshine broke through the jalousies and slid over him like liquid gold, then abruptly he swung to face her with something ferocious in the movement. 'Why do you say there is no future for you here?' he demanded.

'Aren't you soon to marry?' She put the question in a voice that was almost calm. 'I can't imagine your wife wanting *me* here. Besides, you've already intimated that you have plans with regard to Barbara, and I presume you have someone in mind for her to marry. Don Rafael, do you mind if I say that she is extremely unhappy? She knows your intentions regarding Señor Alvadaas and she has talked of running away if you part them.'

He strode back to the bedside, hands thrust down tautly into his jacket pockets, his nostrils tensed, eyes very dark. 'I know that you feel I am being hard with Barbara, but I have her best interests at heart. Her temperament is emotional, and it was inevitable that she would quickly feel an impulse of attraction towards a good-looking member of the opposite sex. It was rather blind of me not to realize that my cousin would be the natural recipient of her first groping favours, but there has been a deeply personal matter on my mind for some time and I failed to notice that the child was becoming infatuated with Ruy. It is but an infactuation, believe me——'

'But she is genuinely unhappy, *señor*.' Vanessa caught at his arm without fully realizing the action. 'She shrinks from the idea of an arranged marriage—as I would myself. Please, won't you try and put yourself in the girl's shoes? Would you want someone who had been deliberately selected for you—as though the business was merely one of safeguarding the *casta*, as in bull-breeding!'

He might very well have shown anger at this, but instead, with a downward glance at her fingers on his arm, he gave a chuckle. It was curiously warm and deep. 'You are not in the least chicken-hearted, are you, my English Miss? So we of Spain select mothers for our sons as we select mothers for the fighting bulls? A novel point of view, and perhaps not totally off the mark. Is it such a bad thing to have regard for the character as well as the look of a person?'

'I think love should come first,' Vanessa insisted.

'But listen to me,' he was laughing a little as he resumed his seat on her bed, 'there is in most Spanish families a hanger-on, as you English would say it. Someone who trades on his charm for the things he will not work for. Perhaps I should be firm with Ruy and cut off his allowance, but knowing him I also know that he would proceed to acquire money in a dishonest fashion. Ah, but this is true, *chica*, and for the sake of his mother's memory I keep him treading a fairly straight course by more or less keeping him. An alliance between this charming rake and my goddaughter would be a disaster and one I cannot allow. He will go away, and now the time of the vintage has almost come, a good-looking fellow of the correct character will replace him and, *caramba*, Barbara will be in love! The time of fiesta, the gipsy music and the dancing, always brings love to the island.'

Somehow he had moved a little closer while talking, and Vanessa grew aware that his hand was holding her right one and that his thumb was lightly pressing the inside of her wrist. 'Your heart, it flutters like a bird,' he murmured. 'Do I tire you?'

She shook her head, while all her senses had jerked into an acute awareness of his closeness and his touch. Pleasure! Unutterable, stunning pleasure was thrilling through her, leaving her limp against her pillows, her great green eyes fixed upon his dark face. 'You have not yet seen the flamenco dancers, have you?' he queried. 'It is most exciting. You will enjoy watching them.'

'But I-I'm going away,' she just about managed to say.

'Not until you are fully recovered, and next week there will be a party here at the *castillo*. You will be here for that.'

A party? An engagement party? Of course!

'It will be something for you to remember when you are far away from Luenda.' He spoke deliberately. 'Come, you cannot wish to leave us without this celebration?'

Celebration! Her heart contracted at the word, for it implied cruelly that he would be glad to see her leave.

'All right, *señor*, I'll stay for the party.' She conjured a smile and with her heart painfully squeezed she knew she would continue to let him think that need of Jack Conroy urged her to Chile—anywhere, so long as it was away from the *castillo* and him, who she really loved.

She closed her eyes and wished him gone. When she opened them, lithe and silent he had left her bedroom and the door was closing behind him. She lay with bleak eyes fixed on the ceiling, while her heart seemed to be beating in every part of her. Fool, fool, not to have guessed sooner how she really felt about the Spanish Don who had saved her life. Oh, it wasn't gratitude—far from it! When a woman thrilled at a man's touch as she had, there was no fooling herself ever again that she wished to be out of his way because she disliked him and thought him overbearing.

The real reason was only too apparent, she wanted to leave the *castillo* before he became the husband of Lucia Montez. She knew Lucia was back here with him. Barbara had told her.

The next few days were a mosaic of impressions Vanessa

would carry away from her bitter-sweet stay at the Castillo d'Oro. One of these was a telephone call from Gary. He was remorseful, and at the same time indignant because Don Rafael, presumably in no uncertain terms, had told him not to show his face at the *castillo*. 'But I've got to see you, honey,' he pleaded. 'I've got to tell you how sorry I am about the crash. Girl, are you a prisoner up at that place?'

'Don't be absurd,' she laughed, but all the same she couldn't help remembering that Don Rafael had threatened to keep her a prisoner here if she continued to see Gary. He *had* taken a dislike to the young Texan.

'How are you feeling, Gary?' she asked. 'They told me you had a couple of broken ribs and some facial cuts. I hope they weren't too bad.'

'I deserved them,' he growled. 'I haven't stopped kicking myself for driving like a maniac just because I couldn't get my own way with a nice girl. Vanessa, that Chile deal —is it off?'

'I'm afraid so,' she admitted.

'Is it your own idea not to come with me, or are you just obeying the orders of that darned Spaniard? Hell, who does he think he is?' Gary was almost spluttering with indignation. 'He tore me off a strip, I can tell you. Said I might have killed you. He's had my driving licence suspended for a year—would you believe it!'

'Well, it will teach you a lesson,' she said equably.

'You're on his side, I see. He's the one who's told you not to come to Chile with me, that's for sure.'

'Don Rafael has nothing to do with it, Gary. I made up my own mind——'

'There's no chance for me, then? You're not going to let me prove that I can be different from the crazy goon who spilled us down that embankment?' His voice was hoarse with feeling as it came along the line, but Vanessa knew that it would be wiser to break clean with him rather than make promises about seeing him in Chile. Every chamber of her heart was filled with another man, and there was no room for Gary. Barely enough for Jack, she realized, and once upon a time she had considered marrying him.

'You'll soon forget me, Gary,' she said. 'There's bound to be someone else—prove to her that you're a pretty nice guy.'

They talked a while longer, then when it really hit him that whatever might have been was now a burned-out hope, he wished her all the best and rang off. The next morning, while Vanessa was reading on her sunlit balcony, a servant brought her a small package that had just been specially delivered. Inside a little white suede box lay a green-stoned shamrock on a slender gold chain. There was also a card on which Gary had written, 'I'm a better guy for knowing you, Red, and next time I meet a gal with green eyes and copper hair, I'll watch my pace.'

Vanessa fingered the little shamrock and felt a dart of pain in her throat. What Gary badly needed was to meet the right girl. Perhaps one day he would.

She wore the shamrock the afternoon Sister Ysabel allowed her to join the family and friends for *merienda*—late tea, which was laid on circular tables down on one of the patios. Barbara was looking doleful, for Ruy had departed for Madrid. His manner had been so gay and carefree, Barbara confided to Vanessa, that it was evident she had been but an interlude in his life. 'I am finished with men,' she vowed. 'They say they love you, but it isn't love at all. They just want to bowl you over. It inflates their ego to have a girl all starry-eyed over them, and directly you are, they're looking round for someone else. I am finished with all of them!'

'They aren't all alike,' Vanessa assured her, out of her own painful new knowledge. 'And infatuation's a good thing. Without going through that, you'd never know that love is something entirely different. Love and infatuation are like time and tide. One is for ever, the other comes and goes.'

Already guests had arrived at the *castillo* for the party tomorrow evening. Among them was a slender, black-haired young Portuguese, and he had such sparkling dark eyes that it was impossible not to take to him. Ah, Vanessa thought, watching him gradually bring back the vivid prettiness to Barbara's face, he's the one the Don has chosen for her! Then as Barbara's laughter rang out for the first time in days, Vanessa smiled herself. But her smile was tinged with melancholy. The Don knew so much about women, yet the woman he planned to marry was surely lacking in certain qualities she would have thought indispensable to such a man. The widow, for instance, always struck Vanessa as rather lacking in humour. She knew her throaty laughter to be seductive and that was why she often used it. But there was about her something of the art and heartlessness of a hand-created camellia.

They had appeared together in the patio, her arm entwined around his like the golden offshoot of an orchid. She diffused femininity like a perfume, courted his favour with flutters of her oiled lashes and seductive pouts of her small red mouth. She wore a sleeveless silver bolero that matched her silver pearls. Her dress of fine black crepe tapered to her slim calves. The fashion Mecca of Comar was written all over her, and though there was no denying that Don Rafael's swarthy distinction was set off by her olive-tinted elegance, Vanessa fiercely wished that such a man could have had the first flush of love from a girl who was all heart instead of mere ambition to be the envied *prima mia* of his impressive castle home.

'My child, you are looking pensive,' Doña Manuela, who shared a cane settee with Vanessa, rested a hand upon her knee. 'Are you feeling still the effects of the accident?'

'No, I feel heaps better.' Vanessa switched on a smile, and couldn't stop herself from adding: 'How elegant Señora Montez is looking.'

Doña Manuela fluttered her fan and glanced across the patio, to where the Don and the widow sat in conversation with several of their friends. Lucia was leaning slightly forward in a charming, listening attitude, wafting to him her perfume, her almond-shaped nails flaming against his dark grey sleeve as she touched it for a moment. An off-white camellia swathed in silver and black tissue, Vanessa found herself thinking. And when the Don looked at her and smiled, jealousy jagged into Vanessa's heart and she wanted to jump up and run away right now, with no delay, no tomorrow evening and that wretched engagement party to get through.

'They make an attractive couple,' she said brightly.

Doña Manuela looked at Vanessa as though about to say something extremely relevant to the couple across the patio, then she patently caught back her words—like someone sworn to a secret she had almost divulged—and remarked instead that it looked as though Barbara had decided to entertain the company with a song.

Barbara played the guitar delightfully well. Scarlet ribbons trailed from the Spanish guitar she cradled, and the company fell quiet in the sunset-gilded patio as she sang *O mar e lindo*.

Vanessa was wafted back to her first morning here at Luenda, when beneath the casuarina trees she had picnicked off crisp little fish and coconut milk, while beside her a tousled corsair had said of love that it was cruel and beautiful.

Oh yes, it was both those things. Cruel as nothing else could be cruel when you loved and knew your love could never be returned.

'*Otra vez!*' everyone called out when Barbara's song came to an end. They wanted an encore and she ran over to her *padrino* to ask his especial pleasure. He passed an arm about her slim young figure and affection gleamed in his dark eyes as he glanced up at the girl. He mentioned a song, and when she commenced it, when all the attention was upon her and the man she serenaded, Vanessa quietly rose and slipped away unnoticed from the happiness and pleasure on the face of everyone in the patio.

Her fingers found a little *cancela* and blindly she pushed it open and found herself seclusion in the big garden where she could weep in peace. It was the myrtle arbour where she had sat alone once before, disturbed in her heart but unaware at that time that it was love she felt, love she hungered for, from the *hidalgo* of Luenda.

She could hear faintly the music of Barbara's guitar—the music of Spain, with its passion and its haunting echo of the glory and terror that made men like Rafael de Domerique. She had striven not to recognize her love for him because, subconsciously, she had known all along that she would be rendered what she was right now, a weeping stranger in his garden...

'Why do you weep?' The voice was ferociously tender; the arms that came round her even more so. She could not have resisted them even had she been in a fit state to do so. She could only let them take her and hold her against a firm shoulder. 'Come, *bellissima*, why are you weeping all alone like this? Does it make you so sad, that you are soon to be in the arms of the man you love?'

She *was* in the arms of the man she loved, but she couldn't tell him, she could only submit to his gentle mopping up like a small girl in need of comfort after stumbling and skinning her knees. 'There,' he murmured, 'now tell me what makes you so sad. Have you perhaps grown fond of us here at the *castillo* and contemplate with regret the inevitable parting for us?'

'Yes,' she whispered, the word a pain; his arms and his closeness a bitter-sweet joy. She had been in his arms before, but never as a woman torn by love. She had touched him before, but never with hands that hungered to feel the crisp thickness of his hair and the lean angularity of his face. She had felt his breath in her hair, but never before had she longed for his lips as well.

She loved ... she loved ... and it was unbearable to be this close to him as a woman unloved. She attempted to pull away, and in that moment the risen moon glimmered through the cypress trees and she saw his face. It was curiously drawn, and the burning darkness of his eyes held her immobile with her hands against his chest. For a long, long moment they gazed like that into each other's eyes, then she felt his chest lift deeply under her hands.

'*Amada*, foolish one, how long must you hate me?' he groaned. His fingers were in her hair, his palm cupped the nape of her neck, his eyes were devouring her uptilted face, famished and strangely hurt. '*Adorada,* do you hate me?' he whispered.

Darling—adored. Was he really calling her those things? Was he actually asking her why she *hated* him?

'I don't, Rafael——'

'You do not love me? Ah, but then——'

'I don't hate you——'

Her faint, last protest died under his mouth. 'Rafael ...' she said, drowningly.

'*Mi almo!*' It echoed through his kiss, the storm and the wonder of it. My soul! Now his mouth was against her neck, his heart thudded into her, his smothered endearments were a Spanish symphony she could not understand, but which was music straight out of heaven.

But no—this was all wrong! Lucia was the woman he was going to marry! Ah, how could he be this cruel to her, when Lucia was to be his wife?

She began to struggle again, and his fingers, as he forced her to stillness, bruised her arms through the chiffon sleeves of her dress. 'Why do you fight me?' His voice was thick with bewilderment and passion. 'Is it so frightening to be adored?'

'You mustn't say all this to me,' she choked. 'I-I'm not the one you love——'

'*Dios,*' his hands grew really violent, his dark eyes glittered into hers, 'love for you has stalked through my blood like a jaguar waiting to spring. It clawed open my heart long ago, and you dare to say to me that I do not love you. Who else do I love? The painted widow who would like to be mistress of the *castillo*?'

Vanessa was quite still now, gazing up at him with enormous eyes that the moon lit to silver. Her heart was beating so fast it was almost suffocating her. 'You love me?' she whispered.

'*Te quiero, amada.*' A tenderness welled into his eyes, positive and overwhelming. 'Time and time again you must have felt it in me, but you chose to think it something else. Often it has been an angry tenderness. Also a driving need—a passion I cannot express in words. A love

185

of the most terrible, and yet I would not have it any other way. Do you understand?' He gave her a slight shake. 'Are you awakened yet from the English schoolgirl who began to haunt my dreams long before she realized that the man who came to see her uncle was a man not quite in his dotage?'

She laughed shakily at that and buried her face in his shoulder. She held her arms around him, she touched his hair, and she could have killed him for smiling so much at Lucia all through *merienda* and looking at her, that night on his launch, as though at someone he wished off of it. 'You weren't behaving like a man in love when you brought me to Luenda,' she said.

'Oh no?' His lips burned against the side of her neck. 'I was behaving very much like a man in love, my English Miss. A man who did not know if he would have strength of will to keep from making love to you. A man who knew that you feared him—the good *Dios* alone knows why! A man who raged inwardly each time the name of the young Conroy cropped up between us. This Conroy,' he held her away from him a moment and raked her face in the moonlight, 'you implied that you loved him, now you are in my arms and accepting my kisses. You say you want to go to Chile to be with him, but it feels very much as though you would sooner be with me. You had better want me, *amigata*. I am a man, I warn you, at the end of his tether.'

'I was running away from you, Rafael, because I thought you didn't want me.' Tears shone in her eyes as he took her passionately close to him again and held all her chiffoned slenderness against his lean hardness.

'I shall never cease to want you, *carissima*,' he whispered. 'If there have been times when I have been on the defensive with you, it was because I was unsure of myself with you as with no one else I have ever known. You—weakened me, made me aware of vulnerability. Also I was aware of the many points of difference between us, the clash of views that could not be helped. I have longed—*bah*, that is a weak word for it!—I have hungered to tell you of my true feelings, but I could not be sure that you would reciprocate them, and so I hid them. Man is clever at fooling his fellow beings, is he not? Animals use a phyical camouflage, ours is more complex, more subtle. The other day in your bedroom, did you not camouflage your love from me?'

'I thought you meant to marry Lucia.'

'Lucia always knew otherwise, but she is of the type who never gives up trying until she actually sees a man at the altar with another woman.'

'But even your grandmother was certain you would marry Lucia.'

'Madrecita has been certain I would marry every woman I have ever known,' he laughed. 'But last week, at the time of your accident, she guessed from my anxiety that I was at last a man desperately in love. She approves of you, my snow-wrapped flame, and watched with much satisfaction when I followed you from the *merienda* festivities a short while ago. You thought yourself unobserved, eh?'

The moonlight showed such a glimmer of devilry in his eyes in that moment that a quick suspicion shot through Vanessa's mind. 'You pirate!' she accused. 'I believe you deliberately used Lucia this afternoon to make me jealous.'

'The situation was getting so desperate, my pigeon. You were talking so determinedly of leaving me.' He fondled her hair with one hand, but his other arm was locked firmly about her, as though never more would she be allowed to talk in that vein. 'But I must vindicate myself a little—it was Madrecita's idea that I pay some extra attention to Lucia, while she kept her eye on you for your reactions. She was to flutter her fan at me if you showed signs of restiveness whenever I smiled at Lucia—often this afternoon the fan of Madrecita has fluttered with extraordinary business. Did you not notice? Ah, perhaps not,' he laughed in her hair. 'You were too busy taking notice of those smiles I was giving another woman, eh?'

He sounded highly satisfied at that thought, and though Vanessa smiled to herself against his shoulder, she said severely: 'You were probably building up that poor woman's hopes. You heartless devil, Rafael!'

'That I am not, *mi mujer*! Feel for yourself.' He took her hand and pressed it to his strongly beating heart. 'It beats in me, but it belongs to you, Vanessa. Can you fear a man who loves you so much?'

Strange that she had feared him on and off, but right now love welled, drowning out everything else. A warm eagerness and anticipation gripped her throat. Wife to Rafael de Domerique, his need, his choice. She gazed up at him and he saw the love in her eyes, felt it in the warm response of her lips when he kissed her ... again ... and yet again. 'I want to shut you in a tower and keep you entirely to myself,' he whispered passionately. 'Is that enough love for you, *amada mia*, to be my fair captive here on the island, until the stars go out for both of us?'

'I know now that I've always been your captive, Rafael,' she whispered back. 'Each time I tried to escape, something held me back.'

'And each time I knew you on the verge of escape, I gambled and left open an exit to see if you would go.' He cradled her face in his lean, warm hands and studied it in the moonglow. 'You will never escape from me once you become mine, *carissima*. I take, I hold!'

'I want that,' she assured him, certain now of what she wanted and no more the bewildered, emotional girl who had liked him one moment, then had felt an uncontrollable urge to flee from him the next. Primitive woman, she thought. A tigress who resented even as she loved her tamer.

In a while they returned to the *castillo* to tell everyone that this year the vintage would be celebrated in conjunction with the wedding of the *hidalgo*. Doña Manuela looked supremely content when in front of his guests her grandson slid a wonderful ruby and diamond ring on to Vanessa's betrothal finger, while she slid a crested gold band on to his. Lucia Montez looked on with a philosophical expression, while Barbara clasped the arm of her young Portuguese suitor. Perhaps she was recalling what Vanessa had said, that true love, like time, went on for ever.

The glow of true love was in Vanessa's green eyes as she raised them to the man at her side. His smile was for her alone as their ringed hands met and clung. The champagne had been poured and handed round and the *sala* was ringing with good wishes. Real Spanish wishes that the couple enjoy a long and felicitous life together—with the added blessing of several lusty *chiquititos*.

Mills & Boon Classics

The very best of Mills & Boon romances, brought back for those of you who missed reading them when they were first published.

There are three other Classics for you to collect this November

SAVAGE LAND
by Janet Dailey

When Coley left the city for a cattle ranch in Texas she was prepared to find certain changes in her way of life. But she was to find that dealing with the brooding Jason Savage was to bring her greater problems than even she had anticipated...

DARK MOONLESS NIGHT
by Anne Mather

Seven years ago Caroline had considered Gareth Morgan unsuitable as a husband for herself. Now they had met again in the African jungle and Caroline's feelings had changed. But the disturbing Gareth told her she would be wasting her time trying to rekindle old fires...

PARISIAN ADVENTURE
by Elizabeth Ashton

It was perhaps because of Renée's resemblance to the famous model, Antoinette, that she found herself transported suddenly from London to the salons of Paris. The famous couturier, Léon Sebastien, needed a replacement for Antoinette and Renée filled the bill. Rumour also had it that Léon needed a replacement for Antoinette in more ways than one!

Mills & Boon Classics

The very best of Mills & Boon romances, brought back for those of you who missed reading them when they were first published.
In
December
we bring back the following four great romantic titles.

THE BEADS OF NEMESIS
by Elizabeth Hunter

Pericles Holmes had married Morag Grant as a matter of convenience, but she had lost no time in falling in love with him. Whereupon her beautiful stepsister Delia, who always got everything she wanted, announced that she wanted Pericles!

HEART OF THE LION
by Roberta Leigh

When Philippa encouraged young Cathy Joyce to elope, she didn't know the girl was the niece of her boss, the formidable newspaper tycoon Marius Lyon — but that didn't stop him promptly giving her the sack. But that was by no means the last of Marius as far as Philippa was concerned!

THE IRON MAN
by Kay Thorpe

When Kim had no news of her fiancé in the Sierra Leone she decided to go and find out what had happened to him. And encountered opposition in the shape of the domineering Dave Nelson who told her, 'Don't run away with the notion that being female gives you any special immunity where I'm concerned.'

THE RAINBOW BIRD
by Margaret Way

Paige Norton was visiting the vast Benedict cattle empire as the guest of Joel Benedict. She had looked forward to it immensely, although she hadn't much liked the sound of Joel's stepbrother Ty, the boss of the station. And when she met Ty, she liked the reality even less ...

SAVE TIME, TROUBLE & MONEY!
By joining the exciting NEW...

WITH all these **EXCLUSIVE BENEFITS** for every member

NOTHING TO PAY! MEMBERSHIP IS FREE TO REGULAR READERS!

IMAGINE the *pleasure* and *security* of having ALL your favourite *Mills & Boon* romantic fiction delivered right to *your* home, absolutely POST FREE... straight off the press! No waiting! No more disappointments! All this PLUS all the latest news of *new books* and *top-selling authors* in your own monthly MAGAZINE... PLUS *regular* big CASH SAVINGS... PLUS lots of wonderful strictly-limited, *members-only* SPECIAL OFFERS! All these exclusive benefits can be *yours* – right NOW – simply by joining the exciting NEW *Mills & Boon* ROMANCE CLUB. Complete and post the coupon below for FREE full-colour leaflet. It costs nothing. HURRY!

No obligation to join unless you wish!

FREE CLUB MAGAZINE Packed with *advance* news of latest titles and authors

Exciting offers of **FREE BOOKS** For club members ONLY

Lots of fabulous **BARGAIN OFFERS** —many at **BIG CASH SAVINGS**

FREE FULL-COLOUR LEAFLET!
CUT OUT CUT OUT COUPON BELOW AND POST IT TODAY!

To: MILLS & BOON READER SERVICE, P.O. Box No 236, Thornton Road, Croydon, Surrey CR9 3RU, England. WITHOUT OBLIGATION to join, please send me FREE details of the exciting NEW Mills & Boon ROMANCE CLUB and of all the exclusive benefits of membership.

Please write in BLOCK LETTERS below

NAME (Mrs/Miss) ....

ADDRESS ....

CITY/TOWN ....

COUNTY/COUNTRY........................POST/ZIP CODE..............

Readers in South Africa and Zimbabwe please write to:
P.O. BOX 1872, Johannesburg, 2000. S. Africa